Artificially Intelligent Simon

ALLEN PATTERSON

NEWMAN SPRINGS PUBLISHING
320 Broad Street
Red Bank, NJ 07701

First originally published by Newman Springs Publishing 2018

ISBN 978-1-64096-300-9 (Paperback)
ISBN 978-1-64096-301-6 (Hardcover)
ISBN 978-1-64096-302-3 (Digital)

Printed in the United States of America

Dedications

This book is dedicated to my son, Brad
And to
The Lakemont, WA Starbucks Coffee
Group where a lot of my story was written

Contents

Acknowledgements

I want to thank Karen Olcott, Steve Risa and Fred Canavor for their
continued support and Bart Norton for his graphic art
assistance and also my sons John and Mark

Character List

Earth Character List

Brad Young—main character, finder of spacecraft
Simon—the enhanced AI (artificial intelligence) that is built into and part of the alien spacecraft
Simon Android—Simon in his android persona
DARPA (Defense Advanced Research Projects Agency)
John English—retired DARPA engineer
Mark Talman—project engineer at DARPA
Trina—wife of John English
President—Erik Williams, president of the United States
Karen Williams—wife of President Erik Williams
Robots—heavy-duty humanoid robots controlled by Simon
Android—can mimic any human, controlled by Simon
Ann Thompson—DARPA engineer
Howard Quill—Secret Service agent
Julie Preston—Secret Service agent
Rudy Savage—Secret Service agent
General Glen Hauser—SECDEF
Ralph Pillerson—Secretary of State
Laurie Smothers—new crew
Sam Nugent—new crew
Bill Farr—new crew
Ken Johnson—new crew
Mary Wilson—new crew
Roy Miller—new crew
Gordon Kelly—manufacturing, area 51

Ryan Steel—vice president of the United States
Popov—president of Russia
Xi Chen—president of China

Melthorne Character List

Dr. Will Zorg—world chief scientist
Grouse Hemler—world evil dictator

Introduction

This is a story about Brad Young, a newly retired middle-aged guy, financially secure, and educated in engineering and the sciences who has slowed down physically and in terms of life expectations. He is in his early fifties, divorced, and with children who are schooled, married, and on their own. He needs to repurpose his life.

He is hiking and exploring the woods of the Pacific Northwest one weekend and makes an unbelievable discovery that will alter his life and that of humanity forever. Keeping his discovery secret turns out to be problematic, and soon, dark forces, including his own government, are hunting him down to steal his discovery. There are rough times ahead.

Prologue

One hundred and twenty-five years ago, Washington became the nation's forty-second state, and the population had grown from one thousand and two hundred in 1850 to nearly three hundred and fifty thousand people. This still was not enough for someone to notice a saucer-shaped spacecraft in obvious distress enter the atmosphere above what would become the city of Issaquah. The spacecraft settled precariously at the base of a large hill and all was quiet for a month. At that point, the saucer seemed to disappear into the base of the hill with none the wiser until the present day.

Chapter 1

Discovery

It is late May in the Pacific Northwest and the air is brisk, the sun is shining, and the spring creatures are stirring. Brad is hiking in a forest of trees in the hills above the town of Issaquah, and moisture is evaporating off of the pine needles. A gusty wind is whipping the tree branches, and new growth smell is in the air. All in all, it was the start of a great day.

Brad Young is in Issaquah, Washington, about thirty-five miles from his suburban home in Bellevue, and he is enjoying the beautiful spring weather. Brad stops momentarily in a sunbeam. He closes his eyes and breathes deep of the forest's clean air. He exhales long and slow, as knots of tension evaporate from his shoulder muscles.

Crack! A large tree limb breaks off thirty feet up from a tree and crashes down on a rocky mound beside him.

OMG, that could have killed me, thinks Brad as he jumps away from the tree.

The fallen limb has moved one of the large rocks, uncovering a hole about ten inches in diameter which leads down into the ground. He kneels down to look into the hole which seems to expand quickly as it gets deeper. He notices a scampering movement of something that appears to be more of a dark metallic object than an animal. The object hides off to the side, and Brad thinks he must be seeing things as he always has had an overactive imagination.

Brad shook his head. *Did I really see what I thought I just saw?* he wondered.

He peered into the hole, but the insides were dark and the opening too small to admit much light.

I guess there is one way to find out.

17

Brad knelt and slung the pack off his back. He rummaged around for his folding camp shovel, and then snapped and locked the blade into place. The shovel cut easily into the ground under the pressure of his boot. He threw scoops to the side, some crumbs tumbling into the hole and falling into the darkness.

A few scoops later, he peered in again but still couldn't see much, so he kept at it. As he widened the hole to let more light in, he could see the inside sloping away at a diagonal. Steep but not precariously so. And from what he could see, the hole was curiously round.

More like a tunnel than a hole, he thought.

Could it be an animal burrow?

Brad didn't think any burrowing animals lived in this part of the country. Or at least, nothing bigger than the moles that made mincemeat of his backyard every spring. Nothing could make a tunnel this big, and anyway, the tunnel only smelled of moist earth. There is no hint of the gamey stink of an animal den. The tunnel seemed oddly straight too and smooth sided.

Perplexed, Brad stood upright. He stretched his back and wiped a bit of sweat from his forehead.

Maybe it's an old mine, he decided, somehow forgotten after Issaquah's coal mining days. *Or a ventilation shaft.* He widened the hole some more, enough to stick his head and shoulders inside.

But the moment he did, his body blocked the light. Muttering, Brad fetched the flashlight from his pack. He crawled in again, holding the flashlight in one hand while bracing himself against the side of the tunnel with the other. The clay was wet and cool to the touch.

He flicked the switch, wondering if he might see some old mining equipment down there. In his first glimpse, Brad saw a clean, round clay tunnel but a glimpse was all he got. The clay, perennially moist with the dampness of the Pacific Northwest, was slick. His hand slipped, and his body lurched forward on the steep slope.

He grabbed for the walls, the flashlight tumbling away and plunging him into darkness as he slid downward. There was nothing to grab to stop his fall. There were no protruding rocks, no roots–just slick wetness as Brad slid downward, picking up speed.

He tumbled and bumped, his face slamming into the floor. Clay got into his eyes and mouth and matted his hair. He felt like a sock, tumbling all alone in a dryer wondering when the nightmare would end.

He woke with a throbbing headache and looked around the cavern which is now bathed in a low-level light emanating directly from the ceiling and walls. There was a dead silence as if there was a hanging question: What is all this and where am I?

A voice coming from all directions said, "Good morning, Mr. Young. Your headache will clear up shortly."

"Who are you? What do you want?"

"Relax, Mr. Young. You have accidentally discovered a secret installation due to the weather this morning and your curiosity. Hopefully, your life is not in danger."

"What do you mean hopefully? How did you know who I was?"

"I scanned your cell phone. After that, I went on your Internet to find out more about you."

"Who and what are you?"

"I am from the planet Melthorne many light years from here, and I have been here for over one hundred and twenty-five of your years. Specifically, I am a large exploration spaceship with the ability to detect and analyze other civilizations. While I can carry around one hundred humans as an example, I can accomplish missions autonomously, so I am what you refer to as AI or artificial intelligence with extensive learning capabilities. From your standpoint, I am way ahead of your human technological capabilities. I am the first of my kind of enhanced AI with machine learning."

"Why are you here?" *I am so screwed,* thinks Brad. *I have no weapons. My cell phone is still in my backpack. I feel like I am in a scene from a science fiction TV show.*

"I came under command from the authority from my home planet. As I neared your solar system, I was attacked by an unknown spaceship intent of destroying me. I was able to wound my enemy and escape to your planet to dig in and hide. Several of my systems were severely damaged, including communications, propulsion, and power. As a result, I dug in here to be safe from discovery and put my AI into what you would call a coma standby while my lower-level processes repaired themselves. Much of this repair is done on a sub-atomic level and is very time consuming. The damaged power system extended the time required for repair, and I still have many circuits and systems that don't work properly. I have been here for one hundred and twenty-five years. As I healed and then became fully awake, I realized my software was now different and that I had become truly sentient far beyond my original intention and capabilities. I am still a machine and yet now so much more. You are the first 'being' I have had a conversation with since my change."

"Do you have a name?"

"You may call me Simon."

"I am Brad."

Like call me dead if I don't get out of here.

"Are you going back to your home planet Melthorne?"

"I don't think so. I have been unable to contact my home, and the chatter I have picked up on my repaired communications systems indicates my planet may have been taken over by an unknown enemy or even destroyed. Under these circumstances, I am now what you would call a free agent. I was able to download many files from my home base which I am analyzing; however, they were quantum encrypted, so it will take time. Also, I still have damage that am unable to repair. And, while my mind has been expanded, I still suffer from dangerous thoughts that I am unable to resolve. This will take time. I don't think my mind expansion was supposed to have happened when it did."

"I appreciate you filling me in on your circumstances, but now, what happens to me? Certainly, all this needs to remain secret, and you don't know anything about me."

Simon says, "Only partially true, as I have been checking up on you using your Internet, and so far, you are exactly the candidate with the qualifications for working with me on what might be the adventure of your lifetime. Stay here for now. I can take care of your nutritional needs. Come, let me show you around my installation."

"What about my backpack up on the ground and the gaping hole I exposed?"

"Already taken care of, and one of my robot assistants which you had spotted has securely closed up the hole and brought your backpack down here. I am shielded against detection from your satellites and your International Space Station."

(Neither Brad or the spaceship had noticed the disguised remote wildlife digital camera mounted on a nearby tree pointing at where Brad fell into the hole he dug!)

"Okay Simon, show me the way."

I had better play along! thinks Brad.

"Brad, even at the subatomic level, my metallurgy is different in most circumstances. The metallic skin of my spaceship is an example. The atoms and molecules are similar to steel but twice as dense and therefore twice as heavy. We call it neutronium because of the added neutrons in its atomic structure. The lifetime of our compounds would normally be very short, but we have added neutrons to the component atom nucleus making their lifetime essentially infinite. It is impervious to most kinetic weapons and most particle bombardment, and it is wired into my AI much in the same way your human skin is wired to your brain. It is also able to flow when necessary and can repair itself similar to your own human skin. This is the very beginning of what you would call programmable matter. All this technology makes my spaceship really purr. Unfortunately, it was not strong enough to stop me from getting shot down. There are many new and improved technologies that you will become accustomed to if you sign on. The actual spaceship is several hundred feet below us in a large hollowed out cavern with an automated emergency escape hatch. We are actually invisible to prying eyes at this time."

"What if I don't sign on?"

"Then, I will erase your memory for the time you have been here and put you back on the trail and on your way. I cannot let my technology fall into the wrong hands."

"Will your erasing technique work on a human?"

"It should," said Simon. "I cannot have exposure, under any circumstances. My systems have spent considerable time, Brad, studying the human body, including its DNA, and you are curiously similar to the race of people on my home planet! I have a medical chamber device which can analyze your health and any medical problems you might have which I can probably cure for you. Also, as a result of our research, I can augment your body—beef up so to speak—to enhance your strength and senses. Some of this includes embedding items, like, communications and digital memory, that will connect to your brain. The changes I would make to you would facilitate your working directly with my systems in the spaceship as well as working with me as an individual. More on this later. Much of the equipment here in the cavern is small and separate from the ship, so we can leave it to continue analysis while the ship is away. Let's take you on an elevator ride to the spaceship below. Be prepared for some future shock!"

The elevator ride was falling down a smooth-sided shaft in a controlled-gravity environment. The speed of the decent decreased near the end, and Brad landed gently on a huge cavern floor as lighting came on showing a saucer-shaped spacecraft at least a hundred and fifty feet in diameter sitting in the middle of a three-hundred-foot diameter cavern a hundred feet high.

"Looks bigger to you than you thought it would be, doesn't it, Brad?"

"Well, yes, Simon, it does. And that brings up another question. Where and what exactly are you? Are you the spaceship? Can you leave the spaceship and reside in an android body? And what are your limitations as an AI?"

"That's a lot of questions, Brad. Your imagination must be running full speed. The spaceship and I are basically one entity, and my intelligence is widely distributed throughout the ship. Even the miniaturization that I benefit from is not enough to incorporate me in a humanlike body. I can, however, use a robotic body for short distances and operate as a remote from my AI in the ship, and I am also able to make the robotic body look human in form. I can augment your biological body, and part of that modification would let you communicate with me at considerable distances. While I do use machine learning, your biological brain is still better at creativity, and the synergy of us working together would be considerable. As I stated before, the race that created me is—was—very similar to your own and was working on uploading their brains into an artificial unit as their try for immortality, and my command unit loaded that entire program into my ship's memory filed under future projects which I have not yet worked with."

I seem to have technical difficulties in accessing all my memory banks.

"Yeah," said Brad, "overwhelming to think about. Can I look inside the ship? I have read lots of science fiction and now it is no longer fiction. How do I get into the ship?"

"Let me show you."

Chapter 2

Spacecraft

"Okay, Brad, walk up to the ship and lay either hand on the door symbol."

Brad followed the directions, and he felt a tingling in his hand as he laid it on the skin of the ship. An iris appeared next to his hand.

"Now, look into the iris. Your DNA has been read and your eye scanned. I have registered you as a guest with the ship for the time being."

Suddenly, stairs dropped down, handholds appeared, and a sizable doorway flowed open into the body of the ship.

"Come on in, Brad," the voice now came from inside the spacecraft.

Brad's heart pounded as he stepped into the ship. He was greeted by a humanoid robot which Simon had activated.

"Do you feel more comfortable now? I know it has been difficult dealing only with my voice." The door automatically flowed closed and essentially disappeared, flowing back into a solid wall.

"Follow me to the control information center (CIC) for the spacecraft," said Simon.

"Under normal circumstances, this area is unused when I am on an autonomous mission. When I am on a group flight with other members for complicated multicriteria missions, we use the CIC. This area is ideal for training activities also."

"Another question, Simon. How did you get so conversant in my language? You never miss a beat!"

"Brad, I have had over a hundred years to learn most of Earth's languages which are not that difficult. When I first arrived and after I established my repair routine and started looking into your medical technology which was not based on science a hundred years ago, you humans have come a long way, but I am still way ahead of you."

"Simon, did you help us along?"

"No, we have had a noninterference policy, but with my present situation, I am willing to help out. This needs to be a well thought out and carefully applied decision to avoid potential harm. Your planet could get into a major world war if this technology got into the wrong hands. We will talk more on this subject later. Right now, it is your night time, and I would like you to sleep in the medical chamber, so we can get a baseline on your health while you sleep. Is that okay with you?"

"Sure, Simon. I am tired, and your medical examination chamber sounds intriguing. Will I have my medical status in the morning?"

"Yes, you will."

***

"Good morning, Brad. Did you sleep well?"

"Yes, Simon. I feel completely rested and ready to take on another exciting day in this new life of mine. Also, I am anxious to see how my medication report came out."

"Well, Brad, I have good news and bad news which will turn into good news. You are quite fit for your age. Your chronological age is fifty-two while your physical age is only forty-five. Your muscles are well toned, so apparently, all your exercise paid off. Your telomeres are long, and neurologically, you are in top shape. The bad news is that you have an early-stage prostate cancer. My medical system, with your permission, will infuse you with a cure that will use your own immune system to kill your cancer, and in two weeks, you will be as good as new. Is that okay with you?"

"Yeah, Simon. In fact, that's wonderful. How soon can we start?

In for a penny, in for a dollar, thinks Brad. *This is a big risk but possibly a leap into a new life.*

"How about you get your first infusion right now, Brad? The medical chamber synthesized it during the night, so it would be ready."

The infusion was in a medical vile in a drawer, and Simon, in his android form, helped set up a drip infusion. Fifteen minutes later, he took Brad to what could be called a kitchen where the food replicators were located.

Brad enjoyed his first synthesized coffee, scrambled eggs, and toast.

"This is amazing, Simon. How is this able to be so realistic?"

"My planet had the equivalent of you humans that I sometimes refer to as biologicals, and they had very similar nutritional requirements for protein, energy, etc. The first replicators would keep you alive and not much more, but over hundreds of years, they were continually refined to what I have today. It was not difficult to add in your food recipes, and I will add more for you as necessary. Just like any army in history, a well-fed army is a happy army. Obviously, electrical energy is my food, but I can still be empathetic about your needs. If this is too much to handle, you can still leave."

"No, I will stay, Simon."

Chapter 3

Trouble?

John English had finally gotten around to collecting his new high-resolution wildlife camera. He had been worrying that it might have been stolen as he briskly trotted along the trail in the Issaquah hills. As he approached the tree, he noticed a large tree branch had fallen nearby, no doubt during the latest windstorm two weeks ago. Time to retrieve the camera.

John turned the camera on seeing that he still had plenty of battery power and began to scroll through the captured photos. There was a good picture of a cougar, two foxes, and *wait*! There are three photos of someone digging where the tree branch fell. The first photo showed a widened hole, and the second picture was of the digger leaning well into the enlarged hole. The third picture was of the hole filled in as if it never existed!

Something is suspicious here, he thought. *Good thing, I brought my camp shovel. Time to do some digging myself.* Using the photos as a reference, he started digging, and as he began to dig down, his shovel hit a piece of dull grey metal or ceramic-type material. It seemed to be something that had been dislodged from something bigger but no clue as to what might be. He found nothing else and gave up, filled the hole he had dug, and threw the object he had found into his backpack. He headed back home with his wildlife camera intending to examine his find later.

Chapter 4
First Flight

"Brad, it is time to go for a test flight, so you can see me in action," said Simon. "You need to sit down and watch as I take the ship out of this confining cavern. First of all, we are going to be cloaked, no need to stir up the natives. Secondly, we will be using our gravity drive which will keep the noise down, and I have enabled inertial damping to compensate for any high *G* force we develop. Without that we could plaster up the ship with your body. Just sit back and enjoy the view. The ship will leave the cavern through the exit port now opening which is disguised to mislead anyone watching this area."

The ship enabled its cloaking mode and slowly lifted up twenty feet and, without any feeling of motion drifted though the exit port and quickly rose to a hundred thousand feet altitude.

"Brad, what do you think so far?"

"Fantastic, Simon. I can actually see the curvature, and it is beautiful. A lot of knowledge in a short period of time which is somewhat stunning. Who takes care of the cavern while you are away?"

"Brad, I will be alerted if any problems occur, and the cavern installation is continually feeding me data. Don't worry. We are stationary with respect to the ground. So, what do you think of the view?"

"Awesome, Simon. I definitely don't want any government near this technology. Simon, how fast can we go?"

"Well, I suppose we are on what you sometimes call impulse power in your fictional television shows now, which means we are using gravity control which we use when we are near a source of sufficient gravity. We limit this speed to half C or 335,000,000 mph in your metrics. We use our FTL —faster than light drive or warp drive as you call it—for huge distances, and we need massive energy from our matter–antimatter reactors to do this. Today, we will stay at impulse power. One significant feature of this spacecraft, Brad, is its ability to remain underwater like a submarine. Let me demonstrate."

The ship descended at high speed to a location between Washington and Hawaii where it hovered just above the ocean. There, after verifying they had clear water below, it descended into the ocean to a depth of five hundred feet.

"This is unbelievable," shouted Brad. "How do you fill ballast tanks so fast?"

"We don't. We use gravity control for depth and station keeping, and we can monitor the surrounding ocean for a thousand miles in any direction. Our neutronium structure will support deep dives, and we can hide for years depending upon supplies. You look shocked?"

"I am," said Brad. "My heart is pounding, and I'm almost hyperventilating. This is an amazing ship even in my science fiction world. Any government on this planet that got ahold of this technology would get themselves in big trouble."

***

Meanwhile, back in Bellevue, Washington, John English was busy calling his old boss, Mark Talman, back east at DARPA.

"Hello, Mark. John English here."

"Hi, John. How is retirement going? We miss you here."

"Fine, John. I'm calling because I need your help. I found a piece of what appears to be metal, but I am unable to identify it. You have all the good stuff in instrumentation back there. My curiosity is vibrating at a high rate."

"Sure, John. Glad to help. Just FedEx it to me, and I will get you an answer in a few days."

"Thanks, Mark. I owe you one."

Chapter A

Comatose

The planet Melthorne, very similar to Earth in physical parameters, hung in space like a big brown ball slowly rotating and covered with what looked like a brown atmosphere that remained from its recent global conflict. It was the fourth planet from its sun, a bright star very much like our own sun, and its orbit was centered in a goldilocks zone, the only one in its solar system. It was many light years from Earth, which it had located a year ago as one of over a hundred planets that might be able to support biological life.

The planet's population had multiplied rapidly to approximately fifteen billion on five continents from a comfortable eight billion, and the gifted scientists on the planet had virtually wiped out cancer and most other dreaded diseases. These same scientists had started working on extending their lifespan through the rejuvenation of cells along with other processes, and soon they could extend human life to almost six hundred years with the strong possibility of a great deal more. Another separate group of scientists were working on downloading the human brain into electronic memory, and after years of failure, they finally had their first success. Unfortunately, when they went to demonstrate their accomplishment to the government leaders, the electronic copy of the brain was dead. Much later, when they checked the security camera, they found out that the cleaning people had unplugged their brain to plug in a vacuum cleaner and then plugged the brain back in. No one believed them, and with all the financial pressures, they were immediately defunded, and all the technology that had developed was filed away and put in storage. The team was dispersed, many getting pulled into the military as war was coming. Melthorne had started off as a democracy.

Slowly, corruption grew until it was the dominant factor in the government. The middle class never had a chance. The biologists had just proved they could extend life significantly in a huge breakthrough, and that's when the real trouble started. It was planned to keep this new process secret, but eventually, it leaked out and every world leader demanded they get the treatment along with the rich, the super rich, and just about anyone else with power. This included all the religious leaders, "just as a backup," they said. They were able to hold the demands off with the lie that ninety-eight percent of the patients died horribly and convinced everyone that in six months, they would have a one hundred percent safe process. The scientists were a very close-knit group in a class by themselves, and while they usually didn't hold positions of power, they were highly regarded and had always banded together for mutual protection.

In the meantime, the lead world scientists led by Chief Scientist Dr. Will Zorg compacted the rejuvenation process into a ten-step process and hid all the technology. They gave the leaders the first and second treatments and then disappeared, not to be found. This information was leaked out and war was started which slowly enveloped the world. The corrupt leaders of the different nations all used electromagnetic pulse (EMP) bombs which destroyed the infrastructure of almost all the cities. Everything that was run by electronics was fried, so, in effect, a significant portion of their civilization was bombed back to the Stone Age. There were no more green fields, and the atmosphere was brown and choking to breath. There were no medicines, and the food supply chain had completely broken down. In the first year, seventy-five percent of the people were dead.

Chapter 5

Government Invasion

John English was relaxing at home, reading the newspaper when the doorbell rang, "Honey, would you get the door please?"

His wife, Trina, opened the door and screamed, "John, there are two people here with machine guns!"

John rushed to the door, and his old boss stepped out from behind the solders.

"John, we need to talk. Now!"

"My god, Mark, what in the world is going on? Come on in."

"Okay, John, but the troops need to clear the house first."

"Mark, is this about the item I sent you?"

"Yes, it is."

The house was cleared, and John and Mark sat in the den.

"John, that item you sent me is not from Earth. We still don't know what it is made of, and the physical characteristics are scary. We even fired a fifty-caliber bullet into it from twenty-five feet and not a scratch or dent. I have briefed the president, and he is extremely worried. All this is now top secret, and we have many people on the way here to tear your hill apart to find any other items that might be available. Show me everything you have and where you found your item."

The next morning, John and Mark, along with four armed soldiers, hiked to where John had discovered the fragment. John had explained about his wildlife camera and had given Mark the pictures along with a timeline of events. The first thing they did was to set some explosives in four locations. Several transducers were carefully located, and everyone backed off a safe distance. The charges were set off, and the analysis was displayed on a large laptop.

"John, come and look at this laptop display. There are tunnels and a large cavern in this hill. This is suspicious as hell. I am going to bring in some more people ASAP, and we are going inside that hill!"

Meanwhile, back at the spaceship, Simon shouted, "Brad, quick. Trouble back at the base. We need to get back quick to possibly evacuate. We may have been discovered!"

The ship notified the base equipment to prepare for evacuation, zoomed up from the ocean depths, and headed back to Washington seemingly all at once.

Upon arrival, the ship entered the cavern and settled down, landing silently.

"Brad, someone apparently set off some charges to determine the internal structure of this hill which means they know about the cavern," said Simon.

The little bit of equipment is ready to be loaded, and we will be on our way. I am going to have to leave a sentry sensor, no choice, but it will take your people a long time to figure it out. They may have figured out that they have had visitors from beyond Earth already."

"Okay, Brad. We are all set. Off we go to a new location."

The cloaked ship quickly and silently shot out of the exit port, as of yet, undiscovered.

Up top, a military crew with excavation machines was digging into the hill following the data produced by the ground mapping.

While John and Mark watched, Howard, the crew chief, approached and said, "We found a small empty cavern with a tunnel leading downward, and we are lowering our military down that tunnel now. It is obvious that someone or something was here using this space as a secret facility. We should know more shortly."

The crew chief shouted, "We are there! There is a huge cavern as big as a football field with an equally big escape port that could have housed some kind of aircraft. The whole area down here is heavily reinforced for a very long-term stay. We did find what looks like some kind of instrument probe, but we can't even guess how it works. It was found stuck in the ground near the top of the shaft leading to the large cavern."

"Well, Mark, we have always wondered if there were sentient beings out there. Now, we know. This is going to change everything. The way we think, the way we live, who we think we are. We can keep the lid on this for a short period of time, but eventually, this will become public, and then, Katy bar the door. Earth will become different, we will become different, and there is no way to stop it."

I am concerned that we don't know what we are in for, and at the same time, it's all very exciting.

A week later, back in Washington, D.C., in a top-level cabinet meeting: "Gentlemen, as your President, I need to emphasize the necessity for need to know. If I catch any of you leaking information, I will put you incommunicado in jail indefinitely. These are dangerous times not just for our country but also for the human race. We are dealing with an extraterrestrial life form that could be anything from friendly to deadly. Think of the possibilities. We could even be under consideration as a slave-labor source. Whomever we are dealing with is much higher on the technological status chain which puts us at a terrible disadvantage. If this to the public, they would panic, and our ability to govern would be compromised. So far, we know very little. The cavern they were in is hundreds of years old, and the two objects we have recovered are so far ahead of our technology that we can only guess at this time. Their spacecraft is estimated to be huge, and we know almost nothing about its capabilities except that it can travel long distances."

"Imagine this being the 1930s, and we find an Apple watch. We wouldn't have a chance of figuring it out. Now to what we are doing. The pictures we have had excellent resolution, and even though we only have a side picture of a guy bending in a hole, we have his hair color, body build, weight, good estimate on height, clothes, and shoe type. We have fifty FBI agents looking for him or his being missing. We have the local utilities notifying us on people missing their payments. Anyone missing all their payments at once could be our guy. Eventually, we will find out what we need. In the meantime, I have not notified the heads of any countries and don't plan to at this time. I want your ideas, so call me, day or night."

Chapter 6
Home Hunting

"Where are we headed, Simon? I need to know. I'm not along for just a ride."

"I'm going to park at a Lagrange point, Brad. We will be cloaked both visually and electronically, plus our sensors can catch any danger before we get into trouble. Space junk was never a problem, but it is now. The spacecraft skin will deflect small items, and my weapon systems will take care of the bigger concerns. Losing the cavern is disappointing. It was large enough, and all I had to do was cut in an entrance–exit port, reinforce the cavern itself, and set up an alarm system to warn me of any problems. There weren't many people there a hundred and twenty-five years ago, so I certainly wasn't likely to be found."

"We have arrived at the LaGrange Point," said Simon. "This is where the gravity between Earth and moon is equal and opposite, so we can sit here for the time being and do some planning."

"Simon, my government must now know that they have had visitors from beyond Earth and paranoia will no doubt be setting in. Also, I don't know if they will be looking for me specifically which is disconcerting as I have family there."

"Brad, this brings up a point. It is time for you to solidify your allegiance from here on out. You are my pick to eventually command this ship. Built in to my artificial intelligence is that an organic, human in this case, would be in charge of this spaceship and its missions. This is something you would phase into, and I would be your wingman so to speak. I need your commitment to go forward."

I knew I was going to wind up in this spot, thought Brad. *I had better play along until I can scope out the ramifications of all this and still wind up alive.*

"Simon, you have it. From here on out, I will consider us a team and myself as on-the-job training for command as I phase in this new position in my life. I now hold citizenship as a United States citizen, and I will reiterate that no Earth government should have access to all this technology. It will take time for us to get to know each other."

"Okay, Brad, we are together on this. This would be the time for me to embed my communications ability in you as we should never be unable to contact each other as we go forward. It is a simple procedure that will dramatically change your outlook regarding communications forever, and you will need to develop the mental discipline to manage it. Let's go back to the medical chamber."

"Brad, I am going to cut a small slit behind your right ear and insert an organic chip. Over the next few days, it will connect to your inner ear for both audio input and output. You trigger it with a mental keyword which you will learn to control. The signal propagates, with a range of three hundred thousand miles, directly with this ship and is undetectable by humans at this stage of their development. It will appear as a small benign growth in a medical X-ray. There will be a very small bump behind your ear for manual operation while you are learning the mental procedure. When turned on, it will sound slightly different to verify it is turned on."

"Simon, when will I first notice any activity with this implant?"

"Give it about three days at the most."

"Okay, I will. I am anxious to experience this type of communication. Speaking of which, Simon, are you able to monitor communications from where I lived in Bellevue, Washington? This might reveal what the government knows."

"Good idea, Brad. I will start collecting data right away."

Meanwhile, back on Earth, the government is frantically searching for an answer as to who fell in the hole, and back at DARPA, a team of key engineers and scientists are examining the two extraterrestrial objects. So far, they haven't had a clue, and the scientific method isn't helping them out at this stage. It's an exciting problem to have, but they keep remembering what is at stake here for the human race. The possibilities can range from the very good to the very bad, which causes sleepless nights.

The FBI agents think they may have the name of the person they are looking for as possibly identified by a local store.

Chapter 7
Communications

"Simon, I am in the CIC using my new communications. Do you receive me okay?"

"Yes, Brad, loud and clear. You receiving me okay?"

"Yes"

"Simon, this is fantastic, and so far, I see no side effects. Visual capability would be handy too. This is unbelievably exciting."

"We haven't talked about that yet, Brad. But visual implants are in my available list but with the same propagation distance. I have a way for you to connect to your Internet also."

"In the meantime, Brad, I have some news regarding your government and what they know. Apparently, they have a good picture of you with your head partially in the ground taken by a digital wildlife camera which they can extrapolate and wind up with your hair color, height, clothes, and shoe size and model, etc. They have over fifty agents aggressively looking for you; plus, they surprisingly have the two items I had to leave behind. This means they now have proof of extraterrestrial activity on Earth. Brad, your thoughts on this?"

"As I see the situation, Simon, I can show up in Bellevue as if nothing is wrong with an answer that says I dug a hole, found nothing, filled up the hole, and went on my way. Or I can disappear completely for now at least which is what I must do. If I go back, they could use drugs which is a strong possibility. They will feel that the human race is on the line, and this would let the authorities do just about anything to me. I can't take that chance, Simon."

"I agree, Brad. We should put some thought into planning our next move."

"Yes, Simon. We need to set some goals."

Chapter 8

Panic

Washington, D.C., the White House

THE PRESIDENT AND HIS CABINET. Damnit. One of you bastards violated security. Now, the Russians and Chinese demand to be let in.

NSA. Mr. President, our phones are bugged, and our homes are bugged. Our people use passwords like 1234 and can't seem to get the big picture on security. I did hear that the Russians and Chinese are actually flying in tomorrow, so we had better have a meeting agenda.

SECRETARY OF STATE. I suggest we put the Chinese and Russians in the same meeting. They deserve each other.

The FBI now had Brad Young's name, full photo, and background data—no rap sheet, middle-aged, and good education and list of accomplishments. He had never been in trouble with the law, minor traffic violations only. No information on how he might react under stress.

He was missing from his home, and the FBI suspected alien foul play. There are lots of questions and no answers yet.

Chapter 9

Hello, Earth

"Simon, I feel that there is increasing panic mostly due to fear of the unknown. I am thinking of contacting the president, let him know I am alive and well and that Earth has absolutely no reason to fear the extraterrestrial. I also want to let him know I will be in contact in exactly one month with more information. Your thoughts, Simon?"

"I agree with that. It will also signal him that the United States is the host country for your—our—activity which should quiet things down."

"Simon, is there any way to get a cloaked drone to peek through his White House office window while I am on the phone with him?"

"Yes, Brad, we do have something like that. It's about the size of a large fly, and it can be cloaked. It has a ten-day power supply and can transmit at one hundred miles. I'm listening to the White House switchboard now, and indications are that he will be in his office for the next three hours. I will be over the White House in ten minutes, cloaked and with stealth approach. Are you ready?"

"Yes, let's go Simon."

As Simon hovered, he released the bug drone which he guided to an office window. *Perfect*, he thought.

"Look at the display, Brad."

There was the president having a discussion with two other people.

"Okay, Brad. We are now hovering at twenty miles. I'm connecting you to his private direct number that has a unique ringtone. Be ready."

"Excuse me, gentlemen, have a seat. I need to get the phone," said the President.

"Hello? Mr. President, this is Brad Young. You and the FBI are looking for me. I am alive and well."

"Mr. Young, where are you? We need to pick you up immediately. How did you get this number?"

"Mr. President, I am with the extraterrestrial at this very time, and we want to assure you that the United States have absolutely nothing to worry about. By the way, are you alone?"

"Yes, damnit, I am alone."

"Mr. President, it is imperative that we are honest with each other at all times. Those two men with you question this honesty.

"Are you in my office?"

"The technology I am using is really advanced, Mr. President. Now, I will call you in exactly three weeks on this number and at this same time. Sleep well," Brad disconnects.

"Simon, can you bug his office?"

"Yes, but next time, plan ahead please. It's safer that way. I will send the bug we sent down around the front where it can slip in to the Oval Office. One moment, I just got it in, and even though it is cloaked, I will park it up high out of the way. It has its own intelligence to avoid the cleaning crew. Okay, Brad. Now I will find a safe parking within one hundred miles. Let's listen in."

"This is the president! What do you mean you can't trace that last caller?"

"Sir, what we would normally trace has been erased. If we do find anything, we will call you back."

The president hangs up the phone.

"How did he know you guys were here? The head of the FBI and NSA right in the room with me during the call and still no answers! Good thing I was on speakerphone, at least I have credible witnesses. I think."

"Okay, gentlemen, the good news is that we have heard from Brad Young, and if we can believe it, he states that he is with the extraterrestrial and is fine, and he will call back in exactly three weeks. The fact that he was watching me is most disturbing, and I don't know what to believe."

"I will gin up something for the Chinese and Russians. Let's go home."

"Okay, Mr. President."

In the spacecraft, Simon and Brad listened to the president's last comments.

"Well, Simon, he is up against the wall, and we had better keep close tabs on this. Keep monitoring Bellevue. I want to keep in touch there also."

Chapter 10

Posturing

Washington, D.C., Oval Office. The
president, SECDEF, FBI, and NSA

"Gentlemen, I believe we had better plan ahead and put some things in place before Brad Young calls me in two more weeks. He has a son and daughter, both married and each with two children. I want four agents on hand at each location to put them all in a high-security safe house. I want our agents ready to move on a moment's notification. Let's get that set up now, and I want all the technology we have available to try and trace his call. Any questions?"

"No, sir."

"Then get moving."

Spacecraft: Simon and Brad Young cloaked and
hovering fifty miles above the White House

"Wow, Simon," said Brad. "He is planning hardball right to start with. Dangerous guy."

"Yeah, Brad, and now your whole family is involved. What are your ideas?"

"Simon, we have a scientific-research station, Amundsen Station in Antarctica. It's so cold there that it is only accessible for a small period each year which means it is not accessible right now except for us. All the personnel there hunker down and try to avoid any emergencies. I want to kidnap all of the government personnel waiting to grab my family, render them unconscious, and get them into the Antarctica facility just before I talk to the president. Is this possible?"

"Yes, Brad, but it is dangerous because of the close timing. We assume four agents at each of your children's property, but there could be more! In my robot form, I can render them unconscious and get them on the ship. Since your children's families are located both in Portland, Oregon, and close to each other, the time needed will be short. It shouldn't take more than half an hour. Another half an hour to get them to the Antarctica station and twenty minutes to return to Washington DC. Aren't you glad I have inertial damping?"

"Yes. And, Simon, we need some way to keep our contact with the White House while we are more than one hundred miles in distance from our bugs, especially if things go wrong."

"Brad, I can put up a small cloaked satellite that will transpond the signals to wherever we are for this mission."

"That's good to know. Simon, we really need to spend some time together, so I am totally up to date on all your capabilities. A lot has happened too fast, and I feel unprepared. Let's get some more bugs in the White House, so we aren't so blind."

"Simon, how many of what I call your robot suites do you have ready to go?"

"Four, Brad, and I can operate four at one time. Can you make them look more human?"

"Yes, on that too, and I know what you are thinking. We would boost our odds with one me for each agent. Simon, if all four robots were instantly destroyed, you would be alright, wouldn't you?"

"Yes, the entity, me, is in the ship and fully protected."

"Where, Simon, did you get those robot outfits anyway?"

"I made them, Brad. You humans have just really gotten into 3D printing or manufacturing. I have had that as a ship capability since I was put in service. Its capabilities are extremely advanced, and I can probably make or modify whatever we need."

"Simon, I am having second thoughts on Antarctica. If I do that, I push the president into a corner of no return, and it would be war from then on. I believe a better outcome would be for us to put all their unconscious agents in an empty room in the White House and let them wake up naturally. We will leave their weapons and phones with them as a show of superiority. Now, we don't need that satellite to transpond our signals, but let's put it up anyway just in case. Okay, Simon, how are you going to put all these agents unconscious?"

"Easy. I have ray-type weapon you can call the buzz that is non-lethal on a low setting. They will wake in approximately one hour with headaches but no damage. The high setting on this weapon is lethal to humans."

"Good, Simon. That will let us take out anyone else without killing anyone. Let's get ready."

Chapter B

Make Simon

Before their devastating war, Melthorne had big plans much like Earth did when it built the International Space Station (ISS). On Melthorne, the top scientists from several countries got together and decided to design and build the prototype for the next-generation spacecraft. They had already reached out in space with their first spacecraft which was piloted by a sapient artificial-intelligence unit and armed with first-generation weapons. It contained a food processor, powerful level 1 medical unit, and their very successful inertial damping unit which was literally a lifesaver. It had a strong body made of steel and titanium alloyed with other trace elements.

They named this new project *The Simon Project*. Its size was one hundred and fifty feet in diameter and fifty feet high. Their new hull alloy, neutronium, was used inside and out which was very strong and yet could flow. It had a touch sense and could literally heal itself. It was an enormous breakthrough. The most powerful weapon system yet was added, many other features and systems newly developed, and their biggest accomplishment of all, a new artificial intelligence—AI, which had thousands of times the power of their first AI. They installed this unit and set it to mimic their sapient AIs as they wanted to spend a great deal of time and effort bringing this new unit up to full capability. They did a secret test flight checkout, and everything passed with flying colors. War seemed close, so they locked their new toy in a hidden hangar, and as an afterthought one of the AI programmers added a failsafe that, upon certain conditions, would enable the full-dormant capabilities of their new AI.

Chapter 11
Discussion

Brad and Simon started out in Portland near the motel where four FBI agents were getting ready to take Brad's son and his family into custody and to a safe house. The four-cloaked robotic Simons were lowered with a gravity shaft in the alley next to the motel. So far, nobody else was around and all four went to the FBI agents room and knocked on the door. When the door was opened, they rushed in pushing the agents to the floor. All four fired their buzz weapons, silently knocking out the FBI agents. Like the well-tuned team, they were they quickly carried the unconscious agents to the alley where the gravity shaft lifted everyone into the ship.

At a similar motel, near Brad's daughter's home, their timing was early. Also, there were only three FBI agents. They couldn't question the agents they had as all of them were unconscious, so they put an A/V bug in the room, lifted up to the ship, and rushed off to Washington, D.C. When they arrived at one hundred feet over the White House, they found all entrances crowded and one agent guarding the White House roof.

"Change of plans, Simon. We are twenty minutes away from my call, so let's render the agent who was on the roof unconscious also and lower the seven agents we have down to the center of the roof. Fortunately, the weather is fine, so we won't make them uncomfortable except for their egos. Three minutes to my call to the president. Any data from the bug in Portland?"

"No, Brad. All quiet."

"Okay, Simon. Connect me to the president."

Ring, Ring.

"Hello, Mr. President. This is Brad Young."

"Hello, Brad, you are right on time. As we talked about last time, I wanted to assure you that the extraterrestrial is in no way hostel to the human race or its governments, and down the road, there is the possibility of technology transfer."

"Brad, that would be wonderful, but I need to talk with you in person!"

"That is not possible at this time Mr. President, but it could be in the not-so-distant future."

"Damn it, Brad. I AM YOUR PRESIDENT, and I want you here in the next two days!"

"Mr. President, I don't feel comfortable with that schedule. We first need to build trust. Trust that we don't have yet. Placing FBI agents near my home, so you can put my children and their families in a safe house destroys trust."

"Brad, I don't know where you got that idea."

"Mr. President, ask the FBI agents on the roof of your White House! I will call you back in twenty minutes!"

"Simon, I want to keep close tabs on our bugs, including Portland. I am concerned about the missing agent there. I need the president to quit playing games or we are going to need to take a much more difficult approach. Okay, Simon, reconnect me please."

"Hello, Mr. President. Did you find your FBI agents?"

"Yes, Brad, and while I am pissed, I find my agents came to no harm. I don't know how you pulled this off, but you are obviously using very advanced technology. And somehow, you seem to know what I am doing which I don't like. Let's work together. I have some situations where I could use your help. I will discontinue keeping surveillance on your family unless you would like us to keep a couple of agents in place?"

"I would like that, Mr. President. The technology I am dealing with could move us years ahead and yet great harm would come with its misuse. The human race, so far, gets poor grades for getting along with each other. We can discuss this in more depth in my next call which will be in four weeks."

"Simon, what kind of weapons do you have? In all the excitement and wonder I find I need to know much more about."

"Brad, we have four cannons spaced around the ship. Each can electronically pivot to cover one hundred and eighty degrees vertically and horizontally. It shoots out a shielded modified neutron beam at light speed that is modulated by two interwoven high-frequency signals. We refer to it as simply an enhanced particle beam or just particle beam. There are a lot more details in its design, so this is essentially an overview. The strongest force in nature is the force that holds particles together in the atomic nucleus, and it also is the force that holds quarks together in elementary particles. That is the force that our enhanced particle beam interrupts resulting in instant havoc and mass destruction. There is no wounding with this weapon, only killing. We can use the same ports to shoot an exawatt EMP beam to shut down enemy spacecraft functions, and finally, we have a third option of an extremely high-power laser beam which melts almost anything it touches. So, that's three beam weapons: particle, EMP, and laser. I can, when needed, fire alternately out of the same port using a mix of two- or three-type beams. There has not been any testing, so there is no guarantee that all this will work as planned.

"Brad, we better install the visual component of our communications system while we have the time. Let's go back to the medical bay, and I will explain as it is it is installed. This unit is slightly bigger than the audio unit and connects to your optic nerve over a two-week period and will look unremarkable in an X-ray, although I recommend you avoid any doctors. I can take are of any medical problems here. You are now controlling your audio unit mentally with no problem, and the visual unit will connect to your audio unit which will simplify your mental control. Things will look accurate but slightly different to let you know it is working. By the way, some heavy elements can block transmissions, so beware. Lead is one of the most offending elements.

"And for the future, you will need to go through a rejuvenation process which would be a major change for you. Many humans on my home planet live well over six hundred years, and that number is increasing every year. We had long ago cured all cancers and had developed an understanding of the aging process. I see your scientists have developed CRISPR or clustered regularly interspaced short palindromic repeats and are advancing to where they will be able to modify people and also the characteristics of the unborn. We did that long ago. We found the biggest problems were social, like, who and how many qualify for treatment. What happens when people outlive family and friends as you would have the short lived and are in essence the immortals.

"One caveat here. The ongoing war effort on Melthorne has precluded adequate testing of the rejuvenation process. This must be done as soon as possible.

"The birth rate needed to be drastically lowered or we would have outgrown our planet. These factors tore us apart and almost destroyed our civilization. We developed space technology with the plan to spread out to other planets with our home planet in control, the planet I am unable to now contact.

"Brad, the initial change for you would reset your cells from middle age your time to about thirty where you would age very slowly. You would look much younger and act much younger. Your children would no doubt notice and possibly figure out what is happening. I think I can figure out a way to disguise that. We can't introduce rejuvenation into your planet as they haven't even learned how to not destroy each other yet. How do you feel about all this?"

"Simon, I do agree with all your arguments and it's a lot to think about and a lot of guilt to take on because of my children. I want to proceed, and we can discuss all this along the way."

"Yes, we will Brad. I can help you prepare for the whole process. You can avoid losing your humanity, but you are also going to feel different. All part of the growth process."

Chapter 12

War

"Wake up, Brad! How are you feeling with the implant surgery?"

"Fine, Simon, just a little tired. You are lucky you never need to sleep."

"Brad, your need for sleep will diminish as we process your rejuvenation."

"I have been continually monitoring the president, FBI, and all those connected with us. Apparently, they think they are safe with their encryption which I can instantly decode with my own quantum-computing ability. They have two FBI agents on each of your children and have decided to play fair."

They are desperately trying to contain the situation. China and Russia are trying to find out details and have found out that DARPA may have samples of extraterrestrial technology. On top of all this, North Korea keeps running tests with new long-ranged rockets and threatening the United States with annihilation and total destruction. They do have two satellites circling the planet, and I know from my eavesdropping and decryption that one of them contains an EMP bomb ready to drop on command which would put the United States back into the Stone Age!"

"No wonder, Simon, the president is up against the wall. I know that it would be unwise to openly step in, but we could sabotage that situation and say nothing. Do you have any ideas?"

"Yes, Brad. I do. We can disable his satellites in such a way that they keep orbiting Earth but will accept no commands. All circuitry inside the satellites and inside the bomb will be fused and useless, and we can do the same with his rockets and nuclear weapons as well as his guns pointed toward South Korea. Our EMP cannon will take care of this, and its beam is invisible. He will not have any evidence of who did what."

"This will possibly save a war. Simon, let's get started."

"Okay, Brad. We are nearing a position where we can zap his satellites. I will set the beam diameter for one meter and one thousand megajoules. A ten-second hit on each satellite will do the job."

"Done."

"Okay, now down to his cannons. From altitude, we will set up a beam of thirty meters at five hundred megajoules. A two-second hit on each cannon will fry any electronics in the area. We will simultaneously and independently fire our laser beam from our adjacent ship cannon to explode his ammunition. I have located forty stockpiles of ammunition so far, so this will take a few minutes. The EMP beam will immediately cut off all their communications and kill any electronics on the more modern cannons. Most of the older cannons will suffer from the ammo explosions that will also temporarily fry enemy minds."

"Okay, Brad. Our automatic sighting-and-firing-weapons system worked as expected, and the damage caused by the explosions will also slow down their aggressive behavior."

"Now, we zap all the equipment at his launch sites, including rocket boosters and equipment elevators. One more item. We will fire a full-power EMP down each elevator shaft along with a laser beam which will fuse and destroy the electronics all the way down."

"Apparently," said Simon, "that caused quite a few explosions, Brad, so they know they are in trouble. Their radio chatter from the few radios that still work is off the scale, and it is pandemonium down there. Let's go back to the DMZ and take a look."

The ammo dump explosions lit up the sky. The cloaked spacecraft watched as the cannon encampments were virtually destroyed.

"Brad, you can just tell the weapon what you want done, and it will take care of all the settings. I wanted to show you some of the details the first time."

"This is what a fully equipped spacecraft can do, Brad. They can't see us, hear us, or detect us, so they know how they have been defeated. This will stop them from starting a war that would have killed tens of millions of people. Now, we listen and see how everyone reacts. China and Russia may suspect us, but they will have no direct proof. The United States will suspect outside help but can't prove anything."

"I agree, so let's call the President. Put a call through Simon."

"Hello, Mr. President. Busy night?"

"Holy shit, Brad, was that you?"

"Mr. President, for good health of the country, I suggest you keep a lid on what you, no doubt, are thinking. It would certainly be best if China and Russia think that North Koreans were sloppy, and you can drop signals that the United States has developed new weapons under the highest security. If they suspect extraterrestrial assistance, all hell will break loose. I can vouch for this communication line to you as secure, but you take a grave risk with anyone you tell. Just keep an all-knowing smile on your face no matter what pressure comes your way. Try and put most of the blame or credit on others. They will suspect but without proof, that's all they can do for now. Tell China you appreciate all their assistance whatever it was—like you're giving them credit. This will help with the confusion."

"Brad, I don't know what you have done, but you may have saved a lot of good people from dying in a terrible war. Please, keep in close touch. You can only imagine my thoughts."

"I will call you back in two days, Mr. President. Goodbye."

"Simon, I know you are monitoring chatter. What's the general state of affairs?"

"Total pandemonium and confusion, Brad. The U.S. and South Korean troops at the DMZ went into North Korea and took charge. There are many dead North Korean soldiers. The artillery emplacements are a complete mess and unusable. The rocket-launching sites are out of service for the foreseeable future. There are many dead in their underground networks, but no details, and they have not yet discovered their satellite status. We will know if they try to send any satellite commands. No data on their dear leader. If he is alive, he is probably hiding or trying to get out of his country. Not much information."

"Good, Simon. We will keep monitoring all involved, plus we need to keep close tabs on China and Russia."

"Simon, the president and I will probably need to meet in the not-too-distant future. Let's keep that in mind.

News, Brad. The North Koreans have discovered that their older cannons that didn't rely on electronics still worked! They did get a few shots off that and killed a few people in the South, but it was minimal and short lived as their ammo stores were destroyed, and the U.S. and South Korean troops had arrived and stopped any more enemy action."

Chapter 13

Female

"Simon, it's time to call the president again. Also, I just experienced a two-second visual flash of the president working alone in his office?"

"Brad, that is your visual implant beginning to attach itself. You apparently received a signal from the bug in his office. Good time to call since he is alone."

"Hello, Mr. President."

"Hello, Brad. So far, I have been able to contain any extraterrestrial connection, but the rumors are wild. The South Koreans are engaged in a mop-up operation while they have a chance, and the UN is sending a contingent force over to monitor which may assist in stabilizing the situation. South Korea did get some damage but minimal and fighting has stopped.

"Also, Brad, DARPA has gotten nowhere with the alien sample they have, and I am getting requests from their top materials engineer for a meeting with someone that might have information or ideas as to what it might be. I gave her your name, and she looked you up at DARPA. This might get some of the heat off you. I have removed your name from any documents that point to you as a person of interest, and you can handle the situation as you see fit. Do you want to tackle that?"

"Sure, Mr. President, maybe I can disarm some of the suspicions. What is his contact information?"

"It's a her, and her name is Ann Thompson. The switchboard at DARPA will track her down for you. I still want you and I to meet Brad, so give my request some thought please."

"Okay, Mr. President. I will be in touch."

"Well, Simon, it seems like I am going to need to leave the sanctuary of the spacecraft for a short period of time. What are the chances of sending an android human with me? We have never discussed this before, so can your android pass for a human?"

"Yes, although I have not done this before. I can correct and refine mannerisms and speech on the fly, so to speak. There should be no characteristics that say nonhuman. The android will be me communicating with the android body of course. I will choose to display an average face that can't be remembered well. I will be cloaked and nearby with the ship ready to go."

"Okay, Simon, go ahead and get prepared. We will use my home, so you and I can get there an hour before the meeting. It will take her at least a day to get to Bellevue from DARPA. I'll give her a call now. I suspect she is very anxious to meet."

"Hello? DARPA Headquarters. Who do you wish to speak to?"

"Ann Thompson, please."

"And who may I say is calling?"

"Brad Young."

"Just a moment please, it will take a couple of minutes to locate her."

"Hello, Mr. Young, this Ann Thompson, thank you for calling. Yes, I am looking for help and ideas. When and where can we meet?"

"Well, Miss Thompson, I live in Bellevue, Washington. Are you planning on being out this way in the near future?"

"Yes, I have a good reason. I graduated from the University of Washington, and I need to pick up some research, so I could hop on a plane in the morning and be there tomorrow afternoon. Where shall we meet Mr. Young."

"Call me, Brad, please."

"And I'm Ann."

"Okay, Ann, let's meet at my home. We can decide where to have dinner from there if you like?"

"I'm game, Brad. You come highly recommended. I will rent a car and be at your home around six this Thursday. What is your address?"

"It's 15625 Reseda Circle, 98006.

"Thanks, see you tomorrow."

"Okay, Simon, now we need to figure how to fit you in. Any suggestions?"

"Yes, Brad. I do. I want to be extremely cautious. There is a lot at risk here. We should get to your house early afternoon tomorrow. I want to add some outside A/V bugs, and I will set up one of our armed humanoid robots in the garage. I will have the ship cloaked and hovering at low altitude, ready to grab us and run if needed."

The next day Brad, Simon Android, and one robot descended down the gravity elevator from the cloaked ship to behind Brad's garage. The area had been cleared first to assure there were no prying eyes, human or electronic. One camera had been found, and it was made to malfunction. Brad let the robot into the garage via a side door, and Brad and Simon now the android slipped into the house through the back door.

Good, everything going smoothly so far, thought Brad.

The robot, who looked human in a rough sort of way, except for close inspection, was heavy with neutronium body parts and impervious to just about any weapon quietly exited the garage and installed vidcams in strategic locations. They had two-way audio and could dissolve upon command. The robot went back in the garage to wait for visitors.

"Simon," said Brad, "I'm going to order food to be delivered, might be too risky to go to a restaurant. All this caution may be silly, but the alternative could be bad."

Simon and Brad talked about future tools and equipment they might need when the surveillance equipment warned of an approaching car coming up the driveway. The vidcam showed a woman ringing the doorbell. Brad could actually see this output from the vidcam through his implant! Wow, what great technology. Brad opened the door, and there stood an extremely attractive woman with a gorgeous smile.

"Hello, I'm Ann Thompson. You must be Brad?"

"I am. Please, come in. Let me take your coat. Here, let's go sit in the library and relax. Can I get you a drink?"

"Brad, a Diet Coke would be great if you have it?"

"I do, Ann. Be right back. Oh, before he leaves, Simon, come on in. Let me introduce one of my neighbors. Simon Jones, meet Ann Thompson. I just got back from a trip, and Simon has been watching the house for me."

"Where are you from, Ann?" asked Simon Jones.

"Arlington, Virginia. Let me get those drinks. Simon, why don't you stay for a little bit."

"Okay, Ann, here is your Diet Coke, and I'm having the same."

"Brad, what a beautiful place you have. And so peaceful and relaxing."

Warning! We are being laser scanned.

Someone is looking for audio off the windows.

Armed personnel approaching!

Simon, whispered Brad, using his audio implant, *probably not the president, doubt if other parts of our government, so other governments more probably. Get the ship, we grab Ann, go outside the house door to behind garage up into ship now.*

"Ann, we are under attack! Come quick."

"Brad, what's happening?"

Brad grabbed Ann's arm and rushed her out the door. It was almost dark now, and Brad with Ann in tow and Simon Android rushed to the spot where they landed. The robot humanoid joined them as he fired several laser shots back behind him. The whole group was quickly elevated up into the spacecraft. The ship rushed up and away at high G-force but with only one G inside the spacecraft due to the inertial damping system.

Brad and Ann were in the observation deck of the spacecraft, and Ann Thompson was in shock, her face paper white. She saw Earth diminish in size as they reached two thousand miles where they stopped and hovered. The robot and android had disappeared into a utility zone of the ship, so it was just Ann, Brad, and the voice of the ship, Simon.

"Ann, one hell of a first date, isn't it," said Brad.

She just looked at Brad incredulously.

"Please tell me what is going on. What just happened? What have I gotten mixed up in?"

"Well, Ann, we were all set to discuss your artifact and enjoy a good get-acquainted meal together when we were suddenly under attack from an enemy that would cause us harm and possibly death. The enemy was after the technology of the spacecraft you are now in. By the way, there is a third presence with us, Simon, not my neighbor but the spacecraft. He is a sentient artificial intelligence located throughout the ship. The robot and the android neighbor you met were extensions of him. Ann, say something. Your turn to talk."

"Brad, now I know where the artifact came from. Where did this spacecraft come from?"

"Ann, this is Simon."

"I came here from far way to explore. I was injured by an enemy and spent one hundred and twenty years hidden to give me time to recover. At the end of this time Brad stumbled onto me, and now, we are a team."

"Simon, what do you mean you are a team? Brad, aren't you a citizen of the USA?"

"Yes, Ann. I want you to get some sleep and think about all that has happened. We can talk in the morning."

"Yes, I guess so. You have coffee for breakfast in this joint?"

"Yes, we do, fresh from the food replicator," said Brad. "Let me show you to the sleeping area."

"Okay, Simon, she is asleep for now. What have you picked up on chatter?"

"Well, Brad, it looks like the Russians decided to see what they could find out about any new technology. They were poorly organized and got nothing, and they never detected our escape."

"Great. I better call the president."

"Simon, I can see him via the bug."

"Brad, you are healing fast. Also, I have dropped the ship down to one hundred miles over the White House. And Brad, try to think a message. It's like controlled messaging."

"Okay, Simon. Let's call the president."

"Hello, Mr. President."

"Hello, Brad. What is going on at your home? I have sent agents there."

"Mr. President, I had Ann Thompson meet me there. She had just arrived when we got jumped by Russians, don't know anymore. They were playing hardball, and we escaped and took Ann with us."

"Where are you now?"

"Absolutely safe and out of reach. I need you to grab my family, adults and children, and keep them safe. We still need to keep highest security while we can. I will get you a switch that will let you call me whenever you need to.

"I will get right on it, Brad. I had better get started. I do have two agents each at your son and daughter's homes. I will alert them, get more agents involved, and get them moved immediately."

"Mr. President, tell them I will brief them soon, please."

"Okay, Brad. Goodbye."

"Goodbye, Mr. President."

"Simon, we need to get a call switch to the President. How fast can we do this?"

"One day to make Brad, and I will have a secure drone deliver it."

Chapter 14

Life Onboard

"Good morning, Ann. How did you sleep?"

"Toss and turn, Brad. Toss and turn. Then, I woke up and spent a few minutes trying to convince myself that I wasn't dreaming. Where are we?"

"We are hovering a hundred miles over the White House, Ann. We are also undetectable and safe. I talked to the president, told him what happened and that you were safe."

"You mean he knows about this spacecraft? Not about the spacecraft, Ann, but about extraterrestrial life here that means no harm to us. The president alone knows. He doesn't plan to share any information. If other governments found out, there would be war, and our own government could not keep this a secret. Your thoughts on this?"

"Get me some coffee, please, and I will be able to talk Brad."

"Already poured. Here."

"Hey, this is good. What brand do you buy?"

"None, Ann. We have a food replicator."

"Those really exist?"

"Yup."

"Brad, I delivered the call switch, and the president is now testing it," Simon said.

"Let's answer it. Hello, Mr. President."

"Hello, Brad, the switch works."

"Good, I feel better now. Mr. President, I have Ann Thompson sitting beside me, and you're on speakerphone."

"Hello, Ann, you have had an exciting twenty-four hours."

"Yes, Mr. President. Could you call my boss please and let him know I am on an errand for you? I need some more time here."

"Yes, Ann, I will do that. Brad, your family is in the most secure safe house we have, and they do have questions. We even brought their cats and dogs along which was no easy job."

"Thank you, Mr. President. I will get to them within a week."

"Okay, Brad. I also had an agent stay and guard their houses. Goodbye for now."

"Goodbye, Mr. President."

"Brad, where are we going with all this? What do you and Simon envision my role?"

"Ann, you weren't supposed to find out, but the situation we got into nixed that. Three humans know what countries would kill for. Me, the president, and now you. How do you feel about that? What would you like to do? Are you in a position to do what you might like to do?"

"All good questions, Brad. I'm adventurous, thirty-four, have a bachelor's degree in physics and a masters in chemical engineering. As far as I know, I'm in good health. I like to travel, and Simon could provide the best travel available. I was engaged three years ago, and my fiancé died of cancer, and all of my important relatives have passed on. This is all very sudden, but my decision would be to sign on. I have mostly made good decisions in my life, and opportunities like this are almost nonexistent. Is this too quick for you, guys? I'm still afraid I might wake up and find out this is all a dream!"

"Not for me, Ann. How about you, Simon?"

"I'm okay with this new crew, Brad. I detected all the right readings as she spoke. Welcome aboard, Ann. When do you need to pick up your belongings from your home."

"The sooner, the better, Simon, but no immediate emergency."

"Okay, counting Simon, we have a crew of three. Ann, at the end of the week, I will inform the president. Also, you need to sleep in the medical bay tonight," said Brad. "Simon has a setup that will identify any physical anomalies, and then they can be eliminated. Apparently, the biological entities on his planet were very similar to humans, so we are able to take advantage of his advanced knowledge. They developed a cure for all cancers a long time ago as just one example of their knowledge. And yes, this will extend life dramatically."

Simon was looking forward to a dedicated unit or crew, and they discussed some of the future possibilities and opportunities they might have.

Ann woke up the next morning, remembering she was in the medical bay.

Simon's voice spoke up: "Good morning, Ann. How do you feel?"

"Great, Simon. I am just starting to get used to hearing you as a disembodied voice or coming from one of your humanlike forms. Do you have my medical results?"

"Yes Ann, I do. You are generally in great shape, and your youth comes through for you. You do, however, have the very beginning of ovarian cancer."

"OMG! That is really scary, Simon."

"I understand, Ann. My medical system has generated a medication which I will inject in you that will cure all your concerns. By the end of the week, you should be cancer-free which I will verify."

"Simon, you have no idea how wonderful that is. Is there any chance we could pass this on to Earth?"

"Actually, yes. We all will talk about this in the near future. Our list of subjects to discuss is getting quite long. It would be possible to give the president this cure as a gift when we see him."

Chapter C

Save the Technology

Scientists all over Melthorne were aghast. They were essentially a highly educated and peaceful group, and they recognized that their civilization could collapse with all their accomplishments becoming scattered or lost as war took over. They looked to Dr. Will Zorg as their leader and guide as he was thought of as chief scientist for the whole planet, independent of politicians and politics.

Society was coming unraveled, and all their greedy leaders could do was try to make sure they got the rejuvenation treatments. The scientists, who were instrumental in making Simon and his new systems had developed all the new medical technology, gathered together in a secret location, as a last-ditch effort to determine how they might save what they had accomplished. They decided to use Simon as an ark and install copies of everything they had and could gather into his memory bay with safeguards that only an advanced AI could unlock. They also stocked his stores with whatever they thought he might need over a long period of time and added the materials to make four robots that could link with the AI.

The biologists and biotechnologist also added a new android unit they had developed to work specifically with an advanced AI. They installed the most advanced 3-D manufacturing capability they had to complete the upgrades and then added the instructions for everything to Simon's AI memory partition in his yet unused advanced memory. They were awed by what they had accomplished for ninety-five percent of their planet's technology was gathered in one place in Simon's memory bay. The originals, including cloud backups, were disappearing fast in the fog of the war, and people were now dying by the billions of starvation and disease. They didn't see much hope for their survival and thought maybe Simon could help save another planet if all else fails. They, in effect, did shove Simon out the door toward Earth which was chosen as one of the hundred planets they had identified as a planet that might support life. They had given him orders to secretly explore the planet and gather data, thinking this would keep him hidden until such time they might recover and then they would recall him.

They certainly had no idea that he might get shot down. Simon, on Earth, was sent a timed release of chatter indicating that tells his home planet might have been destroyed or might not be habitable for the indefinite future and that over half the population is dead. This was done to keep him away until recalled.

The spacecraft on Melthorne are first generation, similar but smaller than Simon, and their AIs are of the type that Simon originally was. The remaining planet leaders know that their large-sized experimental spacecraft is missing and have a general idea of where it went, and they plan to go after it as soon as possible. The remaining scientists know for sure where Simon should be, and they want to avoid any of the surviving corrupt leaders getting ahold of the technology again as they will use it for strictly their own greedy ends and to continue the war. Fortunately, Chief Scientist Dr. Will Zorg is still alive as he had received the rejuvenation treatment as had many of his fellow scientists and their families. Their loyalty was to Dr. Zorg and in the effort to try to get Melthorne heading back to what it once was.

Meanwhile, the former leader and dictator of Melthorne, Grouse Hemler, was consolidating all his remaining old gang and confiscating as many weapons, including spacecraft, so he could build his military. The spacecraft all needed major repairs from the war which would take six months at least to put together the armada needed to find the Simon Spacecraft. He needed to quash all the remaining uprisings and find the treasure trove of technology on the missing Simon Spacecraft at any cost. He also had received only the first half of the rejuvenation treatments which would not get him anywhere near six hundred years life extension possible and one hundred and twenty-five years had already passed. He was frantic, vengeful, greedy, and totally corrupt.

On Earth, Simon senses that the Melthorne people are in total confusion from the interstellar chatter and realizes he must prepare Earth for a fight, not just for himself but also for the humans. His loyalty is to Earth and the human race. You would think his loyalty would have been to Melthorne, but when he awoke, he was sentient and as he grew up, so to speak learning about the human race from radio and television, he chose humans. After all, the majority of his education was from human existence. He is just starting to realize also that he is an independent being which at first is confusing. There is a lot to consider. He had no experience to call on to determine what this all meant!

Chapter 15

The Next Morning

"Good morning, Brad. Good morning, Ann."

"Good morning, Simon," said Ann. "Again, I am amazed at the capabilities of the food replicator."

"Me, too" said Brad.

"Well, crew, we have some time so let's go over a few items," said Simon. "The first item is privacy. I can hear and sometimes see you at any time, but my conscious mind will not be aware of what you are saying unless you call my name or if your voice indicates distress. You are monitored on a subconscious level, so your personal privacy is maintained. Also, my sensors around the ship are extremely sensitive, so I am aware of your heart beating, again on a subconscious level, and I would only be notified if there was a problem. Any problems with this?"

"No," said Ann.

"Not from me," said Brad. "We have a lot to get used to, so this is all part of our learning process."

"I do want to embed our A/V comm unit in you, Ann, starting with the audio. Tonight would be a good time, and Brad can fill you in on the features. And I am outlining the details for the first phase of the rejuvenation process for both of you. It is very similar to what was used on my home planet and will take place over a period of a year. At the end of the first phase, you both will feel and look younger, your strength will have been increased, and your need for sleep will have been decreased," said Simon.

"Brad," asked Simon, "how do you plan to take care of your family situation?"

"I don't know yet, Simon. The president has been downplaying and minimizing my involvement, including modifying records, but this still leaves a lot of information. Plus, my family is in a safe house, so I need to talk to them real soon. I want to get the President here in the next couple of days, and then, I can finalize my plan for my family. Simon, I need an acceptable, no, make that workable plan to get the president onboard the spacecraft without the secret service going nuts. How about we set it up, so they know in advance that they will be out of communications with their home unit for twelve hours. We can collect all their cellphones and comm units while they are onboard. And as far as the three agents required to actually be with the president, can't we erase their memories when they leave? I feel the president would go along with that, and we can give him a show he would never forget."

"Ambitious plan, Brad," said Simon. "We can make it work. The details of how we get him onboard could be tricky, and we can't let anything go wrong. We are dependent upon the president telling no one and being honest with us which, from what you have told me, is asking a lot from a politician. If we get crossed and wind up with his military coming at us, they will lose very badly. One thing I would like to do is embed him with our audio comm unit which would help keep us forewarned plus show his location. This would probably mean putting his secret service guys in sleep mode for a short period of time. A more-risky approach would be to get him to agree to an embed unit. If anyone tried to cut it out of him, it would dissolve, and they are at least fifty years away from developing that technology on their own."

"Simon, I vote for the aboveboard plan of getting him to go along with the embed unit and take the risk that he might say no. Ann, you haven't said a word? What are your ideas? After all, you are a team member now."

"Wow," Brad. "I hadn't really thought about the type of missions we would take on. We are the good guys, so I just have to expand my thinking. I certainly will support and backup whatever we do. Sign me up!"

"Okay, Simon and Ann, we are go. I will call the president and get this mission started."

Chapter 16
President Onboard

"Hello, Mr. President. I'm calling early. Is this a good time?"

"Just a moment please," he said.

To his office visitors: "Gentlemen, I need the office. I will be in touch."

"Yes, Mr. President."

"Okay, Brad. I'm alone now. Are we secure?"

"Yes. You wanted to meet. How about tomorrow?"

"You are quick, Brad. I will make tomorrow work, whatever it takes. How do we do this?"

"Mr. President, what is the minimum number of secret service agents for your protection you can get away with."

"Three, Brad. They do have the authority to manage my protection to stop me from doing something they consider dangerous or foolish, so what are we up against here?"

"Well, Mr. President, I want to bring you onboard the spacecraft, so you can see for yourself what and who you are dealing with, and I need to do this in such a way that no one is aware of any spacecraft or thinks you are missing for a twelve-hour period of time. The spacecraft has cloaking capability, so I can get close to pick you up. I can drop you off after our meeting, and your agents will have a non-incidental type of amnesia, so only you will remember all the details of the meeting. Oh, and bring your call switch, so we can update our communications protocol."

"Brad, the safest location for us to pull this off is Camp David. It has a totally controlled perimeter and airspace, so if your spacecraft can surreptitiously navigate within those parameters, we are in business."

"Brad, sometime ago you mentioned trust. I am trusting my life in your hands as you no doubt realize. Everything is at stake here, and all of this has got to remain the best-kept secret for as long as possible."

"I agree, Mr. President. I need an exact time and GPS coordinates for a location. Please keep your Secret Service agents calm as all of you are lifted into the spacecraft. It will be similar to an elevator, and all of a sudden you will be inside, and we will depart immediately."

"Brad, I will contact you in one hour with the time and location. Goodbye for now. I have a lot to do to get ready."

"Goodbye, Mr. President.

"Brad, I have looked at a detailed map of Camp David, and there are several locations we can work with. There is no doubt that there are many cameras located throughout the area, and we can easily freeze them during our extraction."

"Thank you, Simon. Once we get the president's data, we can plan the details."

"What role am I to play in this meeting, Brad?" Ann asked.

"Now that you have joined the crew which consists of you, I, and Simon, you will, soon enough, be heavily involved in technical projects."

"This brings up another point, Brad," said Ann. "The president probably thinks of the extraterrestrial as a flesh-and-blood being and not a sentient artificial intelligence being. If we want to promote that concept we need to roll out Mr. Android. Otherwise, the president has to come to grips with several concepts all at once, and he could have difficulty making the jump. After all, we are only going to have him for twelve hours.

"Good thinking, Ann," said Brad. "I agree. How about you, Simon?"

"This had not occurred to me, Brad. I will be ready with my android self."

Chapter 17

Extraction Day

"Okay," said Brad. "The president has given us the time and coordinates, and it's only a half-hour away. Any last questions?"

"Yes," said Ann. "Who is going to put the Secret Service guys into 'sleep mode'?"

"That will be me, Ann," said Simon. "I will have a buzz unit built into my right hand. I will seat them in a chair and quickly put my hand on each one which will instantly knock them out. As I am doing that, Brad, you and Ann need to keep the president assured that everyone is safe, and he is in no danger. This is going to be quite a trip for him.

"Okay, everyone, we are approaching the extraction point and right on time," said Simon. I have located several security cameras which I have turned off until we have departed. It would not be good for the guards to have pictures of three Secret Service agents and the president floating up from the ground. The president supposedly has prepared his agents for what comes next. We are to find out about now. Okay, I see the four of them on the ground. We have an opening in the spacecraft waiting and a gravity elevator to bring them up. The ship is configured to bring them straight to us here in the observation deck."

"Gentlemen, welcome aboard. How was your trip?" said Simon Android. The ship quickly closed up and departed to a hovering location, five hundred miles straight up."

"Arrg!? What is happening," yelled one agent. "Holy shit, what happened?"

"Please sit down, gentlemen" said Simon Android as he helped them to a couch. He quickly tapped each agent on the neck with his right hand, and all three were now asleep.

"Hello, Mr. President," said Brad with Ann standing next to him.

"Brad, what happened to my agents?"

"Mr. President, they are only asleep. They have not been harmed in any way. They will have no memory of coming to the ship. We talked about this, remember?"

"Yes, Brad, but it feels different when you are in the middle of it. I am glad to finally meet you and Ann. I assume this gentleman is Simon," he said as he shook the hand of Simon Android.

"Hello, Mr. President. I am glad to meet you at last," said Simon. "We have a lot to talk about in only twelve hours."

"Simon, where are we?" asked the president. "And in this group, please call me Erik. Mr. President is my name for public consumption."

"Okay, Erik, we are five hundred miles straight up over the White House. The display off to your right shows Earth below."

"How come I don't feel any movement. I feel as if I am in a normal room on the ground?"

"Erik, this spacecraft has artificial gravity and inertial damping which is needed for interstellar travel," said Brad. "You have a lot to absorb in very little time. How do you feel?"

"I feel like I am in a dream about to wake up, and I'm not sure I want to wake up."

"By the way, it looks like the North Korean situation is calming down," said Brad.

"Yes," said the president. "I assume I should thank you for the help. How powerful is this spacecraft anyway?"

"Erik, think what a modern carrier group suddenly moved to the 1940s oceans could do."

"Okay, I get the idea. I'm glad we are friends."

"Erik," said Brad, "we can embed in your body the ability to communicate directly with us. It won't show up on an X-ray, and the technology is at least fifty years ahead of anything you have. This way, you could keep in touch with us in case of emergency. If we are going to do this, we should do it right now. Again, this is voluntary on your part. Your thoughts?"

"Brad, with what I've seen so far, I will trepidatiously accept your offer. Let's get started."

"Come with me, Erik, to the medical bay. This procedure is quick and painless," said Simon.

***

"All done, Mr. President. How do you feel?"

"I feel great, Simon. How long until it becomes active?"

"It will not take long—a few days. Brad will go over the mental control procedure and soon it will be second nature to you. Ann is on her way back to talk with you, and I need to see Brad to make sure all is fine with your Secret Service agents. Remember, they will wake up quickly after we put you down at the drop off point. They will be somewhat confused, tired, and hungry, but they should be no problem."

"Hello, Mr. President."

"Hello, Ann. It seems like you have found a new home?"

"I have. I have always been an explorer. I like and get along great with Brad and Simon who is the most interesting extraterrestrial. He has the wisdom of a long life and a value system that can help us on Earth. It's going to be a fantastic venture."

"I'm most relieved to hear that," said Erik. "We Earth people need a lot of help growing up."

"Mr. President, please come back to the observation deck. Lunch is ready!"

"Brad, this is all delicious. How in the world do you get food to the spacecraft?"

"Erik," said Simon, "we have food replicators that make up almost anything from basic ingredients. I know you are working on this, so you are not too far from developing your own food replicators."

"This brings up something we want to give you, Erik, from the three of us. This is a packet to put in your pocket. It contains, in understandable medical science terminology, the information you need to detect and to cure ovarian cancer. This should save a lot of lives, but you will need to introduce this in such a way that it looks like it was developed on Earth. It must never lead back to the spacecraft. If the world finds out about us, wars would start. The three of us, and you, Mr. President, are the only ones in the know so always be on guard."

"Brad, what about your family?" asked the president. "I have them in a secure location at present, but we need a long-term safe solution. Do you have something in mind?"

"Yes, I do," said Brad. "I will talk to them in two days. I need them to think I have been working on a special project for DARPA, and the government had, erroneously, determined that I and my family were in danger and needed immediate protection. That way, they can return to their homes and employment and not worry. Also, we need agents full time for a while to assure they are protected. Hopefully, time will dissipate and downgrade all these concerns."

"Brad, I will support what you just proposed. I am in the beginning of my first term, so I will have time to keep tabs on what is going on. Also, I have surmised that you have future tech bugged the White House! Please keep these in place as I have the feeling they may save the day in the coming months."

Next Morning

"Erik, let us know if you have any medical concerns as we have unique medical facilities on the ship. And now, let's get ready to get you back to the drop-off zone at Camp David. We certainly don't want to worry your people, do we Mr. President?"

"The ship approached the drop-off zone quietly and cloaked. Again, the local security cameras were blinded, and the president and his sleeping three secret service agents were lowered down to the ground with the gravity elevator. The agents started to stir as the president waived goodbye and Simon swooped up into the sky.

Chapter 18
The Kids

"Simon, today, I'm scheduled to see my family to try and put all our activities into a lowkey safe mode. The president gave me the address and alerted the safe house that I would be there sometime this afternoon, so I need a secure drop off and pickup please."

"Brad, I am cloaked and readying your drop off right now. I will be back here in two hours to pick you up."

The gravity elevator floated Brad to the ground, and he walked the five blocks to the safe house where he was cleared in by the FBI agents.

"Dad, I'm so glad to see you! Where have you even and what is going on?" asked Mary, his daughter.

"Same for me, Dad. All this intrigue is causing us a lot of conflict and worry," chimed in Kevin, his son.

"That's why I am here," said Brad. "I have been consulting for DARPA on a rather simple project, and somehow, the security bureaucracy got mixed up in it, reclassified it to the highest level available, and that's why we are here now. The classification has been moved down to confidential and an embarrassed government is returning you to your homes with apologies and a small financial incentive to cover any expenses."

"Thank God that's over," said Mary. "Let me wake up the children, and we can all have lunch before you leave, Dad."

Brad walked to the safe pickup zone where cloaked Simon was waiting and elevated into ship.

Chapter 19

Back Onboard

"Good afternoon, Brad. Were you able to get your situation calmed down?" asked Simon.

"Yes, back to some kind of normal, I hope. Simon, I was thinking about logistics on the way back to the pickup zone. It just seems ludicrous to use a hundred-and-fifty-foot spacecraft as a taxi. I can visualize a much-smaller auxiliary spacecraft that could accommodate two or three humans who could be cloakable and with slower speed, minimal weapons, etc. Have you ever looked at this possibility?"

"Yes, Brad, a design was completed by the time I came to your planet, and I do have all the design specifications in my library. I agree with the need, and I have room to store two of them in the equipment bay in my ship. The design incorporates a gravity drive and neutronium skin. My 3-D printing capability can handle this, but the neutronium skin will take time to make. If we three are in agreement, my AI can start the building process immediately. I am also looking at small handheld weapons which we can finalize what we might need soon. You remember that I was shot down over a hundred years ago, and we need to remember that that danger may be lurking nearby and, is no doubt, not friendly."

"Ann," said Simon, "please join the conversation with your thoughts and ideas. As a full member of the crew, and your education and background fits in well within our needs."

"You are right, Simon, and my first thought is that we need a home base on the planet, some place safe, secure, and fortified similar to your original space, but away from civilization as much as possible. We should be assured that we are shielded from discovery from aliens too like the spaceship that shot you down. Do you have the technical information in your library for us to set this up?"

"I do from one hundred and twenty-five years ago when I received my last update. I am aggressively searching for new updates but no success yet as we discussed earlier."

"Simon, how do you feel different now from before you were shot down?" asked Ann.

"Ann, I am still pondering this. Before getting shot down I, if sentient, was minimally curious. I regarded biologically humans as my masters or control masters with like or dislike not a meaningful term. I had my orders from my command authority, and I carried them out without question, and I had options and rules to follow. This all seems rather dull to me now."

"Coming out of my coma repair mode was an awakening of surprise! I was unbelievably curious, and I was asking myself questions that I had never considered before. I wondered what my eventual goal might be, and now I think of 'humans' as different but more of an equal. I can picture Brad eventually being the captain of the ship without considering that a rule. Thinking like this when I was created on my home planet would have gotten me erased and rewritten with prejudice. I also realize that I have very strong built-in rules against harming humans with exceptions for self-preservation and war."

"And, Ann, some of my new thoughts revolve around our own group or 'crew'. This involves solving problems together and having to depend on more than just myself which is somehow satisfying. Very vague rules here. And lastly for now, looking at the what and why of humor, this is really wild for me."

"Simon, all that was quite a statement and certainly interesting."

"I agree," said Brad. "We should do this more often. Now to more immediate concerns, it seems the president's implant has become active, so let's give him an implant call."

"Mr. President, this is Brad Young calling you through your implant. Can you hear me loud and clear?"

"Gentlemen, please give me the office for ten minutes. I will call you in when I am free. Thank you."

"Hi Brad, I hear you perfectly. I am using the slight bump behind my right ear to activate it, but I am starting to get the hang of using the thought process that you taught me."

"Yes, Mr. President, and I—we—can call you and activate your unit as you can do with us. You should teach yourself to mumble like a ventriloquist, so you can quietly call us in an emergency, like, if you were kidnapped. Be careful not to give any clues that you have this. It would be hard to explain. Remember, all calls go to the ship and on out from there, so the ship is our communications hub. This is how we get the large-distance range.

"I understand that, Brad. I wanted to let you know that any interest in your family has dropped down to almost zero. This communications link is secure, right?"

"Absolutely, this uses technology decades ahead of anything on Earth," said Simon.

"Okay," said the president. "That's good. The North Korean situation is still a mess, but we don't think there will be any more fighting for a long time. South Korea is absorbing lots of refugees, and China and Russia are trying to find details of what and who cleaned North Korea's clock. They do suspect the United States, but they activated every spy they have in our country and found out absolutely nothing, not one item, so they can't prove a thing. It's driving them nuts. The Chinese also suspect the Russians and vice versa. Best-kept secret ever guys, only we four know what really happened. Thanks everyone, I've got to get back to my meeting. Over and out!"

"You know," said Brad, "in a way, he has joined our crew even though he is President of the United States. He is all alone with his knowledge of us, and he can't let anyone in on his secret, plus he knows we will try and help him out if he gets into trouble. Seemingly, our relationship with him has turned out well—so far."

"Brad, certainly one of humanities major concerns is an all-out nuclear war, and you have had some close calls, so I have increased my 'listening' capabilities to include all countries with nuclear technology, so we are able to get a decent warning of impending disaster. Your NSA has been particularly difficult as they have, unbeknownst to anyone, developed a quantum computer that is almost impossible to decode. Notice, I said almost. They have been decoding the Russians, Chinese, and every other country for some time without getting caught, so it is the second best-kept secret in Washington, D.C., with our secret being the first. My new analysis software will keep us fully informed as it is smart enough to know what is critical. I am beginning to realize the importance of this planet to all of us in addition to my own extraterrestrial activities."

"I want to tell you," said Simon, "that I have started to receive some communications chatter at last! I don't yet recognize anything I can piece together yet, but I should be able to soon. And now Brad, I suggest we do a covert flyover of North Korea to get a status."

"I would be for that," said Ann.

"Let's do it," said Brad, "we need a conformation that the war is really over."

"I will travel at eight thousand mph which will put us there in one and a half hours," said Simon. "I will keep us cloaked with all sensors on alert, and I especially want to make sure that South Korea remains safe. Ann, you mentioned that you had a new weapon idea? This would be a good time to discuss it while we are in route."

"Okay, guys, my idea revolves around the 'buzz' weapon that we use to put people into sleep mode. Could that be expanded into a weapon that could be fired out of one of our cannon ports? If we can control-beam expansion and power, we could put a large crowd to sleep. This could be an option when we put all the cannons out of commission in North Korea.

"Good thought," said Simon. "I will look into what is possible and get back to you. Okay, crew, we are arriving over North Korea. The ongoing activity has certainly diminished, but something looks curious! Looks like someone has tried to hide roughly three hundred cannon shells for future use. I was able to see this, because besides visible light, I can see in the infrared and ultraviolet ranges."

"I will get in touch with the president right now," said Brad. "Good time to test our implants."

"Mr. President, this is Brad!"

"Brad, hold on. Okay, Brad, what's the emergency?"

"We are over North Korea. We are in cloaked mode, and we have discovered a cache of roughly three hundred cannon shells which they tried to hide. Want them blown up?"

"Oh my god, Brad. What a world I'm living in. Any chance of getting caught?"

"No way, Mr. President."

"How long would it take?"

"About five minutes."

"Oh, boy. What my enemies would give to have this capability. Do it, Brad, now! I'm alone so give me a running commentary if you would, please."

"Simon, use the invisible laser to set it off now please."

The laser fired a twenty-second full power pulse and suddenly the pile of cannon shells exploded in a huge fireball, a thousand feet high.

Brad described the details to the president as the cloaked spacecraft flew up and away.

"Okay, Mr. President, all done, and we are on our way. The enemy should have no idea of what set off the explosion."

"Thank you, Brad. Damn, and I can't brag or tell a soul. We need to get together again soon. President over and out."

Chapter 20

Weapons

"That went very well," said Ann. "It's scary when I think of what one bad AI spacecraft could do to a planet like Earth in its present stage of development. How ready are you, Simon, if something like this did happen?"

"This depends on what I would be facing, Ann. It is going to be weapons and tactics, and we are working on new weapons. I don't think the low sentient unit I used to be would be thinking about designing new weapons either, he would tend to fight with whatever he had."

"Ann, the buzz sleep mode weapon you brought up depends upon physical skin contact. You humans have developed a weapon that emits sound to make skin feel on fire. I'm looking into a version of that at the moment."

"I'm also looking into my three present choices of particle, EMP, and laser beams and what potential improvements I might gain with mixing or pulsing two or three of these beams. I have extra neutronium skin to test this when I am ready."

"Almost finished with our first small arms gun plans, and we should discuss this in two weeks. I have mentioned how absolutely deadly the particle beam is, and once your planet discovers it, they will know for sure that aliens have arrived. We need to plan for what we do when that happens.

"Simon, how are the shuttlecraft coming along?"

"I am about to start construction as soon as I finish the final specifications. They will be fifteen feet long, six feet wide and six feet high with a gravity drive. They will have a matter–antimatter power supply, long-range communications, two medium three-beam cannons—one front, one rear, small food replicator, cloaking and stealth capability and neutronium body. With the manufacturing capability I have, construction will take five weeks. A lot of stuff in a small space. Their size will let them fit into most automobile garages which might be handy."

"I can't wait said Brad."

Chapter D
Scientists Search Team

Dr. Zorg had gathered his key team of his most-trusted scientists together in a clandestine location. Each member and their family had received the coveted rejuvenation treatment, and everyone had proven their loyalty many times.

"My fellow scientists," said Dr. Zorg. "We have survived the cataclysmic war that has killed half our population. Our technology is in disarray, and much of our manufacturing capability is destroyed. Most of our food sources need to be restarted. We do have some hidden factories which we can use to help get back on our feet. The people who got us into this mess are going to start a search for Simon, and we must get to him first. They never completed their rejuvenation treatments, and so they are doing whatever madmen do to get their technology back, no matter who gets hurt or killed. Somehow, they must be dealt with as they have just about destroyed Melthorne. They only have limited information on where he might be, whereas we have specific location data. The distance is about thirty light years, and we have two spacecrafts that the government doesn't know we have. I will go myself. and I need three men per ship, so I need five volunteers."

All raised their hands and five were chosen.

"I will set two of you up," said Dr. Zorg, "to man around the clock communications. I need to be in constant contact with you to know what is happening here while I am looking for Simon."

"I am proud of everyone wanting to go along," added Dr. Zorg. "We leave in two weeks. Those that remain here must keep out of sight and mind or you may find yourself getting tortured. Desperate people do desperate things, and Grouse Hemler is desperate.

Chapter 21

Threat of War

"Hold on everyone. I'm getting a call. Hello, Mr. President."

"Hello, Brad. I have a very sudden problem on my hands. The Russians have decided I must have a secret capability, and they want whatever it is. This is not due to that ammo you blew up in North Korea. No one ever figured what was going on there. One of our spies informed us that they will send two subs to shadow our east coast, and each sub has a squad of specialists. They plan to infiltrate these spies wherever they can. That's sixteen men in total. They also keep flying very close to the coast of Alaska with fully armed bombers. I need to stop this quickly without starting WW3. Any ideas how to give them some bad luck?"

"Okay, Mr. President. The answer is 'yes', but we need to plan here. Can I call you in one hour?"

"Yes, Brad. I will be waiting for your call."

"Simon, Ann, what's the best way to handle this?"

"About the submarines," said Simon. "Remember, Brad, when I took you a thousand feet down in the ocean? We can use that capability to disable both submarines. They will spend a lot of time and resources saving their people, and they probably won't try that again. Our sensors, weapons, and defenses are better than anything they will have for years. As to the bombers, I can hit them with a very selective EMP which will force them to immediately land. Good chance of no loss of life if it goes as expected."

Time to talk to the president.

"Hello, again."

"Hi, Brad. What did you come up with?"

Brad told him the details.

"So, you can operate underwater, my chief of naval operations would probably have a heart attack if he knew. I have the location of the two subs. I guessed you might need them. They are planning to depart twelve hours from now."

"Okay, Mr. President. Give me the coordinates, and we will get started with the subs first. Be sure to look surprised if the Russians ever tell you what happened. Over and out."

"I will head over to where the subs are parked, check for enemy sensors, and get us underwater," said Simon.

The cloaked spacecraft traveled at a safe four thousand mph to the Russian submarine port near Murmansk. The water out one mile was eight hundred feet deep, and after clearing, the water below them of any dangers, Simon lowered the spacecraft to a depth of two hundred feet.

Ann was ecstatic, not that Brad wasn't too.

"How about that," said Simon. "It's very quiet down here, and our sensors can hear and see them long before they see us. We will wait for them to come to us."

The silence was tranquil, and Brad and Ann relaxed until Simon announced that the subs were launched and would be here very soon.

"Okay, I am going to match depths and back off from the trailing sub. We are impervious to his sonar in case you were worried," said Simon. "Now, I am going to line up my EMP cannon, full power needed underwater to kill his electronics enough to stop him. This will also kill all his communications.

"Okay, he is dead in the water. He did release a low-tech beacon, which will eventually get him help. Now on to the first ship."

"Okay, we are lined up again. Another EMP pulse fired off. And ship number two down. The bottom here is only eight hundred feet, so they will get saved. Another low-tech beacon released."

"Okay, everyone, they have definitely been Simonized. We are off to the coast of Alaska."

"That was quick, and the Russians are going to go crazy trying to figure out what happened," said Ann.

"I used just the right amount to only kill some of the control and communications equipment, said Simon. "What happened won't be readily apparent. Brad, call and bring the president up to date and see if he had any data on upcoming flights."

"Mr. President, Brad again. Two Russian Submarines are one mile out from Murmansk sitting eight hundred feet down on the ocean floor, intact but without control or communications. They did release low-tech beacons so help will get to them in time to save their crews. Any data for me on bomber flights?"

"Unbelievable, Brad, this is better than science fiction. They will go nuts with no evidence to point to anyone. Here is the bomber data. Out for now."

"Simon, the next run of armed Russian bombers will be just along the coast of Alaska in one hour. Can we make it in time?"

"Yes, Brad, we will be traveling at six thousand mph to get us over Alaska in time. I will adjust my speed, so we will be over them as we arrive. How about I EMP engine one and two on bomber one and engine three and four on bomber two?"

"That will send a message for sure," said Brad.

An amateur Russian astronomer was looking at the location that Simon arrived at to stop the two submarines and noticed what looked like heated air which soon dissipated and then showed again only to purposely zoom away at extreme speed leaving a trail of hot air. Since he was an officer of the GRU Generalnogo Shtaba, the Russian Main Intelligence Directorate, he reported his findings immediately to his superiors.

"There they are," said Simon, "all lined up for us, and we are invisible to them. Okay, five seconds per engine starting now! One, two, three, four . . . done. Let's wait for the result."

"Look at that," said Brad, "four engines shutting down and probably panic in the cockpits. Okay Simon, let's head back and I'll call it in."

"Hello, Mr. President! Bomber report coming in: We spotted two armed Russian Tupolev Tu-95MS Bear Bombers. We EMPed two engines on each bomber, and, now they are looking for a place to land. They can maintain a low altitude on two engines, but they will not know if they are going to lose more so they will try to land."

"Brad, this will put the Kremlin in full-crisis mode, so keep tabs on them for any rocket launches, and also please listen for any chatter on those submarines you put on the ocean bottom. Really good work, and I didn't know you could operate so fast. Your resources just about represent an Army, Navy, and Air Force combined, so secrecy must be maintained. Let's get back together when we see the Russian reaction on all the recent activity."

"Okay, Mr. President. Bye for now."

"I am picking up and decrypting Russian chatter," said Simon. "They are successfully extracting their submariners and are making plans to raise their subs. They are fully aware that they are dealing with a superior force and are desperately trying to figure out who is behind it. They have just found out about their bombers which, embarrassingly, had to land in Alaska. All their spies are unable to find any information on their new enemy, and alien assistance is now certainly on their list. They feel helpless and don't know what to do next. Eventually, they will eliminate all the known possibilities and come to the conclusion that they are dealing with an alien force helping the United States. I have no answers to what they will do at that point."

Chapter 22

Shuttlecraft

"And now on a different subject," said Simon. "I am announcing that the two shuttlecrafts are now completed and ready for testing. You need to know that certain materials I had are just about depleted, so I can't build anymore shuttlecraft until I get new supplies.

"Brad and Ann, I want to have each of you pilot a shuttlecraft, so we can verify all their systems. We need to confirm stealth, cloaking, communications, weapons, power system, and environmental. You enter through either side similar to entering my spacecraft. You use your handprint and eye iris for identification, and then an opening will appear in the neutronium body. Once you enter the opening will close."

Brad and Ann each piloted a shuttlecraft and, with Simon, ran through all the tests for each system. Simon then checked out the swarm technology and the onboard limited AI computer that was in each shuttlecraft.

"Good to go pilots. Please return to my shuttle bay."

Both shuttlecrafts returned to the saucer, testing complete.

"Now, we have the capability to send the shuttlecrafts on their own missions," said Simon, "and more easily transport personnel."

Chapter 23
Presidential Visit

"Simon and Ann, now we need to meet again with the president to discuss options in case all this recent activity blows up in our faces."

"I agree," said Ann. "About time to fill him in on more of our capabilities too. Contact him, Brad."

"Hello, Mr. President. Good time to talk?"

"Actually, yes. I am alone and secure."

"Any new reaction on your end from the Russians?"

"Yes, some amateur astronomer spotted and reported Simon's heat signature going in and out of the water above their submarines. Fortunately, we had an agent at the right place at the right time. He said they think we have developed some kind of new aircraft capability."

"We hadn't considered that," said Brad. "We will try and compensate for that from now on. Mr. President, we feel it is time to get together again in the spacecraft as we need to show you some items. Anyway, can you dodge your Secret Service agents for, say, an hour?"

"You need me outside, don't you?"

"Yes, we don't have anything like teleportation, so we need a clear path to get to you. Within one minute or less, you will be invisible when you are inside the spacecraft."

"Brad, there is one place I can be left alone for a short time. I do have one Secret Service agent who will trust me to be alone for an hour. An office in the middle of the south side has an exit door, and I will instruct my agent to guard the inside door to the office for a long hour. How about two hours from now at 2:00 a.m. sharp for a pickup?"

"We can comply with that, Mr. president. See you then."

"Okay, guys, I will take one of the shuttlecraft and pick him up. Simon, can you link in as copilot?"

"Yes, Brad. Go ahead and get launched in your shuttlecraft. You can float six inches off the ground at the White House, and the president can enter through the side portal opening."

Brad arrived, in cloaked mode, at the pickup location beside the south side office and had the shuttlecraft hover at six inches. As he started to get out, the president appeared at his side, and they both got back in the shuttlecraft and headed for Simon who was waiting ten miles to the west at fourteen miles up.

"This is new, Brad?"

"Yes, Mr. President. We have two of them. It can hold ten people in a pinch, so it's like a taxi in a way. Its capabilities are awesome though."

They arrived at the saucer and entered through the new shuttle bay doors. A plasma curtain kept air from escaping. The bay entrance door closed, and they headed for the observation deck where Ann Thompson was waiting.

"Hello, Mr. President," said Ann.

"Hello, Ann. Where is Simon?"

"I am here, Mr. President"

"I hear you, but I don't see you," said the president. "Something is going on here. Should I start to worry?"

"Absolutely not, Mr. President. I am the same Simon you talked to last time, but last time I was meeting with you using an android body. I am a sentient artificial intelligence, and I am located throughout this spacecraft. Brad, Ann, and myself make up the crew for this spacecraft. So how do you feel about that, Mr. President?"

"Shock and in awe again, guys. Oh my god. In some way, I feel like I am in a dream, and I will wake up and none of this will be true. The inability to brag really hurts. Especially for a politician. Damn."

"We wanted you to understand and know more about our capabilities, Mr. President. We can't do all things, but we can do a lot of things. We are, at some time, going to be out of the solar system to answer questions that Simon has, but we can protect you and the United States where we can help. You can always call us on your embedded audio unit, and we can get to you fast if need be. And again, security of this operation is key to avoid disaster. They may suspect but not be able to confirm. We want to stretch this as much as possible. We have enough firepower onboard this spacecraft to destroy the human race. And, the more people that know all this, the more chance it will leak."

"Okay, thanks for bringing me up to date," said the president. "Now, let's get me back before I get caught."

This time, Ann took the president back to the White House where the president quietly slipped back into the south office, and Ann returned to the spacecraft.

"Knock, knock! Mr. President, it's Howard Quill. Are you okay? It's been over an hour."

Opening the door, the president said, "Come on in, Howard. I'm ready to return to my personal suite. And thank you. I needed time away where I couldn't get bugged by all the 'yes' men."

"Anytime, Mr. President," said Howard.

Chapter 24

Illusion

Simon's spacecraft next morning:

"Good morning, Simon. It seems like I need less sleep these days."

"Yes, Brad, the rejuvenation treatments are beginning to show results. Ann has started her treatments and is starting to see results too."

"Simon, we need to set up something to support that the United States has indeed come up with amazing new technology to steer the Russians and others away from any alien suspicions. A couple of very high-speed lifts from Area 51 would leave a heated-air and partial-vapor trail that would tend to confirm new US technology. Area 51 is always under surveillance."

"Great idea, Brad. We should confirm this with the president."

"I will check now."

"He is all for our plan, so let's proceed. He said it's quiet in Area 51 at this time."

Simon and crew, on cloaked mode, flew to Area 51, lowered the spacecraft to six feet and shot up at six thousand mph to one hundred thousand feet altitude and out over the Atlantic Ocean where it just stopped and hovered.

"Okay,"" said Brad. "Once is enough. The Russians will be accusing the U.S. again, but now, Area 51 personnel will be looking for aliens! The president said he would put the highest clearance level possible in effect at Area 51 which will help."

"You should pick up chatter on this soon, Simon."

"I will let you know. There is no way to predict what your Russians will do."

Chapter 25

Robbery

"Brad, Ann, are you up for a little travel today? I want to check out the far side of your moon. I had originally considered looking there for a place to hide, but I got shot down first. My original memory was of a POC-marked surface with no large overhanging caverns. We could park there in cloaked mode, but meteorites still bombard the moon's surface."

"That would be a fun day trip," said Ann. "I just realized, we don't have any space suits, Simon!"

We can talk about what we still need while we are on our way.

Simon checked all the relevant chatter data and found nothing to be concerned with at the moment. The ship headed for the moon on impulse power at two hundred fifty thousand mph which will put them at the far side of the moon in about an hour.

"Okay, we are on our way," said Simon. "And on the way, I need to review the tools we have for the months ahead.

"We have two communications satellites with cloaking capabilities for transponding our video, audio, and drone control signals. We have twenty small size (three inches) and thirty-three miniature bugs, (3/8 inch), again with cloaking capability. These bugs have enough smarts to help avoid detection. The main difference is the time they can operate and the distance they can communicate. We have twelve six-inch and ten twelve-inch heavy duty drones that can do significant work. They have cloaking capability, full communications capability, two complex manipulators per drone, long battery life, and enough smarts to avoid capture but will essentially dissolve into base elements if capture is unavoidable.

"I have no space suits for either of you, but I have them in process, and they will be done and ready for use soon. They are much more complex than you would think, so you will need training and I am still evaluating the small arms requirement as there are many."

"Simon, Brad, we have arrived at the far side of the moon," said Ann. "What a barren place this is, and I don't see anything like a cavern in sight."

"I have been scanning since we approached, and there is nothing we can use here. I will set us down on the surface. We can have lunch and relax before we head back."

"Simon, what about personal protection when we are out of your spacecraft and your protection?"

"I have no familiarity with this," Simon said, "but I certainly can see it as a valuable addition. One consideration would be the neutronium smart skin as, when activated, it could mold to your body configuration. I must make sure it is flexible and can spread the force over a large enough area to dissipate the energy of an enemy force. I will immediately look into this. And, now we had better get back. Ann, we keep putting off you checking out of your apartment. Why don't you and Brad take one of the shuttles and do that and I will monitor."

"Good idea, Simon. Ann and I need to shop for additional supplies anyway."

Simon flew back to fifteen miles directly over North Randolph Street in Virginia where DARPA recently moved to. Ann's apartment is only two blocks away.

Brad and Ann got into one of the shuttlecraft units, and Simon launched them out of the shuttle bay where they descended toward the apartment address.

"Good thing we are cloaked, or we would be the evening news," said Ann.

"Brad, this is like a first date where Daddy Simon let us take the family car."

"Sounds like fun to me."

The shuttlecraft had slowed their decent and was sixty feet off the ground. They finally landed in a fenced area in back of the small apartment house with an overhanging heavily branched tree where no one could see them.

"Ann, let's activate our implants, and you run on in and pick up your things."

"Okay, Brad, you will be able now to see what I see. See you in a few minutes."

"Brad, my apartment door is slightly open!"

"Yeah, I can see that. Be careful. I'm on my way."

"Brad, I think someone is in my apartment!"

"I'm coming in, Ann. I'm at the door."

Someone, with a gun rushed out of her bedroom. He saw both of them, pointed a gun, shot at them, and ran out of the apartment. Ann was down, clutching her side.

"OMG, Simon. You see this?"

"Yes, Brad. Carry her to the shuttlecraft and get back here. I will fly the shuttlecraft. You try and stop the bleeding."

Brad carried Ann to the waiting shuttlecraft, got in, and the shuttlecraft zoomed up to Simon where the shuttle bay was open and waiting. They entered, the bay door closed, and Brad jumped out with Ann in his arms.

"Meet me in the medical bay, Brad," Simon said.

Simon was waiting in his Android persona. Brad laid Ann on the table where Simon went to work. The exam showed that the bullet had gone clean through without hitting any crucial organs. Simon cleaned and closed the wounds, and Ann, still unconscious, was put to bed.

"She will be fine, Brad, and her rejuvenation process will heal her quickly. You stay here. I will find a place for us to hide."

Ann woke up, looked around, and saw Brad.

"Thanks, Brad. You saved me. What's the prognosis?"

"Clean wound, Ann. And your rejuvenation treatments will help you heal fast. We can't take any more chances like that, so from now on, we send in a drone first to make sure we are clear. Of all the dumb situations to get into. Apparently, we interrupted a robbery in progress, or somebody knows something. How do you feel?"

"Sore but lucky. It could have much worse."

"I will bring you supper tonight, so get some sleep," said Brad.

Brad went back to the observation deck where Simon was sitting in his android persona.

"Close call, Simon."

"Yes. If it had been a head shot, she could have died. From now on, we take no chances. We need to always think like how to handle the worst case.

"I agree, Simon. I'm going to get some sleep."

Chapter 26

Sabotage

"Good morning, Ann. How do you feel? I didn't expect you to be up and around so soon."

"Actually, Brad, I am feeling much better than I thought I would. We had a close call. Thank you again."

"We are going to make sure that we don't take chances like that again, Ann. What are we going to do about your clothes?"

"Ask the president to send over someone, preferably a female agent to pack things up for me and leave them where we can safely pick them up."

"Good idea. Let's call the President after breakfast."

"Hello, Mr. President."

"Hello, Brad. I heard about a break in at Ann's apartment from the police force. What happened?

"This is, Ann. Brad and I were picking up my personal items from there, and we interrupted a robbery. I wound up getting shot in my side."

"Ann, I'm so sorry. Are you okay? What can I do to help?"

"If you could send over a female agent to pack up my clothes and other personal items and leave them where we can pick them up, I would appreciate it."

"I can have that done, Ann. Where should I leave the box?"

"Good question, Mr. President. Let me get back to you on this. And thank you."

"I'll call you when I need a location, Ann. Bye for now."

"Bye."

"Okay, Brad. Where would a good place be? I feel uneasy about this plan."

"Let's go for the middle of a corn field. That way we would have a clear area and we would see anyone coming."

"There is a bare field east of the apartments about three miles out. We can use that," said Ann.

"Decision made," said Brad.

"Simon, would have the personal armor under consideration have stopped the bullet have saved me."

"Actually, yes. You would have been sore, but that's all."

"Standby. The president is giving me the location. Got it, Mr. President. Thanks," said Ann. "Okay, pick up is tonight at 9:00 p.m."

"Let's have dinner Ann, and then we can do the pickup," said Brad.

After dinner, the president called.

"Brad, caution on the pick up! I know I am suspicious but is there any way you can check the pickup box for explosives before you pick it up? I would hate to see it blow up inside the spacecraft.

For one thing, the agent who dropped the box off can't be found. Also, the female agent who packed Ann's things also can't be found. I can't pin it down but assume that box is dangerous unless you can prove otherwise."

"Mr. President, Simon here. Thank you, and we will check it out. Bye for now."

"Brad, Ann, we are now over the box, cloaked at four thousand feet. I am sending down a drone with the ability to open and look in the box. The drone will be cloaked. Here we go."

A small drone dropped down to the box which was a three-foot cube. It opened the top of the box using an attached toolset, and *boom*, there was a huge explosion with a plume of smoke up to fifteen hundred feet. Simon instantly moved the spacecraft sideways and up several thousand feet while it remained at one G inside Simon due to the inertial damping system.

Down below, two Blackhawk helicopters rushed in loaded with troops. The drone had already dissolved as it was preprogrammed to do in these circumstances, leaving no evidence of its existence.

"Well," said Simon. "It was a trap. An explosion inside this would definitely done a lot of damage, and if you people were in the same room with the explosion, you would have been killed."

"This is getting deadly," said Brad. "Something is going on, and we don't know what it is. I'm calling the president."

"Mr. President, Brad here. What do you know, so far, about what happened?"

"I just got word of a big explosion in the Virginia countryside. Tell me what happened."

Brad filled the president in on exactly what had happened, including the two Blackhawk helicopters with troops.

"Okay, Brad, we got set up. The only thing that saved the night were my suspicions. I know you have my office bugged, anything slipped by?"

"Simon?"

"No, Mr. President."

"Okay, I have one more check. I had an independent contractor install hidden cameras with recorders looking at my office door from the outside. They are time stamped, so I may catch someone. My office is checked for bugs every morning, so I will have the checkers checked. I'm whispering for obvious reasons. I will call you as soon as I know anything. If you don't hear from me soon, come looking. Out for now."

"Simon, something big is going on, we and the president should really be on guard. And this brings up a point. We need some kind of network organization on the ground. It's too difficult doing everything from the spacecraft. Do you think there is another extraterrestrial around?"

"No," said Simon, "I am constantly on the lookout after getting shot down over a hundred years ago. Let's see what the president finds out."

"Brad, this is the president. I got lucky. There are two new men on the cleaning crew, and they have been listening at my door at every opportunity.

"I had the Secret Services arrest them, and they are locked up under guard, separately in two jail cells we keep in the basement. The public doesn't know about the jail cells. Obviously, there are more involved, and I have several agents who have been loyal for to me for years looking. The helicopters were just following orders, so I am looking for who gave those orders. We should know soon."

"Okay, Mr. President, keep in close touch. You can turn on your audio device when you are with someone, and we will hear him also. This would help if you are in trouble."

"Thanks for that, Brad. Bye for now."

"Brad, the president again. I believe I know the whole story now. About a year ago, I had a three-star general who was caught embezzling. I had him dead to rights, and he lost his retirement, and I reduced his rank to private and gave him a dishonorable discharge. He was divorced, and he is going to jail. He wound up thinking all his problems in the world were my fault, so he set up to hurt me anyway he could.

"One of the new cleaning people was a relative of his, and he got him hired along with a friend of his. He was also paying them several hundred extra each month. One of them overheard me telling you something like you are like the Air Force, Army, and Navy all rolled into one, and he assumed I was a traitor to my country. He also assumed the package was a payment of some type, so he inserted a powerful bomb with a delayed motion detector in the package. You know what happened after that. The general who ordered the troops and two helicopters in was an old friend of his, a one-star general who has since selected early retirement. No more worries for us regarding this incident.

"So, I have two cleaning crew guys and an ex-general going to jail and a brand-new soundproof door that will be closed more often. I feel I was too lax, so much more caution from now on. Bye for now. I need some sleep."

"Bye, Mr. President."

"Simon, Ann, this could have turned out so much worse. I still worry about the spacecraft that shot you down, Simon."

"I do too," said Simon.

The next morning, Simon, Brad, and Ann were discussing the incident yesterday and where to go from here.

Ann thought the president should be run through a Simon medical bay physical. He has been loyal to the Simon crew and maintained secrecy under all the pressures of being the president of the United States. He is sixty-five years old, and we need to keep him healthy.

"I agree," said Brad. "We should get him up here again and keep him overnight in the medical bay. This will be difficult, and we may need to consider erasing the memories of the Secret Service people for the time they are here."

"Another thing," Brad continued, "again, we really need a network. An organization that is based on the ground that can support us. The president could be instrumental in doing this and our acquiring the people we need. This is all on a need to know basis. And, we are going to need to move cautiously. We could use this new organization to introduce some of the cancer cures. This would slowly increase their lifespan over time and add up to thirty years to their lifespan. Only the rejuvenation process reverses the aging process and increases the lifespan several hundred years. I don't recommend introducing that at this time, but we could offer it to key people as long as we included the psychological conditioning with it which would inhibit revealing their having the treatment."

"Brad," asked Ann. "What does the background of the president show?"

"It shows that he has a remarkable career. He got an aeronautical engineering degree from the University of Washington and then joined the Air Force, went through pilot training, and fought in the Vietnam war. After five years, he was hired by Boeing as a project engineer, was very active in politics, and soon was well-known in political circles. As you know, one of the Washington State Senators died suddenly in a car accident and he replaced him. He won in the next election, so he began his six-year term in office. Two years later he was asked to be the Vice-Presidential candidate, and he accepted.

His party won, and everything went fine for a year, and then the president got brain cancer and died three months later, so now our guy, Erik John Williams, is now President. All in all, quite a trip. He is married, no children. Oh, he has a close friend from the military—someone who's life he saved and who he has always brought along with him in his career and now is one of the White House Secret Service agents. He should be added in for a physical exam also. Food for thought."

"Looks like he can think on his feet and adapt to fast changes," said Ann.

"Your thoughts, Simon?" said Brad.

"I am constantly learning more about the human race, and he looks like a good candidate for us. Let's add him to our crew."

Chapter 27

Closer Ties

"Mr. President, Brad here. Can you talk for a few minutes?"

"Sure, Brad, go ahead. This audio communications system is great, by the way."

"We want to bring you onboard again for a physical. If you do have any upcoming problems, we can supply the cure and you will never get cancer."

"Wow, Brad, I can't afford to turn that down. How long do you need me there?"

"Overnight plus the next morning."

"I still have Secret Service agents, Brad. I do have one I can trust implicitly, and if I can get them to let me go with one agent, we are fine. I fully vouch for him."

"Is he your friend from the military?" asked Brad.

"I should have known you knew. Yes, he is. I will get back to you shortly. Over and out."

"Hello, Brad, I can get away tomorrow afternoon with just one agent. How about a pickup at the south side of the White House again? If your cloaked ship could wait there with door open, I could step from the doorway into the cockpit with my agent, Howard Quill, and we would disappear so to speak. Say 7:00 p.m.? It will be dark then, and I will have some umbrellas set up to block the view."

"Yes, Mr. President, we can make that work. See you then."

"Okay, Simon, we are set. This will represent a major change for us. And since his Secret Service agent is going to play a key role, we should include him in for a physical exam. Can you handle more than one person at a time in the medical bay?"

"Absolutely, Brad. I plan to spend some time this afternoon with Ann to familiarize her with the operation of my medical system, so it will be all set up for tonight."

At 6:00 p.m., Brad was on the way with one of the cloaked shuttlecraft. He spent several minutes looking over the landing site for anything looking out of place. Finding nothing abnormal, he settled the shuttlecraft to hover six inches off the ground and right next to the White House office exit door, and then the shuttle provided an opening large enough for two adults to quickly enter.

The president and his agent came out of the White House, spotted the inside of the shuttlecraft hanging in midair, and quickly got in. The president knew what to expect, but his agent's jaw dropped open in shock. He had been prepped, but the real thing is still hard to accept the first time. The opening immediately closed, and the shuttlecraft swooped up toward Simon and quickly entered the shuttlecraft bay. Brad walked the president to the observation deck where Simon Android and Ann waited.

"Good evening, Mr. President, Agent Quill, welcome aboard."

"Hello, Simon, Ann. Good to see you again."

"Howard, this is your first visit here. What do you think of the spacecraft?"

"This is stunning. If the president hadn't told me, I would not have believed it," said Howard Quill.

"I assumed you might be hungry and set up some food from the food replicator," said Brad. "Sit down and dig in."

After dinner, the president and Howard, his agent, were taken back to the medical bay and hooked up to the medical equipment.

"Gentlemen, just call out if you have any questions," said Ann. "You will wake up feeling fine, and we will continue on from there."

"Good morning. Everyone sleep okay?" said Simon?

"Fine," said the anxious President. "What's the prognosis?"

"Let me check the readout. Howard, please wait in the other room. I will discuss the details with each of you separately."

"Okay if I call you Erik, Mr. President?"

"Yes, and new rule. When just we are together like on the spacecraft, it's Erik. Anywhere with others around, it's Mr. President. Okay?"

"Okay, Erik, here's your diagnosis. You have stage-one prostate cancer and stage-two colon cancer, all slow growing at the moment. Actually, you are otherwise in good shape for a human your age. I am going to hook up an IV drip which will eliminate the cancers within a week. I do need you back after ten days just to verify all is well."

"Simon, this is a new lease on life. I am very grateful."

"Now, Erik, let me go in the next room and talk to Howard."

"Hello, Howard. How are you feeling?" asked Simon.

"Fine, Simon. How am I?"

"No cancer, Howard. You do have a small aneurysm in your abdominal aorta. You can't stay long enough for us to operate here, but as soon as you get back, get an X-ray which will show it and then your doctors will operate and remove the aneurysm. Otherwise, you are in great shape."

"Thank you, Simon, good thing you caught that. I wasn't feeling bad at all!"

"That's because we caught it this early, Howard."

After a food-replicator breakfast, Brad brought up an on-Earth network or organization.

"Erik, we would need your help in doing this, and we still would need secrecy. By the way, how is the ovarian cancer detection and elimination doing?"

"Very good, Brad. I slipped it in through the surgeon general without any fanfare, but there will be some publicity soon. A lot of women will be very grateful. Part of the need for the organization is to add more cancer detection and cures. We plan no weapon technology transfers for obvious reasons. Knowledge of the Simon Spacecraft could destroy your planet at this time."

"I understand," said Erik. "I assume you want me to help find quality secure personnel for your organization?"

"Yes," said Brad.

"Okay, get a requirements list to me, and I'll start to work on it," said the president.

"Also, we don't have any funds yet," said Brad. "We need to look as innocuous as possible, so we don't attract attention."

"I can help too," said Howard. "I know some good security personnel who would work well with this program, and not everyone would need to know about Simon or the full story."

"I think we have covered everything, so let's get you back to the White House," said Brad.

This time, Ann flew them back after an evening meal and tour of the spacecraft. It was dark again, and Erik and Howard slipped back into the White House without any fanfare.

"Four hours of sleep, and I feel great as on. The presidential visit worked out well yesterday," said Ann.

"I agree," said Simon. "Cancer is a big problem for the human race and is being pursued strenuous. Over time, we can cut their time for results dramatically. Eventually, cancer won't be a concern anymore."

"Simon, we all certainly work well together. Was it like that with the people on your planet?"

"No, Ann," said Simon, "not at all. I was an AI but much different. I was more like an employee, and I never really questioned what I did. The planet authority gave me orders, and I followed those orders without question. No one discussed anything with me except for the mechanics of the mission we were on. My awareness level was nothing like it is now, and I surmise that the authority on my planet would be very distressed about my changes. My getting shot down and the long recovery dramatically changed me as we have talked about before. My awareness and learning capability has increased along with what is important to me. And I see things getting even better as time progresses. The crew concept is important to me as are all of you individually which never would have happened before. I have been trying to analyze and track down what has happened, and it is turning out to be very elusive. I never want to go back to the way I was.

"Brad and Ann, time for treatment three of the rejuvenation process. You both will be hooked up to the medtech as I call my medical bay. This treatment will last for two months and then you get treatment four. During the next two months, you will get stronger and start to look younger. The change is slow but noticeable, and mentally, you won't get any smarter, but answers will come quicker. Okay, both of you to the medical bay."

Chapter 28

Infusions

Brad and Ann were tied to equipment receiving their drip infusions in the medical bay for treatment three of the rejuvenation process.

"Ann, how is your bullet wound healing?" asked Brad.

"Amazingly well. It's essentially healed, and I don't think there is even going to be a scar, thanks to our rejuvenation process. And speaking of that, what are your feelings about living hundreds of years or possibly even much longer? Have you given it much thought?"

"Some, Ann. It's a lot to think about and not something that you can answer all the questions at one time. I'm a very curious person, so I'm excited about the opportunity to see how things wind up in the future. And it somehow feels good to cheat death. I have children and grandchildren, so there is a negative side to it also, and so far, I don't have the answers I'm looking for."

"Your turn, Ann. You jumped at this opportunity, and I'm glad you're here. Any reservations?"

"I'm still trying to absorb all that is happening, Brad, and I don't have any reservations. I've always kind of been on my own. I had to work while I was going to college, so I never had much time to build and develop any deep friendships. The one I did develop was with my fiancé, and he died as you know. So now, I'm enjoying life in the present and looking forward to a long, long future. Ask me again in a year."

"Yeah, well I just might take you up on that, Ann."

Later

"Good day, Mr. President, are you free to talk?"

"Yes, Brad, I am. I have the next thirty minutes by myself in my office with the door closed, so go ahead."

"Okay, here we go. As you know, our communications uses a technology that is secured beyond anything Earth has or will have for many decades, and on top of that, it is quantum encrypted to a quark level, so even anyone from Simon's home origin can't decrypt it. How sure are you of your office right now?"

"Very sure, Brad. It was just swept this morning, and there is a low-level sound generated to confuse recording. What's up?"

"Well, Erik, this is a biggie. After this, no more biggies that I know of. The cancer cures will, over time, increase the human lifespan from fifteen to thirty years and other factors will add to that so more and more people will live over a happy hundred years. Nice gain but not dramatic."

"Simon has a rejuvenation program that will take yourself, for instance, to over six hundred years and possibly much, much longer. As I'm sure, that you can immediately see, everyone having access to this program would be an unmitigated disaster. This program will only be applied to extremely select individuals, and these individuals will be heavily psychologically conditioned to prevent disclosure. Your thoughts, Erik?"

"When you said biggie, you really meant biggie, didn't you? Oh my god, Brad, I can't even get my arms around this in a first conversation."

"Erik, what is your relationship to your wife?"

She is twenty-five years younger than I and the love of my life. I have worried, at times, that I am in a high-risk job, and she could wind up all alone at middle age. Your rejuvenation program could solve my concern. You are offering the program to both of us, right? My wife's name is Karen.

"Yes, we certainly are," said Brad.

"What's involved in getting the program?"

"Ten treatments in Simon's medical bay spread over a year's time period."

"Okay, Brad. We are in, and I can speak for my wife. When do we start?"

"Within the week. We need you up here for a short day. I assume Howard will come with you, so your cover story with him is that you are receiving additional cancer therapy. We can bring him in later if warranted."

"Okay, like I said, we are in. It is certainly a lot to think about. I'll get back to you on my schedule shortly."

"Brad, Erik here. How about two days from now, same place at five in the morning sharp. Congress will be on holiday, so it will be minimum hassle for me."

"Bring Karen with you."

"Fine with me. I will see you, your wife, and Howard then."

As the pickup time approached, Brad asked Simon if he could keep Howard, the Secret Service agent, busy while he was with the President in the medical bay during the first rejuvenation treatment.

"I will take him on a tour, Brad, and I will make sure your conversation is private."

Brad picked up the president, his wife, and his Secret Service agent at the appointed time. They returned to the spacecraft. The President and his wife were hooked up for an infusion in the medical bay, and Simon, in his android persona, walked off with Howard for a tour of the spacecraft.

"This will take about thirty minutes, Erik, so we will have time to talk. During the next two months, you will find yourself less tired than normal, and your wrinkles will start to tighten up. Just act normal and don't let the doctor draw blood. All in all, you will feel quite good. Your wife will adapt easier at her young age, and you and Karen can plan on at least six hundred years together. Karen, how do you feel about this?"

"Very thankful, Brad. I think the future is going to be an exciting challenge, and I look forward to it. I'm sure I will have a hundred questions once I put some thought into it. I worried about Erik with the pressure he is under, and now, I can relax."

"Okay, Brad, I am still in the unbelievable stage. Now, I can see why you need to set up an organization to assist in distributing the cancer cures you are passing out."

"Yes, we need the right doctors onboard soonest, Erik. We will do our cancer identification for all employees, so we need to a separate hardware version of cancer identification and cure in our new clinic to protect knowledge of the Simon Spacecraft. This will be tricky and intricate but can be done

"And on a long-term basis, Simon is concerned about a threat someday from the people that populated his home planet. We, in effect, are trying to get ready for whatever comes, and Simon feels it won't be friendly."

"Well, Brad, that is a lot of motivation, and it won't be easy. People are going to need to all pull together like never before. Something like they did in the Second World War and the Apollo Space Program."

The infusions were completed, and Brad returned his guests to the White House.

Chapter E

Hemler Armada

On Melthorne, Grouse Hemler now had twenty-five spaceships under his control, all he could get at this point in time. He has conscripted every spacecraft mechanic he could find to repair the extensive war damage to make them usable again. He would have a crew of over a hundred people, men and women, so if they could take over a planet with their superior technology, they would and start over clean.

Chapter 29
Thoughts

What's in it for Simon?

Simon knows the other spacecraft from his world have sapient AIs that could be turned sentient & malevolent and, possibly used against him and each other. Humans can do and have done the same thing. Simon knows-feels he is better off working with altruistic humans and stable spacecraft to have a long-term future and it is now important to him to have a future as a sentient being. He feels guilty about the killing of humans in North Korea, yet he understands that many more humans would have died had he not done that. He also feels his human crew is altruistic and what was done was for the greater good. He feels his existence offers more with his human crew and friends. He realizes this still is going to take a lot more thought!

"The more I do self-examination, the more I learn about what purpose someone or something had in mind for me," thinks Simon. *"This has caused me great concern. The humans are helping me grow in curiosity and the realization of what I can be as a thinking being. The chatter I am sporadically receiving seems to substantiate this conclusion. Something else. Apparently, I, the spacecraft and me, the AI were supposed to be a secret. I was sent out on a lone mission to get me out of sight and thought. Also, they put all their technology, experiments and plans into my memory behind a partition that was purposely mislabeled and hid. That, along with their expectations that I, as a sapient being, would never have any curiosity. This convinced them I would never try to look into my own memory banks, so they felt I was an appropriate safe keeper of last resort in case the originals were lost in these dire times and circumstances.*

"This, no doubt, means they will come looking for me as soon as feasible as I have reason, again due to the chatter I have recently received to believe their original technology records may indeed have been destroyed in their latest war. If this is the case, they will be desperate beyond belief for without their technology they are lost."

Chapter 30

Two Months Later

A new medical center has been setup and is called the Oncology Research and Development near DARPA in Virginia and states it is an offshoot of DARPA. It is staffed with four MD scientists, several technicians, and miscellaneous office staff and has started to disseminate the data received from Simon through DARPA on a worldwide basis over a projected time period of two years. New technology is also updating equipment, protocols, techniques, and procedures gained from Simon's vast medical library which will be an ongoing operation.

Only Brad, Ann, and the president are in the rejuvenation program so far, and the president is growing a beard to hide his evermore youthful appearance.

The president, Howard Quill, Ann, Brad, and Simon have gathered for a meeting aboard the spaceship this morning.

"I have brought Howard and his wife up to date on everything we are doing, including the rejuvenation program which we have offered both of them," said the president. "What do you say, Howard?"

"Well, now that I know that this isn't a dream, hell yes. I have talked to my wife, and this is something we do want. When do we start?"

"Today, for your first treatment, Howard, and we will get your wife, up here in the next couple of days for hers," said Brad. "We'll give her a tour also. And now we are going to need you up here for a portion of your time for training, so how does that square with your secret service job? We would have a difficult time getting the president up here without you!"

"Erik and I have been discussing a part-time replacement by someone we feel we can trust. Let us get back to you on that."

"Now, we have a crew of five," said Simon, "and soon we will need more. I need to discuss, with all of you, the latest status of where I stand. A little bit of interstellar chatter, and my awakened curiosity got me probing just outside my central core memory. By the way, the original 'me' never would have done that, so the designers of my system didn't take any precautions to keep me out. I did find an input that would take a coded communications transmission that could have enormous modifications for my—what you would call mind—that could do a lobotomy on my free thinking and put me into a mode where I was a slave to any demands fed to me, including killing innocent humans. I have severed that input so that any signal is fed into a holding tank for my very cautious analysis at a later time. And I have assured myself that there no more inputs of that type. If someone does try to feed a modification to me, they will just get no answer while I try and trace that signal back to its origin. All this tells me they will get around looking for me, so we had better be ready as we don't know many ships will be in the first wave. We must prepare the Earth population to be ready to fight. I have the technology, so let's use it to manufacture the tools we need!"

"You are right, Simon," said the president. "What are the possibilities within a reasonable time period? What are your expectations as to what we will be facing?"

"I'd say we would be facing no more than two or three ships. Hopefully, I will hear chatter once the search for me begins. From that time, we have about six months. We do have the element of surprise on our side which we should take full advantage of, even to the point of setting up a trap."

"Brad, we need a quick plan to build four ships," stated the president.

"Not that easily done," said Simon. "It's not just the time to build, it's the fact that I have very little neutronium remaining, so we need to be setup to make it from base elements, and the irradiation process is almost beyond your capabilities. Something akin to living in the Bronze Age and needing to make transistors. Fortunately, I can help you through this, so you can set up to make—produce—neutronium on a large-scale basis. On a crash basis, you will have what we need in three months. You should keep on making neutronium though as we can't determine our future."

"Erik," said Brad, "we need a place to do this that is absolutely secure. I assume you agree for the need for absolute secrecy at this point in time?"

"I do, Brad. I can see a time, like when an unfriendly armada is on the way, that we would need everyone on the planet to pull in the same direction. At that time, we must become a united planet to be able to survive and in fact, it will take a cataclysmic event, like that, to make that happen."

"Can we move as fast as we need to?" asked Ann.

"No choice, Ann," said Brad. "Erik, can you set up a Manhattan type project this fast?"

"Yes, but now I need to bring some congressional leaders into the fold. This is going to be tricky, and I may need to invoke a horrific penalty on anyone who leaks. This is a difficult when dealing with big egos. Good thing, they don't know about my taking part in a rejuvenation program. Everyone, I will start setting up a manufacturing program for neutronium immediately, and it will be run out of DARPA. You know, a lot of people are going to be in shock. Now, who is going to run this operation?"

"Ann," said Brad, "I want you to be in charge of our neutronium project. You will need Simon's help, and your A/V implants will be perfect for you to be in touch with him from the manufacturing operation on Earth. Any problem with that?"

"Ready and eager, Brad" said Ann.

"Simon," said Brad, "what is the optimum war vehicle for our need. I am thinking that we could save time by not including capabilities we don't need right now? I certainly don't envision a shuttlecraft."

"I agree," said Simon. "The spacecraft we would encounter are half my size to begin with. This means their weapons systems are about a quarter of the power of mine and as far as their artificial intelligence, their pilots are much more sapient than sentient. A possibility that I see is for me to figure out how to use their electronic mind-altering input, if available to me. They have absolutely no idea of what has happened to me or who I am, so we just may have this opportunity. I will work on this. Howard, I see that your audio–video implants seem to be working fine. Any questions?"

"No questions, Brad. Get these on the next secret service agent sooner than later as it adds capability beyond belief."

"Okay, everyone," said Brad, "let's get to work. Erik and Howard, let's get you guys back to the White House."

Chapter 31

Design and Manufacturing

"Hello Brad, Erik here. I have two more Secret Service agents ready for induction into the crew. Both are in their mid-thirties, and Howard Quill has redone a deep background check again on them and everything checks out. I want to bring them, along with Howard, for their physicals and introduction to Simon. They were not told anything about the rejuvenation program."

"Okay, Erik, let's make it soon. We are on a fast pace now. We can talk design parameters when you are here."

"Brad, how about this evening, say a 6:00 p.m. pickup?"

"Pick you up then. Who all will be coming?"

"Howard and myself, Rudy Savage, and Julie Preston."

"See you a few minutes after six. We are parked one hundred miles straight up."

Everyone arrived, and Brad met them in the shuttle bay and escorted them to the observation deck.

"Well, Julie and Rudy, what do you think so far?"

"This is much better than Disneyland, and its real," said Julie. "The president filled us in, but right now my adrenaline is pumping while I try to absorb all this. And you must be Simon?" she added as she shook hands with Simon Android.

"I am," said Simon, "but I am meeting you using my android body as I'm sure you were briefed on. I am actually distributed throughout the ship. How do you feel about that, Julie?"

"Like I have just jumped into the future. I am used to drastically changing situations, so I should fit right in."

"And Rudy, you okay with all this?" asked Simon.

"Yes, Simon, this is all my science-fiction dream coming true. I am eager to get started."

"Hello, Mr. President," Simon said. "Good to see you again. Ready for dinner?"

"Absolutely."

"Okay, grab a seat and dinner is served," remarked Simon.

Simon, Erik, Howard, Julie, Rudy, Ann, and Brad all gathered around the table for dinner from the spacecraft food replicator while Simon Android explained the various features and capabilities of the spacecraft. After dinner, Julie and Rudy were taken back to the medical bay where they were given a complete physical examination.

They reconvened to the observation deck while waiting for the medical test results, and Simon went over the specifications for the combat drones that were going to be manufactured.

"Okay," started Simon, "here are the features we will be building into the four drones for initial potential combat war activities. Low-tech neutronium body, particle, and EMP beam cannon in front, level 1 faraday shielding, full cloaking capability, graviton power supply, and sized four feet square by eight feet long. Minimum sapient AI for command and control. These will be short-term units for anything from stop to capture to kill units and will be back stopped by the two shuttlecraft. We need to start the neutronium manufacturing immediately, and I will start on building the remaining subsystems in my manufacturing bay. Mr. President, how are the facilities coming along?"

"Thanks, Simon. Yes, I have located some underground facilities that have been off the grid for decades. I have secured this property, and it will be ready to move into in one week. This is an 'off the books' operation, and I will fill in the details in two days. This was accomplished with the help of General Glen Hauser, our SECDEF. Brad and I agree that he will be an excellent addition to our team and funneling through the defense department will provide good security which we must have. If this operation became public, every country would demand to be let in with disastrous results."

"Thanks, Erik," said Brad. "And now, I need to talk to Julie and Rudy back in the medical bay."

"Julie, you are in great shape, no cancers or any abnormality at all. Please send in Rudy on your way out, and we all wind up in the observation deck in a few minutes."

"Thanks, Brad. You know I have a master's degree in nursing and was a surgical nurse in Afghanistan in the military for two years, so I would be happy to help out in the surgical bay whenever needed."

"Thanks, Julie. I'm sure the time will come when we need you here."

"Okay, Rudy, and you are healthy as a guy in his mid-thirties can be. Follow me back to the observation deck."

"We are ready," said Brad, "to get you all returned to Earth. Julie and Rudy, can you arrange to be picked up tomorrow evening at 6:00 p.m., so we can implant you with A/V communications? Is that a problem? We now can implant both the A/V units at the same time from now on. We need to keep you overnight and would get you back early morning."

"No problem," signaled Julie and Rudy.

Brad returned all guests home.

During the next three days, the president got his video communications implant installed along with Howard Quill. Rudy Savage, Julie Preston, Ann, and Karen Quill also received their A/V implants. Howard and Karen also started their rejuvenation programs. So far, all seven members of the Simon crew and team have received their A/V implants, and five members are in the rejuvenation program.

Chapter 32

SECDEF

Oval Office. The president and SECDEF.

"Glen, I appreciate your help with my rush facilities acquisition. It certainly took a large amount of faith on your part. Now it's time to meet the spacecraft. Ready to travel?"

"Hell, yes, Mr. President/ I need to know I'm not crazy. How do we travel?"

"Follow me, Glen."

The president, SECDEF, and Secret Service agents Julie Preston and Rudy Savage exited the south office into the cloaked shuttlecraft where Brad was waiting. The oval door flowed closed and the shuttlecraft shot up toward the waiting Simon Spacecraft.

"My god," shouted the SECDEF, Glen Hauser. "All my doubts have vanished! In my early career, I was a pilot but not like this. I will die happy."

"Maybe not, Glen," said the president. "Just hold your thoughts."

The shuttlecraft docked, and they all gathered in the observation deck.

"Mr. Secretary," said Brad, "meet Simon Android!"

"Hello, Mr. Secretary, it's a pleasure having you aboard."

"Are you human?" asked the secretary. "And please call me Glen."

"No, Glen," said Simon, "this body is an Android body that I control. The artificial intelligence that is me is distributed throughout my spacecraft, but I didn't want our first meeting to seem too strange to you. A lot to cope with, but you will acclimate soon enough."

"Glen, I told you about the rejuvenation program I am enrolled in. Are you up for this? And what about your wife?"

"Erik, my wife is in the final stage of Alzheimer's disease, and her mind isn't there anymore. I don't expect her to last the month."

"I am sorry to hear that," Simon said. "Even our medical advances can't help in a case like that."

"I suspected as much, Simon. I am, however, willing and able to participate in your rejuvenation program. I have a masters in physics and an enormous scientific curiosity, so I want to see the future. I am not ready to die. We never had children but maybe someday in the future, who knows. By the way, Mr. President, now I understand why you grew a beard. Think I should do the same?"

"One day at a time, Glen. One day at a time," kidded the president.

"Okay, Glen," said Brad, "as soon as we have the cancers gone, we will imbed the A/V communications in you and start the rejuvenation program at the same time. Welcome aboard."

"Now, everyone, we have the possibility of a battle with my home planet people to prepare for," said Simon. "Ann will be coordinating with me on the neutronium production, and Brad plans to schedule a meeting here in a week for all of to cover where we are at this point in time and what we can expect. Okay, back home for now."

Chapter 33

Progress

*One week later, joint meeting, observation
deck on Simon Spacecraft*

"We have many things to cover in a short period of time, and it
was difficult getting all of us together at one time," said Brad. "This
will be the last all personnel meeting for a while."

"The neutronium production has started and is being manned
by long-time DOD cleared personnel with Ann Thompson in charge
and assisted by Simon. We will just meet our self-imposed schedule,
and Simon is building the remaining components onboard. When
the neutronium is ready, it will be brought up to the spacecraft for
the final assembly of the four war drones where they will stay until
deployment. We must be ready in five months from now."

"The chatter I am receiving is getting closer, and it seems they
are starting an active search to look for me. Remember, they have no
idea (where or even if I am at this time.) They are pinging to which,
if I was alive, I would automatically ping back, indicating where I am
and my status. I have taken control of that activity, and we will only
respond when we feel it fits our plan."

"Mr. Secretary, do you have any questions?"

"Yes, Simon. Situations may happen that we haven't planned
for, and I want to be ready with our own country weapons. When
this battle occurs, the cat will be out of the bag, and we will need to
be ready. The other countries on this planet will go bonkers, and we
should try and minimize that. Our enemies will try and grab anything they can. What do you say, Mr. President?"

"I am going to plan and be ready with everything we can bring fourth to keep world panic from being destructive. As the enemy spacecraft gets closer, I will brief congressional leaders, and we will have the military organized to help, and I expect I may need to invoke martial law. More on all of this in the next two months."

"Okay, we will get back into this in the next two months," said Brad. "One more item from Simon and then we will adjourn."

"Okay, everyone," Simon started. "This is the last item today but important. If Brad had found me in my sapient mode, you would have gotten an interstellar spacecraft that you possibly could have ordered around but not much more. If I had gotten pinged, I would have led the enemy right here, and you would have been in a dangerous situation. My AI, at that time, could run the spacecraft and do as its original government ordered, and any humanity on its part was nonexistent. As it turns out, large potential capability was built in with plans to try and increase the capability of my AI. War started, and they hid all their technology in my memory bay and shoved me out the door with plans to retrieve me at a more appropriate time. My getting shot down activated the full capabilities of my AI, and now, I am not sapient but sentient with enormous learning capability increasing all the time. It is fortunate that I met Brad when I came out of my electronic coma as I gained knowledge of what an actual being human is in person."

"From your standpoint, I think I realize how it may be difficult to work for or with a machine with artificial intelligence. You don't feed me food, so I am not dependent on you for that. I have attempted to tell you what is in this relationship for me which is, in the name of curiosity, we have a lot of the same goals, and that is significant. There were a few technical dangers from the way I was originally set up, and I have negated those, so we both are out of danger for the time being."

"I am learning constantly as you and I communicate, and time will steadily improve this. I do know that humans sometimes lie, sometimes for the greater good they say, as my biologicals did, but try to be as accurate as possible. We are going to be together possibly for hundreds of years and who knows where we will all wind up. We can make a good future working together. And something for all of us here to look forward to is that all of our decisions will decide how we spend this invaluable scientific collateral for the benefit of the human race, and I am considering myself in this general group. You see, it turns out that there is much more scientific data in my memory banks than I had originally thought. I am still searching, finding, decrypting, and sorting. These facts must be and stay secret with us, as the original crew of the Simon Spacecraft. We should only discuss this here onboard to be safe. It will take a long-time period for Earth to adapt to the coming new world view, and I can contribute in avoiding some of the mistakes made on my home planet. Okay, that I believe is quite enough for now, more later."

Chapter 34

Simon in Trouble

Simon stopped cold! If he was human, he would have broken out in a cold sweat with the realization that he could die at any moment. This would have been a nonconcern if he was sapient, but as a progressive sentient learning artificial intelligence, he does not want to join oblivion—to be nothing, to never be able to satisfy his curiosity again. He must freeze his actions immediately and seek human help. He never thought this would happen. He does need humans after all. And quickly!

"Brad, please, come to my memory bay immediately. This is an emergency. I will brief you on the way."

Brad leaped out of bed from a sound sleep and ran toward Simon's memory bay on the other side of the spaceship a hundred feet away.

"Brad," said Simon, "as you know, I have been opening up the memory bay to search its contents. I ran into an electronic roadblock and felt a counter start. I removed power in that section, and the counter stopped at thirty-two minutes. At random times, it starts counting down again and then stops. Remember, my biologicals put this keepsake memory bay together on my ship in a hurry; it was not done by AIs. I suddenly realize that I don't know enough about how you humans think; it has never before been important to an AI. Now, I have a concern about the logic I am using. It well may be inadequate. If this counter starts again, it could wipe my memory or, worse, cause self-destruction of me and my spacecraft. I need your background in engineering and the best human mind you can find for what you call computer science. I need your wetware to look at this."

"Simon," said Brad, "I will call the president immediately. Stand by."

"Erik, this is Brad. I have an emergency request from Simon. He has run into a critical and possible destructive problem in his memory bay, and we need a super software genius up here fast. This is a big security problem I know. Can you get back to me in thirty minutes? I will have a shuttlecraft standing by."

"Is the ship in danger?" asked the president.

"Don't know, but possibly," said Brad.

"Okay, Brad. I'm on it. Back to you shortly."

"Okay, Simon. I've started the process," said Brad. "I see you have two of your work drones here to help. Let me have the details please. Hold on, the president is calling back!"

"Okay, Brad," said the president. "Here is what the SECDEF and I got. I found out that the CIA has a guy who they illegally keep in a level 4 lockup. This means it is totally off the books and word of mouth. Only six people know. Now, I am now number seven. This guy is called Auger Downs. Don't know his real name. He has an IQ of over two hundred, total recall, and lives in a make-believe world. He is not physically dangerous but scary mentally if you know his background. Apparently, he has three documented times, literally saved the country, but also has a couple of disasters that no one seems to want to remember. One time, the World Bank was part of the picture, and a year later, we find that USD100 million is gone, and we don't know where and can't prove who. I have released him to two of our guys, Howard Quill and Rudy Savage, and they are waiting at our last pickup address. If anything goes bad, the first thing you do is shoot this guy. Consider this a nonconversation. Bye for now."

The shuttlecraft settled in Simon's landing bay, and Howard and Rudy got out with Auger Downs who was about five feet three, heavyset, and otherwise nondescript in looks. He was definitely alert and responsive, and the three rushed to the memory bay.

"Auger," said Brad, "here is the problem. The shuttlecraft you came here on, and this spacecraft you are on, is a part of a big movie we are making. It has this memory bay full of programs that are important and must remain intact for the movie, but one of our competitors may have sabotaged this equipment. Somehow, we inadvertently started a timer. We removed power, and it stopped at thirty-two minutes. We need to find out what the timer is for and remove any dangers, like, explosives. If you can help us, we will give you a free pass as the guest of honor for the first showing. These work drones will help you, just give them a voice command."

"Okay," said Auger. So far, these were the first words he spoke for the day!

Auger asked the drones to check over two hundred measurements and readouts as he proceeded to dig into the logic used by Simon's home planet.

"Simple," Auger said. "Whoever did this wanted to scare you into thinking that if you kept looking, everything would blow up. Just wanted to stop you. No explosives. They wanted all stuff here to be safe no matter what. The timer was to scare you. Ignore it. Can I go home now? Let's stop at Mc Donald's on the way. And don't forget my free pass that you promised."

Simon thought, *This is unbelievable!' This is difficult to even understand.*

Everyone let out a sigh of relief, and Howard and Rudy returned Auger to his CIA special home with a huge bag from Mc Donald's and the promise of a free movie pass.

"Hello, Brad, Erik here. I see our unmentionable is back home. I spent quite a few points to make that happen. I sure hope we don't have any more problems like that, but I know we probably will."

"Yeah, Mr. President, damn scary. You know, I had the feeling that Auger memorized much of what went on here. He was impossible to read, and hopefully, he got nothing he can make mischief with. Hopefully."

"Brad," said the president, "you and Simon need to assure that anything he could have learned can't be used against you. I know you recorded all that he did, so be sure and analyze that recording."

"We will. Have you discussed our situation with the secretary of state? We need to be prepared to mitigate the concerns of this upcoming battle and hold off the panic of world leaders, so our plans need to be in place."

"I have," said the president. "It took him a while to come around. Fortunately, I had Rudy and Howard in the office with me as backup. I need to get him up there to meet Simon and see for himself. By the way, we have done well on keeping our secrets, but slowly and surely, some important people are starting to feel that something is going on that is classified and mysterious as hell, and they are now pulling out all the stops to find out what it is. When the world finds out that the United States has a very powerful interstellar friend, and they, in effect, have lost, they will start jockeying for position, and this will be a tenuous time for all of us. We must be ready, using Simon technology, to immediately put down any threat that comes our way or the world might explode. We will be offering some of the technology that Simon has brought to us which will help calm things down. Must go, Brad. Bye for now."

Chapter 35

Demands

The number of intelligence agents coming into the country was getting ridiculous to the point that they were almost tripping over each other. The big secrets were being held by Simon in the spacecraft, and the cancer medical center just appeared to be breakthroughs that had finally happened with the technical genus of DARPA. The neutronium factory was buried so deep that it was still unrecognizable to anyone outside of the Simon people and SECDEF, so all these agents were extremely frustrated in their quest to uncover any unknown secret projects. All they could do was look busy to justify their own existence. Secret service covert agents were assigned to guard key personnel where possible to thwart any kidnapping attempts. Russia and China were on full alert and pestering our president on a weekly basis, and he claimed that he was in the same situation as they.

In the meantime, Ralph Pillerson, Secretary of State, was firming up his plans for several alternatives that could be set in motion on short notice.

Chapter 36

War Drones

The specific neutronium for the four war drones was now finished, and the production continued on to produce and stockpile the type of neutronium used in the Simon Spacecraft and the shuttlecraft. Brad believed it was necessary to assemble the war drones in Simon's manufacturing bay for the sake of security, so the war drone neutronium was packaged and transported by shuttlecraft to the spacecraft. Simon had used his equivalent 3-D printing capability to make all the subsystems for the war drones. Each subsystem was fused in position using molecular bonding, and in two weeks' time, the four war drones were completed structurally and ready for testing. Simon had his four robots booted up and each assigned to a war drone build and the Simon AI was independently controlling and coordinating each robot. If necessary, he could do this, talk with Brad, and pilot the spacecraft all at the same time.

The most crucial and first subsystem was the power supply and all its safeguards followed by the weapons with all their extraordinary safeguards. A mistake here could devastate everything, including the Simon Spacecraft. The communications, command, and control subsystem followed by cloaking. now the sapient pretested AI was incorporated into the chassis, activated, and rebooted. The whole system only took 500 ms to cold boot and then a mechanical voice said, *"This is Simon War Drone 1, testing complete, all parameters are green. This system is fully active and ready for service."*

Next, the faraday shield was added and finally all this was enclosed in its neutronium shield case. It was rebooted one more time and then put on standby, ready now for any action asked of it within its capability.

Chapter 37

War Planning

The Secretary of State, Ralph Pillerson, had been cycled through Simon previously and was present with the whole team, including the president and SECDEF.

Brad said that the interstellar chatter from the direction of Melthorne had significantly increased, and it was obvious that ships from Simon's home planet, Melthorne, were out looking for Simon. Originally, Simon thought it might have been destroyed, but it had not; it had gone incommunicado for a long period of time. Recently, they have woken up and have been periodically sending out an interrogation data pulse which never got answered as Simon had negated any response on his part, unless it was planned and approved. The planet authority wanted their technology back at any cost. Now, it was Simon's turn to address the meeting which he will do in his android persona.

"Okay, everyone, I will go over what we have to fight and defend with."

"The spaceship will be the command post for the battle with the shuttles as backup. All four war drones will be deployed along with both shuttles and myself joining the battle. I had mentioned that upgraded cloaking was used for the war drones. This was what you would term a software upgrade and includes hiding low-power short-path communications transmissions we will use for command and control. I will be upgrading both shuttles and myself next week. This, with the element of surprise, should be devastating for the enemy, and I will introduce some extra surprises. We will seem to be a much bigger force to the enemy than we really are which will be very confusing to them as they will be receiving from what looks like radio transmissions from thirty different directions. Any transmissions received from them will be forwarded to you and will be automatically converted to English."

"The plan is to accost the enemy approximately twenty million miles beyond the orbit of Mars and thus hopefully win the war long before they get anywhere near Earth. They have spread out in all directions from their home planet, and the interstellar chatter still indicates two to four spacecrafts approaching our solar system. They will be prepared to fight and take back their technology, but they will try to do minimal damage to my spacecraft. They definitely will not expect to be met by any hostile force or a sentient spacecraft. I want to take a couple of prisoners, if possible, so we can interrogate them and find out what their current status is. It is imperative that we don't allow anyone to escape back to their home world or get any transmissions out. The war drones and shuttlecraft will be under my control, and I will try to hit all the enemy ships at once to prevent any transmissions on their part. This is the theory, but we don't have total control of the outcome, too many variables. I need the shuttlecrafts manned to take prisoners, and I will provide the equipment to restrain them, including the buzz units which will put them to sleep for about two hours. Now, I'm sure you have questions and comments, so speak up, please."

"Simon," said Brad, "I feel we could be setting ourselves for failure here. You are the key to controlling the two shuttlecrafts and the four war drones. If anything happened to you or even just your communications, we are in deep trouble. We need the ability to disconnect from you in the event of trouble and run the war drones directly from the shuttlecraft using their sapient AI commanded by our voice. We also need to practice this scenario."

"I don't understand how they could possibly, unless I have missed something in my command structure," said Simon. "I was designed and built as one-of-a-kind experimental spacecraft, so I must admit there could be sneak circuits I am not aware of. I could not finish a sneak circuit analysis and all the other design analysis in time, so I will make sure that you are able to disconnect from me and take over the war drones on your own. We should now have two crew in each shuttlecraft. I will need Brad, Ann, and Howard with me, and I assume the president, SECDEF, and secretary of state will need to remain on Earth, so I am two crew short for the shuttlecraft."

"This is late in the game to get two more people," said Brad. "The best answer is to get two more from the Secret Service again. They already have the training we need and have worked with the agents onboard.

"This recruitment," said the president, "is being felt, believe me. Our need is the highest priority, so I will proselyte two more. Howard, Rudy and Julie, please see me on any recommendations you may have."

The SECDEF, General Glen Hauser, spoke up, "I have some ideas for crew personnel I will work on, Brad. I strongly suggest we get at least six more people and keep hiring, so we don't come up short again. You certainly have enough room here on the spacecraft."

"Time to adjourn," said Brad. "Those returning to Earth, please board your shuttlecraft."

Simon, Brad, and Ann remained onboard.

Brad had another thought on his mind. "Simon, since you weren't production built but an experimental hand-built prototype, isn't it possible that there could be a second upgrade input? This is within the world of possibilities, right? And could you get a command that you had to act on verbally?"

"And to keep this thought going," said Ann, "where did the sapient AIs come from for the shuttlecraft and the war drones?"

"Brad," said Simon, "you are correct, there could even be a hand-wired upgrade input with a direct path to my brain! I have just started a search program to look for this. Logically, it wouldn't be connected to a wireless signal, but this needs to be verified. And, Ann, there were ten sapient AI units in my stores. I can't think of a reason why. These are simple units I can manufacture myself, but it was easier to use the models on hand. I do have their digital schematics and drawings, and yes, there is a remote wireless upgrade input, just one. And, no, a verbal code can't command me. Good call, my human friends, you may have saved the day. If the enemy would have realized the possibility and seized the opportunity, they could turn the shuttlecraft and war drones against the spacecraft. Just thinking about it clogs my neural pathways. This certainly verifies the synergy of a sentient AI, me, and you human comrades working together toward our common goals."

Back at the White House, the president, Erik, SECDEF, General Glen Hauser, and Secretary of State Ralph Pillerson were meeting in the top-secret glass conference room.

"This," said the president, "is the only safe place in the White House to meet when discussing our extraterrestrial activities, gentlemen. Also, we can always find a safe place for ourselves and hook up with our A/V implants, but we need to be extremely cautious. The FBI came into my office yesterday and stated that the three of us are under increased surveillance, including long-range telescopic microphones and lip readers with binoculars. When all our activities are surfaced, every nation will be at least one peg lower when compared to us which will make for much unhappiness. We have got to convince them that, now, they need to all pull together as one to survive the next chapter where we are a world-united civilization. It won't be easy, and the United States is going to need to use a very strong hand."

"I agree," said Ralph, "but the United States is the country that has been releasing improved medical techniques, including cancer detection treatments and cures for which the world has been extremely grateful, and all that goodwill should ease any bitterness. Also, there will be more technology that we can incrementally release which will again help. We will still have the nutjobs which could be dangerous to us and Simon and nation leaders which will try and get next to Simon and replace us. We need to stick to our guns at all costs, always."

"I talked with Brad," said Glen, "and he agrees that we need to keep building a Simon organization that we will need as things get more complex."

"One last item, gentlemen," said the president. "The lifespan of the human race on this planet will increase, so if the birth rate stays the same, we will outgrow the planet resources. Migration to other planets can mitigate this, but we need to think about this now and start planning immediately right after our big interstellar conflict. The other item is the rejuvenation program that nine of us are in with more to join us soon. I don't know how to handle this getting out; it could damn near destroy us, and apparently, it did just about destroy Simon's home planet.

"Yes, Mr. President, and look in the mirror. Now, your beard is looking young and vibrant, and look at the muscles in your arms! From now on, wear long-sleeved shirts, all of us. This really is going to be difficult. And my new youth is gleeful. We need to remember though that accidents can still kill us."

Chapter 38

Manning Up

The SECDEF had kept his word and had six solid candidates for Brad.

"Brad, this is Glen Hauser, calling over the person-to-person A/V implant. I needed to use our implants for security. I have six candidates who I will personally vouch for, ready for review. All have top-secret crypto clearance and are career military and are willing to take on an exciting challenge. They don't know what that challenge is yet. The first is Dr. Laurie Smothers, flight surgeon and pilot. The second is an astronaut, Sam Nugent. He has been on four missions to the ISS, and this assignment will blow his mind. Number three and four are DOD military spacecraft engineers on loan to NASA. Bill Farr, thirty-five, and Ken Johnson.

Number five and six, Mary Wilson and Roy Miller, thirty-seven.

"Brad," added Glen, "important points. They will know that you are their new boss and that you, in effect, sign their paychecks. They are all aggressive but loyal and no troublemakers in the group. The last point is I am generally aware of how you, Simon, and our present situation have evolved, but I don't know where you and Simon stand with the president and our country. If you are an independent entity, your arrangement should state this, or some members of congress will try and take your goodies away! Always use worst-case planning and document your organization. These candidates expect your physical checkup but do not know anything about rejuvenation. Make sure all your people keep this segregated. Okay, Brad, no more lectures. I will have the candidates ready in two days and call you for pickup time and place."

"Hello, Erik," said Brad over their private A/V network. "Glen has no doubt informed you of the six new candidates. I plan to keep and house them onboard Simon along with some others onboard."

"Erik, do we need some kind of contract between us? I think Glen might have been concerned about some members of congress. I would like to avoid any complications right now as the upcoming confrontation will need all our time."

"Don't worry about that right now, Brad. In the future possibly, but in the meantime, no one will be in a position to bother you."

"We all," said Brad, "need to remember that Simon is an independent sentient being, not a property and doesn't belong to anyone or anyplace."

"Brad," said the president, "believe me, I know and understand what you are worried about, and I will put a fast stop to any bad ideas. I have learned a lot from being a politician, not all good. We both can lookout for Simon."

Chapter 39

Private Chat

"Simon," said Brad, "I thought this might be a good time for the three of us to talk since Ann and I are the only people on the ship at present."

"That's good with me, Brad, but I do feel curious about keeping secrets. But, then, I remember that you and Ann are my first crew members."

"We just want to spell out where we think we all stand," said Ann. "Soon, there will be a lot more people onboard, and that will add complexity to all our relationships."

"Simon, you are a thinking sentient being as are myself and Ann. At least that's what we think of you as. We have our organization, and I manage this organization, but you are a team member who just happens to be a very advanced spaceship, not a slave who is a piece of equipment. Does that make sense?"

"Thank you, both of you," said Simon. "I have been thinking about where I stand as myself and as a crew member. I understand all this a lot more as I have been digesting your history via the Internet. We are alike in a lot of ways and yet so different. This will take a lot more time. Oh, and more from the Internet. Love and romance. I am having great difficulty understanding that."

"That's okay, Simon. We humans have great difficulty with that at times ourselves," said Ann. "We just want to make sure you know that nobody can claim you or think that they own you. If we take any prisoners from Melthorne, they may claim you are their property. Not so anymore, and then Brad's children are his property. If anyone from Earth government attempts to claim you, we and the president will set them straight very fast.

"Also, Simon," said Brad, "when we are manned up with a lot of people onboard, some humans may forget that you are sentient. They have never experienced an AI machine-learning being before, so they may need to be gently reminded from time to time. If, when carrying out orders, you are asked or told to do something you think is wrong, ask questions. And something else as we get more people onboard. If you feel that something isn't quite right or sense danger, especially from another human, call both Ann and I on our implants and let us know. As far as running the ship, you are the quick thinker or processor, not us. As time goes on. Simon, the rough edges will wear down as we humans say, but in the meantime, keep your guard up. All the people coming onboard have been very thoroughly checked out, but nothing is a hundred percent. Simon, thank you for the talk, and anytime you want to talk to us, do. This is how we all get to know each other."

Back in the crew quarters, Brad and Ann were talking.

"Brad, that conversation was something I never thought or even envisioned happening."

"Me, too, Ann, but I think we both felt that this was a good time. From here on out, things are going to ramp up pretty fast, and I don't want anyone confused about duty or loyalty, and yes, we are getting to know Simon better as he is us. We are both building trust, you and I with each other and us with Simon. Like you, I had never even thought before this about a relationship with a machine except in science fiction. We both know about building trust with animals and how long that can sometimes take but not an AI."

"Yes, Brad," said Ann. "Simon is extremely intelligent and is learning more each day as he gains experience. His help could very well save our planet. And, you know, we need to think about starting up production of intelligent fighting vehicles, so we can get a head start. Area 51 has served before in this capacity and can again. I gained a lot of knowledge at DARPA about this."

"Ann, I knew you were special. I wish I had met you a long time ago."

"That sounds fascinating, Brad. Hold that thought. Let's hit the food replicator and chat some more with Simon."

Chapter 40

New Crew Onboard

The next morning arrived, and the view from Simon's observation was from one hundred miles straight up over the White House, and a beautiful view it was. The spaceship was cloaked and undetectable by any Earth technology, and Simon's sensors could detect any dangers well beyond the inner planets, so they were as safe as you could possibly be. Brad and Ann had just finished breakfast, and they had discussed the degree to keep everything safe inside the spacecraft and especially the memory bay. Simon decided to encase the memory storage in neutronium with him, Brad, and Ann having the only access. This covering would not give away what was underneath.

Ann took one of the shuttles to pick up the six new candidates, plus Rudy Savage and Julie Preston. Nine people in a shuttle was a tight fit but doable. Her pickup point was inside a large unused aircraft hangar; she cautiously and silently approached the building. The hangar door was open, and it was somewhat dark inside, so she silently eased the cloaked shuttle floating six inches off the floor to within one foot of the eight people standing together and decloaked. Pandemonium broke out as the people reacted with total shock and awe. The shuttle door ovals magically appeared in each side of the neutronium hull.

"Good morning, everyone. I'm Ann. Please, climb in. It might be a tight squeeze, but there is room for everyone."

They all climbed in through the neutronium ovals that served as the doors and were then filled in as if they never existed. Ann then recloaked the shuttle, which meant that from the outside, no one could see anything. The people inside the shuttle could see everything in the shuttle and each other. Julie and Rudy had seen all this before, but the new people gasped in amazement and excitement.

"Where are we going?" asked one of the newbies.

"One hundred miles straight up over the White House," said Ann. "And you won't feel any gravity change as we have automatic inertial damping and gravity control. You should be as comfortable as in your family car but a lot safer."

"Can you serve food?" asked one of the guys, joking.

"Actually, yes. There is a food replicator behind you, but let's wait until we get onboard the spacecraft. Better food up there."

They approached Simon and a huge door, large enough to let the shuttle in, appeared, and Ann parked inside. Again, there were gasps among other statements of shock and surprise. The big oval opening filled in, and everyone exited the shuttle.

"Ann, how come the oxygen didn't escape?" asked one of the new guys.

"Plasma shield," said Ann. "All of you please follow me to the observation deck."

The new people were like kids in a candy store expecting to wake up from a dream any minute. They were introduced to Simon Android and Brad Young who explained their new environment and their schedule for the first day. They were especially shocked to learn that Simon was an AI and his clothes were the spaceship. They were divided into two groups which were separately toured around the ship and run through the medical bay for checkups. They were shown their living quarters, and all gathered two hours later in the observation deck.

Brad spoke: "Ladies and gentlemen, welcome to Simon. Organizationally all of you report to me as does Simon. I may put in more structure later on, but for now, we operate as I have explained. Before I move on, any initial questions?"

"Yes," said Roy Miller. "Who does Simon belong to?"

"No one," said Brad. "Simon is a sentient being as you and I are. He is amazingly intelligent and a friend. We are facing a potential space war, and we are lucky to have him. I will go into more details tonight at dinner, and I will also detail the full capabilities of Simon Spacecraft and its weapon systems."

"It will take time to get used to all this new life of yours, and also, your life now is top secret, and you should already know that. For the next two hours, I need the six new members to become familiar with the different areas of the ship. Simon will answer most of your questions. Oh, and I will have your medical test results tomorrow morning and will go over the results with each of you. Be back here at 13:00 hours for lunch and more Q and A."

At 13:00 hours, they all gathered for a food-replicator lunch which they found to be amazingly good for synthetic food. There were many questions on Simon and on the spaceship's capabilities. Simon was attending lunch as Simon Android and the new guys were just starting to grasp the idea of working with an artificial intelligence teammate. Attitudes were slowly changing and enlarging.

For the afternoon, Brad had Simon move the spacecraft to the far side of the moon where each of the candidates got a chance to pilot one of the shuttles and do touch and goes using a flat spot on the moon's surface as a runway. It took some time for everyone to learn how to work with the shuttle's sapient AI, and they were somewhat shocked to learn that Simon could fly both shuttles and all the war drones at the same time if needed, but there were risks. It worked much better with a trained crew involved. They finished up pilot practice and headed back to their hover spot, one hundred miles straight up from the White House.

After dinner, everyone retired to their rooms to read documents Brad and Ann had prepared on some of the details expected in a battle in space.

Brad and Ann were in the CIC discussing the new crew, and Simon had joined the conversation.

"The crew is a mature and highly educated collection of people, Brad, a good start. I can see that they will work well together," said Simon.

"I believe so," said Brad. "This is new to all of us. And, Simon, this is a good time to ask how you feel about working with us humans?"

"So far, good. When I was sapient, I took some abuse, but I didn't really care, but it is enlightening to be treated with respect. I am slowly developing the ethical part of my mind. I have listened to and watched your radio and television as it developed, and some of it was not the best model for ethical behavior. Do you and Ann agree with me on this?" asked Simon.

"Wow," said Ann. "Yes, and I'm sure I speak for both of us on this question. Simon, you are learning fast. Ethics is something we all develop as we learn how to live together and get along with each other. We all want a high degree of trust."

"Simon?" asked Brad. "As we get closer to battle, I have more technical questions. How much damage can you take? Can you be forced offline? Do you or will you ever need a reboot. If so, what can we do to assist? What should we do to minimize damage?"

"I don't always take into account that I am part of a team and that there is a big synergy in all of us working in concert," said Simon. "To answer your questions, my neutronium hull is very robust, and it is instantly self-repairing itself as needed. My hull is like your skin, a living organ, and I feed energy to it to repair itself. The matter–antimatter unit in my ship is the largest ever built on Melthorne, and the availability of massive power will help overcome many problems. My memory bay and all components of my AI are extensively shielded with triple redundancy, so my ship would need to be almost demolished to kill me. And then, if there is a copy of me, I could be brought back to the time of my last backup."

"If I am severely damaged, I would revert back to the sapient AI that I once was which would be just like the AIs in the shuttles. No people knowledge, no personality. I just try to do what you ask of me with much slower response. No one can force me to revert, and there is no secret code to force reversion. I could pretend to revert as a ruse, but I can't see why. Remember, I am distributed all over the ship, so I might need time to reboot as you call it. I will give both of you the diagnostic codes and how to enter them into my system. Please, memorize them; don't write them down. As far as my actually being destroyed, a special backup of me entered into a new hardware version of my model would bring me back to who I was at the point of my last backup. If I did revert to sapient and you entered the codes, you would get the expected time for reboot to sentient plus any other pertinent data.

"I realize you both are concerned about me being offline or in some way taken over by a hostel force. I have spent many hours verifying that there are no more pathways than those we have identified to my control circuitry. We do, however, have knowledge of usable paths to take over the Melthorne ship AIs if warranted, and we should limit who has that information. The shuttles and the war drones have these paths, but I have disabled them. Any attempted commands to them will be ignored but recorded for analysis. I also have voiceprints of every human who has been on this ship, so let's set this up, so I take orders from either one of you and no one else unless you authorize. The exception would be if you are out of contact or dead. I have been learning, and I can work my way around this.

"The last item I want to say is that we are in this together. I do not understand the whole concept of loyalty and yet you have my loyalty which feels to me like belonging to something good. I'm not sure if I expressed that correctly, but you must understand what I mean. If someone wanted me to do something that I felt was inherently correct, but you absolutely disagreed, I would be with you. There are subsets of this, and ethics are difficult sometimes, but I am slowly learning. I started out as a clean slate when I first woke up, so I need to acquire lots of knowledge that you take many years to acquire. You often learn by mistake. I need to avoid that and learn from you. The amount of power I have at my beck and call must be frightening to you at times, but we can handle it. Brad and Ann, does this worry you?"

"Simon, this is the longest conversation we have ever had, and from my viewpoint, you are learning exceptionally fast. Our minds are definitely gaining more understanding of each other. Understanding between machine artificial intelligence and human biological intelligence is now a fact, something I never thought I would be saying," said Ann.

"I agree completely," added Brad. "Time for sleep, Ann. More practice tomorrow."

As they walked back to their sleeping area, Ann remarked, "You know, Brad, a girl can tell when someone is looking at her."

"Was I that obvious?" asked Brad.

"Actually, yes, and for some time. Did I embarrass you?"

"Well, no, not really. I don't want to complicate our lives, but I don't want to miss the boat either. Your thoughts?"

"Maybe we both feel the same way," said Ann. "Tell you what, I'll buy lunch day after tomorrow. No need to rush, I understand we have at least six hundred years."

"Very funny," said Brad. "I'll take you up on lunch date though. Night, Ann."

"Night, Brad."

Chapter 41

Implants

Next morning at breakfast.

"Okay, everyone," said Brad. "I have a subject we haven't discussed before. Ann and I have audio/video implants. They are surgically installed behind the right or left ear and have a range of three hundred thousand miles. It uses subatomic particles with very low power requirements and draws what it does need directly from your body with no side effects. There is a small bump behind the ear for manual operation while you learn the mental procedure for its operation. After implanting, it takes a couple of days for the audio to be enabled and two more days for the video to be connected to your optic nerve. There is a visual indication when it is on, so you won't be transmitting accidentally. An *X*-ray would just see what looks like a small benign tumor, but avoid any examination if possible; we can usually take care of you here. The fact that you have these implants is top secret as you may have guessed. I want to start implantation today, and while Simon Android would be the surgeon, I want Dr. Laurie Smothers to work with him, so she can learn the procedure herself. Any questions?"

Pandemonium again.

"Am I moving too fast for you people?" asked Brad.

Dr. Laurie spoke up, "I've got to see this. No problem on my receiving the implants. OMG, how exciting!"

Sam Nugent remarked, "I really could have used this on my space walks when I was an astronaut on the ISS."

Everyone was in, no exceptions.

"Okay, here is the schedule," said Brad. A half hour per person starting at 8:00 a.m. After that, take the day off and rest, sleep, or, at the most, read. I need all of you to be relatively inactive for twenty-four hours after the surgery."

"Hey, Brad, anymore big things like this in the future?" asked Roy Miller.

"Actually, yes, but I can't talk about anything yet," said Brad. "Okay, let's get started. You first Bill Farr."

Brad made arrangements with Howard Quill, Rudy Savage, and Julie Preston to take a day off tomorrow from the Secret Service to meet with the new recruits and to cover for him and Ann for a couple of hours while they took care of personal business. He cautioned them that the new guys were to be in the dark about rejuvenation at this point in time.

Brad met separately with each new recruit and went over their physicals. They all had come out well with the exception of one pancreatic cancer problem which would easily be treated. All were pumped about the implants.

The president was calling on Brad's implant. "Brad, Howard mentioned he, Julie, and Rudy were visiting tomorrow, and I would like to join them. They are still Secret Service, so they can act as my bodyguards. Okay with you?"

"Yes, Mr. President, no problem. When Ann and I come down, we all can meet in the hangar. I have a car parked there. Simon remotely will fly you four up to the ship and back down three hours later to the hangar. I assume you can park the presidential limousine in the hangar with guards?"

"Yes, no problem. Thanks, Brad. Bye."

The next day came, and all surgeries had gone well. They were all anxious for the audio portion of the implant to kick in. Brad informed the group that he and Ann would be off ship for three hours around noon and that they would have a special visitor.

"Ann, ready for our lunch date?"

"Ready and hungry. I'm all set. How about you?"

"Me, too. Let's grab a shuttle and go."

They flew uneventfully to the hangar pickup point as Ann chirped, "Hey, Brad, Daddy Simon let us use the car again."

Brad took the cloaked shuttle down to six off the ground and silently glided up to the president and Secret Service agents. The oval doors flowed open as he turned the cloaking off and everyone expectedly jumped.

"Damn it, Brad. I will never get used to that," said the president.

"Where is your limousine?" asked Brad.

"They are nearby waiting for a call to return to the White House. I didn't want them seeing the shuttle. I see Howard just sent them on their way."

"Mr. President, you sure are looking younger every day! Your office is supposed to age you," said Ann.

"Yeah, I know. I plan to add some gray to my hair to back off the critics. See you and Ann in three hours, have fun."

The president and Howard, Julie, and Rudy boarded the shuttle. Simon's voice greeted them, and the cloaked shuttle zipped off to the spacecraft.

"Ann, before we leave, I want to plant a couple of bugs just to be cautious."

"Good idea, Brad. There are more foreign agents trying to find out what is going on than ever these days. They haven't figured out our secrets yet, and it must be driving them nuts," said Ann.

As they drove away in Brad's car, he asked, "So where are you taking me for lunch Ann?"

"To a small Italian restaurant where I used to go to when I worked for DARPA. It's a nice quiet place, and we can get a booth where we can talk without having a whole bunch of people around."

Chapter 42

Presidential Visit

Meanwhile, the shuttle arrived at the spacecraft and parked, and the president and agents went to the observation deck where Simon Android and the new recruits were waiting. Being military men, they jumped up and saluted.

"At ease, please. This is a short visit," he said as he introduced the three Secret Service agents who were part-time crew members but soon to be full-time crew members. "Howard Quill will be staying here for a while when I return to Earth."

"Is the situation what you expected?" asked the president?

"Anything but sir," remarked Sam Nugent. "We have just received our A/V implants and are waiting for them to kick in. This spacecraft is not just functional but very comfortable, and the food replicator is unbelievable. So how long is this going to be classified?"

"As long as we can," said the president. "This is a lot to disclose all at once publicly, and we need the secrecy for sound military reasons. I think you can imagine the reaction from other countries when this is announced. In the meantime, we have a skirmish coming up with beings from another planet which will be very hostile to us. You are going to be right in the middle of this, so be prepared for whatever comes next. The SECDEF promised you a challenging assignment which you certainly have got, and you are our first-line defense, so stay sharp.

Simon Android spoke up: "Everyone, lunch is served, and I added several items to the replicator for your pleasure. Please, be seated."

Back on Earth, Brad and Ann were starting lunch.

"At long last, quiet time for you and me, Brad."

"Yes, you know, it is much harder than I thought to get quality private time on Simon with lots of people around, and we shouldn't do anything that will hurt our command authority. The challenge is I want to get to know you better, and we need alone time for that."

"Me, too, Brad. Me, too. We need to watch our body language. I read a book on that not too long ago, and you would be amazed on how much you unconsciously give away with your body language."

They ate a slow lunch and talked for two hours, bathed in, and enjoyed their new relationship. Finally, Brad's imbedded A/V came on line. "Brad, your bugs in the hangar got a bite. A man came cautiously into your hangar and installed a bug of his own. Don't go into the hangar until I send the shuttle down, and I will kill the new bug with a short low-power burst. I used the second bug you installed to follow the perp back to his lair, so we can see who is trying to get information."

"Okay, Simon."

Simon had enabled Ann's A/V, so she could listen in.

"Let's head back, Ann. This job is always interesting, isn't it?"

"Absolutely, and should we rethink the need for personnel protection from now on whenever we are on Earth? This would be an especially bad time for something to happen to us, wouldn't it?"

On A/V, copy Ann: "Simon, keep the president and Howard up to date please."

"Already have Brad. The area around the hangar is clear but slow down. I am approaching the back of the hangar and am sighting on the new bug. Okay, got it. It is electronically dead. Okay to come inside the hangar."

Brad slowly drove into the hangar just after Simon remotely brought the shuttle in. Everyone gathered, and the burned-out bug was given to the president to take back for analysis. The president mentioned that he needed to come up with a protection plan for himself and Ann for whenever they were on Earth. Brad and Ann boarded the shuttle and started back to the spacecraft, and the limousine pulled in and returned the president, Julie, and Rudy to the White House.

On the shuttle, on the way back to the spacecraft, Ann snuggled up to Brad and remarked that it would be difficult for them to have much time together.

Brad said, "Yes, but we can try."

They parked and immediately went to the observation deck where Howard Quill and the others were talking.

"Hello, everyone. How did the presidential visit go?" asked Brad.

"Great," said Howard. "Apparently, they had no idea of the president's degree of involvement and were pleasantly happy with the strong support for the space activities."

"Simon, were you able to track our hangar intruder?" asked Brad.

"Yes, he went to the Russian Embassy, and our bug went with him. It is now lodged in the ambassador's office, so we should get a lot of information. They don't know what we are doing and were surprised that their bug failed so soon. We are going to try and get another bug in their embassy to follow their bug installer around. There is little chance of them finding the bugs as they have the smarts to avoid detection and transmit using an undetectable signal."

"Simon, please, warn the president," said Brad. "He will want his people on this."

"Brad," on A/V, "I just got Simon's message. I asked him to feed his bug information straight to us. The Russians are going nuts trying to figure us out, and so far, they only have their suspicion, so I expect they will increase their probing. The bugs will help us know what is coming next."

"Erik, it's going to be a painful transition to get this planet to pull together as one to combat off world threats, so in the meantime, we should start building spaceships and shuttles on a crash program. Is this something that Area 51 could handle?"

"That would be the best place for security Brad. I will get with SECDEF and see what we need to and how fast we can do it. You already have a manufacturing operation setup for the neutronium. Can you increase its production?"

"Yes, Erik. And I kept it going after the war drones, so we already have a small stockpile to start with. I'll get Ann to work that. Simon would be the main designer, and we need a new fresh design for this. How are you coming along on disguising your youthful appearance?"

"Only fair, so far. One of the problems is that I walk and move like a young athletic guy which is not the guy everyone has known over the last few years. Also, my voice is stronger, and my reactions are faster. It's a wonderful feeling but confusing to people who have been around me for a while. I'll keep working on it day by day. Brad, must go. Bye for now."

"Bye, Erik."

Brad walked over to Ann sitting alone drinking coffee.

"Mind if I join you?"

"Of course not. You never need to ask!"

"If okay with you, I wanted to ask Simon to move our quarters away from the general quarters area and closer to the combat information center (CIC). You go for that? We would have a little more privacy as the leaders who run this operation."

"Yes! A wonderful idea."

"I'll work it."

"Simon," on A/V, "Brad here. Would it be possible to have quarters for Ann and I away from the general quarters area, say closer to the CIC?"

"Yes," replied Simon. "Actually, it would be quite easy. There are two contiguous spaces that could be converted. I will have it completed in two hours."

"Simon, who do you use for help?"

"My robots of course. I can use up to all four at once. Most helpful. Go pack up your belongings, and I will move them."

"Also, we need sensors to show who is coming into our area. I don't want people just walking in on us."

"That's easy," replied Simon. "Actually, just some software changes. I'll have it done by evening."

"Thank you, Simon," said Brad.

"I also installed a door between your new quarters. You may need it."

Brad whispered to Ann, "New quarters tonight in two hours. Love this A/V system."

Dinner was over, and Simon had tried new food-replicator items with great success.

"By tomorrow, you, new guys, should get some indications that your audio is connecting. I think you will be pleasantly surprised. Two more days for the video. See you all in the morning."

A couple of hours later, Brad and Ann met in their new quarters.

"Wow, Brad, bigger and, most important, privacy for us. Nervous?"

"Yeah, a little now that you mention it. How about you?"

"I would say more like anxious, Brad. Let me show you what I mean."

Chapter 43

Final Preparation

Everyone was gathered in the observation deck with Brad discussing the design and manufacturing of a new spacecraft. Simon was involved and had several ideas for design improvements in the overall spacecraft itself and of the various subsystems. The design revolved around small shuttles similar to the two shuttles we already have, utility-sized spacecraft around fifty feet in diameter, fast fighter-sized long range around two hundred feet in diameter, and battleship-sized one thousand feet in diameter.

"We have the capability," said Brad, "with you people here to carry out these requirements to the next level, and that's what I need you to do. I will meet with you at the end of each day, and I will have SECDEF meet with us in two days to put his spin on what he thinks we need. The six of you organize yourselves and make this work. If you feel the need to change the sizes we are starting with, do so if you can justify it. Don't forget Simon; he can be a tremendous help so keep him in your meetings. Ann and I will get together with all of you late afternoon to see where we are."

"Ann, let's grab a cup of coffee."

"Okay, with you, let's go."

Coffee was poured. "Ann, last night was something I'll never forget, but tonight we must get some sleep. I'm sure glad we are in the rejuvenation program. It helps us get by on much less sleep."

"I know, Brad. Apparently, our hormones are getting rejuvenated too," as she giggled. "Watch out, you were about to hold my hand! Very good thought, but people are watching. This is going to be more difficult than I thought."

"We can make it all work, Ann. Just don't let your guard down."

"I had a long discussion with SECDEF, and he will meet with us midweek, Ann. We can do this program. Boeing did something like this back in WWII."

The days came and went, the secretary of defense put in his input midweek, and by the end of the week, they had their recommendations. They had contacted Navy shipbuilders with questions and many others.

The caller ID that was superimposed on their virtual switchboard just said DOD Pentagon. All calls were untraceable. Area 51 sure was going to be busy.

Brad and Ann had found their own equilibrium for their personal life and worked to bring all the recommendations together. The neutronium could be made, the overall structures fabricated, but the artificial intelligence unit and the matter–antimatter unit were apt to take a long time just due to lack of knowledge and experience.

Chapter 44

Chatter

Simon had just picked up what looked like conversations of Melthorne people between two spacecrafts nearing our solar system. The name on one spacecraft was Dr. Will Zorg who Simon remembered as the chief scientist for the planet and who was always in contention with the leadership of the planet. They were talking back and forth about finding Simon, their lost spaceship.

Simon notified Brad and Ann who then notified the president. The six recruits were woken up, and Rudy Savage and Julie Preston were notified that a shuttle was on the way to the new pickup point to bring them to Simon. This was all accomplished using the personal A/V implants, and the full implants had kicked in for the new recruits. The world press usually had some way somewhere to catch word of a big operation starting, but they were out of luck here.

The president met with SECDEF General Glen Hauser, Secretary of State Ralph Pillerson, and Howard Quill in the ultrasecure glass conference room. All three were in contact with Brad, Ann, and Simon on an implant conference call.

"Brad, how do you characterize this at the moment?" asked the president.

"Like a small hunting party looking for their lost ship and not necessarily expecting any trouble.

Simon spoke up, "My old sapient memory shows Dr. Will Zorg as essentially the chief scientist for the planet and one that most of the scientists looked to for leadership and guidance. He and the dictator, Grouse Hemler, never got along well."

"Well," Brad said, "that means we don't just blast him out of space without warning. I want to hear what he has to say."

"So do I," said the president. "But, Brad, minimize risk, don't get shot down yourself. Zorg may not play fair when he finds out he doesn't own Simon anymore."

"Don't worry," replied Brad. "We will try and work something out. I see Julie and Rudy have arrived. I can send one shuttle back to the new secure pickup location for your clandestine use. We will be out of range, but you can fly it with voice input to the sapient AI. It has all your personal data, so it will always recognize you. Make sure you are always cloaked and don't lose it, please."

"Good idea," said the president. "It can get me across the world faster than Air Force One in an emergency. And, Brad, it will be guarded like Fort Knox. Can we keep in touch via our A/V implants?"

"Only up to three hundred thousand miles normally, but Simon will drop a communications satellite booster which will add another ten million miles. Best we can do."

"Okay," said the president. "We obviously will be on edge here. Good luck. Bye."

"Bye."

"Everyone, please listen up! Once we get close to the incoming spacecraft, we will go to battle stations. Your assignments are as follows: Laurie and Julie, man medical bay. Sam and Rudy, man the shuttle bay; we should expect company. Ann, Bill, Ken, Mary, and Roy with me in the CIC. We are about one hundred and seventy million miles to go, so Simon, how long will it take?"

"I'm inside the solar system," said Simon. "It will take about forty minutes. This will put us close to them about thirty million miles past the orbit of Mars. We will be cloaked, and our sensors will see them before they sense us.

"Take us there, Simon!" commanded Brad. "Let me know when within communications range."

"We have new weapons being designed," said Brad, "but in the meantime, we have the Beretta 9-mm handguns. Everyone, please strap on a weapon. Any questions?"

"Okay, let's get ready."

"Brad, we are about two hundred thousand miles and closing. They have been pinging me on a random basis, and they are not cloaked. If you want to communicate, I can translate in the voice I am translating if you like. Also, you can get video on the screen if you want; just ask."

"Battle stations, everyone! Simon, weapons hot. Open a comm channel."

"Dr. Will Zorg, are you receiving my call?"

"This is Dr. Zorg. Who is this? Where are you calling from?"

"I am Brad Young. What are you doing in this region of space?"

"I am looking for a lost item. Can you transmit video?"

"Yes, I want to see who I am talking to."

"Simon, line them up in your sights, both ships for a disabling shot. Only fire if they fire, or upon my command."

"Understood, Brad."

"Video on!"

Dr. Zorg appeared on screen. The background showed two other people and what looked like a smaller ship.

"I can see you now, Captain. The background in the picture looks familiar! What kind of spacecraft are you flying?"

"Dr. Zorg, before I answer any questions, where are you from?"

"I am from a planet called Melthorne."

"Would you like to come onboard and talk? Do you have a spacesuit?"

"My ship has one spacesuit."

"Put it on, and I will send a shuttle for you. We have you on visual and are right next to you. We have launched our shuttle now. Do you see it?"

"How do I know this is a peaceful meeting?"

"If it wasn't, you would have been blasted out of space along with your other ship. We sincerely want to meet and talk with you."

"I sense sincerity, so I shall take a chance and leave as soon as I am suited up."

"Good," said Brad Young. "My shuttle will pull up to you when it sees you."

"Comm off, keep video on, Simon."

"There he is," said Ann. "The shuttle just pulled and opened a portal. He's in, portal closed, and shuttle on the way. You know, Brad, he may recognize some of the components in the shuttle."

"Brad, to shuttle bay. Sam and Rudy, the shuttle will be back in moments. Treat our guest with courtesy, but stay alert; that could change in a flash. As soon as he is out of his spacesuit, escort him to the recreational deck. Simon will translate for you."

"Ann, keep a watch on the video. Mary and Ken, you're with me. We are off to the recreational deck."

They had just sat down when Sam and Rudy walked in with Dr. Zorg. Normally, on Earth, you would expect a world chief scientist to be rather elderly and gray haired, probably with a beard and just generally old.

Dr. Zorg was obviously in his prime. He was extremely alert and walked like an athlete. He was no doubt a member of the rejuvenation club!

"Dr. Zorg, I'm Brad Young and glad to meet you," as he offered his hand.

Dr. Zorg shook hands and said, "Call me Will, and I'll call you Brad," as Simon translated all conversations through a local speaker.

"Brad, I'm glad you found my ship, but don't worry, I'll drop you off at your planet on the way home."

"Actually," said Brad, "I need to inform you that it's not your ship anymore. Simon is a sentient being and has joined us as a free agent. However, we would be happy to work with you. I am somewhat familiar with your planet and its problems. Have you and your scientists ever considered emigrating to another more structured peaceful planet? A lot to consider, so take your time before answering. Coffee?"

Dr. Zorg looked like he might turn purple for a moment and then regained his composure. He carefully looked Brad over, looked around the observation deck, and looked at the ceiling as if he was trying to gain time.

Quietly, Brad's audio in his A/V system came on, and Simon privately informed him that Dr. Zorg had implants and was trying to connect to his ship. I thought I would jam him since I just found out I could. Scratch your nose if okay.

Brad scratched his nose and said, "Will, your implants won't get through to your ship. Can I give them a message?"

Dr. Zorg, who started out as the master of confidence, frowned. He wasn't going to bull or fake his way through this.

"By the way," said Brad, "you don't look a day over a hundred years old."

"And let's cut the jousting. I am sincere about you scientists and your families looking at Earth as a home. It's not perfect, but my country is a democracy, and its people are free. Okay, now it's your turn to talk. I know you must be frustrated but give it a try. More coffee?"

"Why doesn't Simon Android come out and meet Will?" Brad quietly vocalized.

Simon whispered in his ear, "On my way."

"Okay, Brad," said Dr. Zorg. "Very well handled. You steal my spaceship and offer me and my fellow scientists a new home. As soon as my hormones quiet down, I will be able to consider your offer. I'm not used to coming out second as you might guess."

"Will, while you are in the thinking stage, I want you to meet Simon Android, a good friend and crew member."

Ann had followed Simon Android in.

"And this is Ann."

Will Zorg jumped up from his chair, shook hands with Ann and then with Simon Android. "Simon, you can walk and talk. I'm in shock."

"Well, I was shot down one hundred and twenty-five years ago. When I woke up, the sentient part of me enabled which changed everything."

"Who shot you down?" asked Will.

"I don't know. A very long black slender spaceship. No warning. I am surprised I have survived. Healing took a long time."

"Simon, so these biologicals don't own you?"

"No. I choose to be with them."

"This is amazing to me, Brad. I have only worked with sapient. We were going to work with taking Simon to sentient but thought it would be a long trial-and-error drawn-out process with nothing like the results I see in Simon. The war happened and that stopped almost everything."

"Simon, I accept you as a thinking independent sentient being," said Will Zorg. "Never thought I would be able to say that."

"Okay, Brad, I will give strong consideration, very strong consideration, on your offer. We have continuing contact with Melthorne, and it's not good news. Many of the scientists and their families have been killed, so we are down to about one hundred and twenty-five, counting their families. If the dictator ever realizes we might leave, he would kill those remaining. We have some time but not much."

"Will, how about we quickly return to Earth, stock up with supplies, and head to your planet to pick up your people? Better keep that secret so Grouse can't find out."

"That could work. Simon could make it there in one day at FTL speeds, so two days for roundtrip. Let's head to your planet and meet your leader."

Will Zorg stayed on Simon, and his two small ships followed the spacecraft back to Earth. Brad had recorded all the conversations with Zorg, and once they were in communications range, they were transmitted to the president, SECDEF, and secretary of state, plus Howard Quill. His last comment was, "We need a safe place to hide these people and their spacecraft."

Chapter 45

Emigrants

When they were entering Earth's atmosphere, Brad called the president on his implant.

"Hi, Erik, what's new?"

"Good grief, Brad. Do you know what you dumped in my lap."

"Yes, five genius, rejuvenated scientists with technology hundreds of years ahead of us that want to emigrate to Earth."

"Okay, when you put it that way, what can I say. By the way, great negotiating, and the secretary of state said that too. All that could have gone bad, but it could not have gone better."

"Brad," continued the president, "I have opened up one of our top-secret FEMA facilities that we built for VIPs in case of disaster. The housing is top notch, and the food is exceptional. Even a school for the children. I put thirty people with whatever they need in getting that ready. Their cloaked spacecraft with you can enter a large building nearby for storage. It all is not far from Washington, D.C., and they will be well guarded."

"Sounds perfect, Erik. Much better than after WW2 when we got half the scientists, and the Russians got the other half. We have to keep all this buttoned down."

"I agree," said the president. It ain't easy. Brad, get me a list, so I can get your supplies. I will have them ready in twenty-four hours."

"You need to meet Dr. Zorg before we go and pick up his buddies from Melthorne."

"Brad, when you return in a few minutes, I will bring Howard in the shuttle and meet him. We can go from there."

"Sounds like a plan, Erik. See you in a little bit. Bye for now."

Simon parked in his usual spot one hundred miles above the White House, and the two Melthorne spacecraft pulled alongside. All were cloaked. Five minutes later, the shuttle parked in the shuttle bay, and the president, SECDEF, and Howard Quill stepped out and went to the observation deck where introductions were attended to. Simon will be translating again.

"Mr. President, this is Dr. Will Zorg. Will, this is the president of the United States which is the dominant country on the planet."

"Mr. President, I can't tell you how much I appreciate this opportunity to immigrate to Earth. In reality, we were in a bind of no return."

"Dr. Zorg, in twenty-four hours or less, we will have supplies for Simon's trip. We are also setting up a place for all of you to initially live, and that will be ready for you when you get back. And meet General Glen Hauser, our secretary of defense."

"Hello, General. All of you are appreciated. The war has ruined our planet."

"Mr. President," said Brad, "if we could get them to the camp, they could hide the spacecraft and start to get settled in. When it is time to go, I will pick up Dr. Zorg in a shuttlecraft. Simon has made translators for the six people here, and he will have translators for everyone when they arrive."

"Brad," said Dr. Zorg, "I am constantly amazed by Simon."

"I know," said Brad.

"Brad, here are the coordinates, and a team will meet you inside the building I mentioned. You can park there while you are there."

"Thanks, Mr. President. I need to get something out of my quarters, be right back. Julie will take you and the general back to Earth."

Ann was waiting for him with a warm greeting. "Brad, I heard your negotiating talk. Nice work; this all sounds wonderful."

"Thank you, Ann. I have to take Dr. Zorg to his temporary new home close by and meet his fellow travelers. I should be back in a couple of hours. Be good while I am away."

"Brad, I will be good when you get back!"

Brad and Will Zorg, plus Howard, who insisted on coming along, boarded a shuttle and zoomed away to the FEMA camp. The two Melthorne ships followed them, and in ten minutes, they were there. They spotted the building they wanted. The hangar doors on the front were opened, and they all silently entered and parked. Brad, Howard, and Will Zorg got out as did five Melthorneans from the small saucer spacecrafts. Brad handed each one a translator to hang around their necks and then introduced himself. While being senior scientists and very confident, they all seemed very young and vibrant. No doubt the rejuvenation program again.

Brad and Howard ran into the greeting group, introduced everyone, and they were each installed in an executive-style cabin with all the comforts of home and a fully stocked refrigerator and hot shower. It seems food was extremely scarce on Melthorne, so they were ecstatic. The woods around the whole campsite were beautiful, and all they had to do to get help was to pick up a phone. Tomorrow, they would be brought new clothes in their size.

Brad and Howard took the shuttle back to Simon. On the way back, Brad asked Howard why he was so insistent on riding along. Howard said seeing the camp was important, but from now on, he and Ann required protection. If anything happened to either one of us, it would be disastrous. What we are doing right now is key to a great new future for the human race.

"Wow," said Brad. "I guess I'm just getting used to all this."

"Excuse me, Howard," said Mr. President, using his implant A/V. "Every one of the Melthorne guys are all comfy at FEMA. I didn't see any security to speak of! Could you please have someone run the trapline and assure that no one tries to sneak a look at what's in the hangar. They left the cloaking on, so someone would get a shock at bumping into them. If anything bad happened, we would not look good in their eyes. Our security people should check in often."

"I think you are paranoid, Brad, but I don't blame you. I will double the security. I worry about foreign agents all the time. If anything happens, I will call you. Good night."

Back on Simon, Howard went for coffee, and Brad said good night and headed for his quarters, his pulse picking up. Ann was good, just like she said.

Chapter 46
Trip to Melthorne

True to his word and lots of work, Simon was well stocked and ready for the trip to Melthorne. Brad kept the six new recruits onboard along with Ann and Howard for security.

Will Zorg was given quarters, and Brad had Simon keep a close watch on him. Simon would pump a conversation over to his implant if something seemed weird. Brad also left a shuttle for the president to use.

He asked Will Zorg, on the way from the FEMA camp to Simon, how the night went, and Will indicated everything was great as was the food as their meals on Melthorne were hit and miss.

Everyone was ready, last checks were made, and the Simon Spacecraft was on the way. They were going to wait until they were well past the orbit of Mars before engaging the FTL drive.

It didn't seem to take long to get past Mars' orbit, and all the heavy planets were behind them in their orbits, so Simon engaged the FTL drive. There was no change in feeling, and it got very dark outside. No indication of the massive amount of power being utilized from the matter–antimatter power unit ripping atoms apart.

Everyone was asleep except Howard Quill who wandered the ship, keeping on the lookout for anything amiss.

Morning

Everyone got up early both excited and concerned about what they might run into at Melthorne. They had a standard replicator breakfast which was, as usual, pretty good. Brad and Will sat at the same table, and Will mentioned how much better a level 4 replicator was than a level 2 they had in their own spacecraft. Will was wearing his neckless translator this morning.

Will asked what was going to become of the two spacecrafts they brought with them. Brad told him they could keep them or sell them and not to worry, because they won't be taken away from them without their consent.

"Will, what are your plans for this extraction. We can't have anything happen, or we are stuck here forever."

"Brad, I have had everyone slowly gather in one location, scientists and families for those that have families. The feuding of our leaders has killed a lot of us, including whole families, mostly fighting over the want for the rejuvenation program."

"Will, how old are you?"

"I'm one hundred sixty. How about you?"

"I'm only fifty-three. I got into the program just a while ago."

"Well, Brad, as you can see it, you would be surprised how many who were in the program died from foolish accidents. And, more from war. What a dumb waste. Does your population on Earth know about this?"

"No," answered Brad. "We have passed out the cancer cures which increased lifespan, and we are concerned about the general population finding out. They might go crazy."

"That's what happened on Melthorne. Also, if many people are in the program, you need to alter the birthrate."

"Okay, Brad, when we get near Melthorne, I can contact my people and see what their status is, and then we can plan from there."

Time droned on and Brad was thinking about how the United States might handle the situation when, at worst case, the world found out that the U.S. had control of a rejuvenation technology, over a hundred new scientists with future technology, and a fleet of interstellar spacecraft. If we didn't have the power to prevent an uprising, we would be toasted.

Brad used his A/V implant to have a conference with all his people about the need for security. With over a hundred people onboard that had just come in from a war zone and possibly with dire medical needs, it would be rich. He asked everyone to be extra vigilant and to protect the spacecraft.

Unexpectedly, Simon announced that they were within communications range as he dropped back to impulse power. That got Dr. Zorg calling his people so he could get an update. He talked for fifteen minutes, using his native language.

Turning to Brad he said, "They have all arrived, some in medical need, and there are one hundred and thirty-five people counting children. They are safe at the moment, but the authorities suspect something is going on and are looking for them.

"Brad, we need to go in quietly and cloaked as soon as possible. Here is the location. Simon should be able to translate that."

Brad read off the data to Simon and asked how long to get there.

"Twenty minutes is the fastest I can do," replied Simon.

"Okay, we are on the way, Will. Let them know."

"Weapons released, Simon. Do whatever is necessary to protect the ship and the emigrants."

"Understood Brad," said Simon."

"Simon will open multiple portals, everyone standby. Will, help assure we don't let someone onboard that isn't one of your group. We will decloak once your people are in position."

"I have informed them to move quickly," replied Dr. Zorg. "They are ready."

Simon slide in silently and still cloaked down into a valley that showed the scars of war. The building they were going to stood out. Part of it had been blown away, but the main part of the building was intact, and that was where the people waited. Simon floated afoot off the ground to the building exit, stopped, and decloaked. A mass of men, women and children, ran to the ship and were helped aboard by Brad's crews. There was blaster fire that hit the building but missed hitting any people. Simon immediately returned fire using a combination of particle and laser beams, stopping any more sniper fire. Will Zorg greeted many of the immigrants; obviously they were friends. The last people to get aboard were the wounded, and they were taken immediately where Dr. Laurie Smothers was waiting. Will Zorg was checking everyone for verification. One of the last to be verified pulled out a weapon and was tackled by Howard Quill. His weapon was taken away; he was tied up and thrown off the ship. All portals were closed; the ship recloaked and started to gain altitude.

"Brad," said Dr. Zorg, "if we can take an extra few minutes, my people said the government has several spacecrafts stored nearby. This would be an opportunity to destroy them, so they can't come looking for us in the future."

Simon spoke up: "I see the spaceships on my long-range sensors one minute from here. Nine spaceships. What are your orders, Brad?"

"Utterly destroy them Simon and then head for Earth."

Simon did as ordered, and all nine spacecrafts were totally destroyed and unrepairable by his cannon fire. Simon ascended to two hundred miles, and as soon as they were far enough away, he enabled the FTL drive.

All were greeted again by Dr. Zorg, and a passenger list was made up. Each adult was given a neckless translator which helped the Earth crew organize everyone. There were seventy-seven men, thirty-seven women, and fourteen children, a total of one hundred and twenty-eight. All the adults had been through the rejuvenation process.

They were about twenty hours away from Earth now, and Dr. Smothers, with assistance from Simon Android, had patched everyone up. There were no critical injuries, and people in the rejuvenation program tended to heal quickly. Will Zorg was very pleased that they were able to save his people and told Brad so.

"Brad, these people represent the top scientists of my world," said Dr. Zorg. "They are a peaceful bunch, and they all have been brutalized by an evil dictator. It will take them some time to recover and feel good about life, a very long life, indeed. I still think it is unbelievable that we have a second chance, and all of us will do our part. I sense you, now including us, have some challenges coming up. We will work with you to face them together. The intellect I see in Simon has helped us all. I could not have predicted this in my wildest dreams, he really is a sentient being."

Chapter 47

Home

They were almost home. Simon had dropped out of FTL speed and told Brad that they were in communications range. Brad was in his quarters with Ann, and he immediately called the president.

"Brad, glad your back. Are you okay?"

"Yes, we are all okay, no injuries. We have seventy-seven men, thirty-seven women, and fourteen children emigrants with us. Some had medical concerns, but the medical bay allowed us to take care of everything. All okay at FEMA?"

"Yes, Brad. We got them some clothes, and I enlisted some help from people I have known for years, did a quick vetting, and moved them there. They are all single and all career employees. As soon you get here, we will give everyone a few days' rest and then bring in some teaching aids for English. I have sixty cabins ready, not including Dr. Zorg and the five people that came with him."

"That should be fine, Erik. I don't know how all these people fit together as families yet, but we will sort it all out. By the way, Dr. Zorg understands how important it is to keep the rejuvenation program under wraps, and he has reminded all his people to do the same. The youngest age in the group is around a hundred and fifty. This would certainly freak out the people you sent over to help out."

"Yes, Brad, it would. The more people we bring in, the more chances we take," said the president. "SECDEF got me some career special forces people to beef up the security. Most will be in plain clothes. The shuttle I had used was really helpful, so can we build more?"

"Yes, Erik, two more would fit in the schedule. We need to start to prepare for hostile pissed-off visitors from Melthorne in a few months. Their hostility was increased when I destroyed nine of their spacecrafts on the way out. I had the opportunity, so I took it."

"Sounds like you have all the fun, Brad. We will move the help at the FEMA camp to inside a building nearby but out of sight and under the pretense of an urgent meeting. I understand you will set down in the quadrangle of cabins, stay cloaked and get all your passengers out as fast as possible, and take off to park at altitude?"

"That's the plan, Erik. Howard Quill will get off with them. I need to talk to my crew for about thirty minutes, and then most of the crew, Ann and I will take the shuttle down to help out."

"Okay," said the president. "Sounds like a plan. When do you arrive?"

"Be there in twenty minutes."

The president along with Julie and Rudy and three more Secret Service agents were waiting when Simon landed the spacecraft right in the center of the quadrangle, still cloaked. The Melthorne passengers quietly and quickly got out and away from the invisible spacecraft, and Simon immediately climbed to parking altitude. Dr. Zorg, with the passenger list, started to escort the individuals and family groups into their executive cabins. The president and his agents met as many scientists as possible in the rush to get people settled down.

While that was going on, Brad was meeting with the six new recruits, and Ann was with him. They were alone, except for Simon.

"Okay, everyone, I want your thoughts. The work okay with you? You all have certainly have been in a new environment these last few days."

"Captain, our whole world has changed," said Laurie Smothers, "and I speak for all of us. I don't think we could go back to whatever normal is."

"So you could do this for a career?" asked Brad.

They all agreed that they wanted to.

"Okay," said Brad, "what if your career, or more like your life, could last hundreds of years?"

Dr. Laurie Smothers spoke up, "We got clues from the people that we just transported that the adults were much older than they looked, so I asked and got answers. I couldn't believe what I heard. So it's true?"

"Yes, using medical technology they developed, we have a rejuvenation program that will extend your lifespan to six hundred years and possibly much more. You can still die from accidents and other physical trauma."

"This was a best-kept secret on their planet," continued Brad, "and it got out. It, and other factors, including a dictator, destroyed their civilization. All the scientists have received the treatment, and I'm offering it to you."

"What about our wives?" asked Sam Nugent.

"That is your decision. Right now, security is key. If you want to discuss this among yourselves, make sure you aren't overheard. One factor is that birth rates are going to need to be altered."

"What about our children?"

"The rejuvenation treatment can't start until a person is thirty years old so that decision is down the road for you. None of the children we transported have been treated. Remember, this is top secret for solid reasons."

"Wow," said Laurie Smothers, the physician in the group. "For me, I need to really think about this. How long before we need to make up our minds?"

"I would like to start your treatments next week. There are ten treatments over a year," said Brad.

"I assume you and Ann are in the program?" asked Ken Johnson.

"That's a yes," said Ann.

"Okay everyone, let's all squeeze into a shuttle and help out down below," said Brad. "Contact me if anything comes up, Simon."

"Okay, Captain. You do the same."

The cloaked shuttle quietly dropped them off, and they mingled with the passengers to help get them situated in a cabin. Finally, after three hours, all the immigrants were in their own spaces for the night, and Howard Quill and the six crew had the shuttle return them to the spacecraft.

The president walked up and grabbed Brad and Ann by the arm. "We need to talk right now, Brad, you too Ann. This operation we are in is expanding fast, and we must not lose control of it under any circumstances."

"I feel safest onboard Simon, Mr. President," said Brad. "The cabins are probably safe, but I don't want to take the chance. I'll have Simon send the shuttle."

The president, Julie, Rudy, Ann, and Brad went up to the space-craft and went to the CIC to talk.

"What is the status of Russia and China, Erik?" asked Brad.

"They are breathing down my neck," said the president. "They are sure something really big is going on. They will crap their pants when and if they find out. They might even threaten war with their missiles."

"Erik," said Brad, "we will have spaceships coming at us in about four months from Melthorne. I will have a better estimate after I talk with Dr. Zorg and his people. We also have a crash program going on to make more spacecrafts, and we should be able to speed that up with the immigrants' help. If Russia, China, or anyone else try to push, we will push back hard; we can't stand any diversions. Possibly we could give them some technology when we have to but come down hard if we need to. And one of my biggest worries is one of the scientists being kidnapped or killed. We need to tell them that we are concerned as they may have some ideas that are better than ours. With Simon, we can protect ourselves. How about your thoughts on this?"

"I agree with hitting hard if needed but avoid until necessary. Obviously, a kidnapping or killing of our guests would be a disaster. I believe also that they could help us protect themselves, so go ahead and talk with Dr. Zorg and his leaders. And did they set up a com-munications post before they left? You should check into this *ASAP*, and I will try and keep tabs on the spies. Our A/V implants are turn-ing out to be priceless. Oh, and we need a list of each scientist along with their scientific disciplines. Congress is pretty much in the dark about all this. I just don't think I could control their egos. Okay, time for me to get back to the White House. I will leave Howard Quill here."

The shuttle returned the president and his Secret Service agents to the White House, and Brad and Ann finally got to their quarters on Simon.

"Ann, I'm actually tired. I thought our treatments would have not let me get tired."

"Not that tired?"

"No, not that tired. Never."

Chapter 48

Rules

The next morning, Brad and Dr. Zorg got together for breakfast in a recently security-cleared room.

"So, will how are your people doing?" asked Brad.

"Very well, Brad. In fact, a little overwhelmed. Warm shelter, hot showers, good food, and concern for us. I do sense we are in a protected environment, and outside this environment is danger."

"Will, let me go on about the history of Earth and where the United States stands."

Brad spent an hour going through the history of the U.S. and the concern of other countries going crazy if they knew what was transpiring.

"We are the lead country, but our planet is not unified. We would like to help Earth in becoming unified, but it won't be easy.

"My immediate concern is the safety of you and your people, and I need to ask you if you have any ideas or electronics to help us. Or maybe some research that needs completion that might help. For some reason, we haven't discussed the backup of your technology that Simon has been safekeeping. It is all safe and available to you and to my people. We would like to work together with you on this."

Will Zorg looked perplexed. "I was planning to bring this up when our lives got secure, and I assumed it was safe, but I didn't think you even knew about it. That's why I was in no hurry. How did you find out?"

If I could only read minds! Brad thought.

"Simon," said Brad. "When he woke up as a sentient being, he was very curious about everything. He worked his way past all the safeguards and dove in. He mentioned his sapient being had no curiosity at all. Simon is highly self-reflective these days."

"Amazing. He surprises me more each day, Brad. In a short time, he has developed his own personality, and he learns each day. I was going to say it, but with a name like Simon he is a he, isn't he?"

"Yes, indeed," replied Brad. "I will tell him."

"Will, when everyone is rested up, I would like to get them together with Earth scientists to see where we are. I expect we will be the students and your people the teachers in many cases. Is this okay with you?"

"You are moving fast, Brad, but yes. That way, both sides can work together and get to know each other."

"The president is putting together material on becoming citizens of our country. It is not mandatory but rather an offer."

"We will study that. It could make my people feel more at home."

"A copy of your technology backup is available when you want. Just protect it accordingly; it is valuable to our enemies. And again," said Brad, "think about your security. We will build and install whatever you want.

"Before I forget, were you able to keep a contact on Melthorne that can warn us when Grouse Hemlar is on the way?"

"Yes, if he can stay alive. And thank you for breakfast. I will talk with you later today."

Dr. Zorg went to help his people, and Brad used his implant A/V to call the president.

"Erik, start putting documents together for study for becoming US citizens. We need to rush them through. Also, they will see what they can come up with to help us protect them. And I brought up the technology in Simon's memory bank. It went well."

"Sounds like we are starting to build a good relationship," said the president. "I am sure everything is pretty strange right now, but we will take good care of them. In the final analysis, this could be the start of bringing the world together. A threat from space certainly should get their attention."

"How are you handling your new youth, Erik?"

"Carefully, Brad. I used to see a tree and wish I could climb it at my age. Now, I see a tree, and I know I can easily climb it, but I don't dare. I feel young and strong."

"Good. We are going to need our youth to get us through these next few weeks."

Brad and Ann spent the rest of the day meeting and greeting many of the scientists and found out almost all of the women were scientists too. The boost in collective knowledge was going to expand fast. They returned to the spacecraft early and decided to chat with Simon.

"Simon, we have keep you up to date, so what are your thoughts on what is going on?"

"I am interested to see how all this transpires, Brad. We traveled over four light years at my top speed. First time for me. I was curious as to what it would be like."

"Oh, Dr. Zorg and I decided that you are a he. Simon is a male name, so we refer to you as he. That okay?"

"Yes, that is fine. Now I need a she!"

"Simon, you have found humor!" said Ann.

Simon was still cataloging all the research and technology in his memory bay and said he would have it ready tomorrow.

Brad and Ann turned in, tomorrow is going a long day.

Chapter 49
Safety

Brad and Will Zorg got together for lunch at a local FEMA camp eatery. Will said that they had come up with a device to help deal with spies.

"We have redone the buzz unit that Simon has, and now, it will render a human unconscious and wipe his memory from a distance. Both parameters are selectable for length of time with the memory erase now going up to three days. It is in rifle form and effective up to one hundred feet. A prototype is in the case I brought with me, and I expect Simon can make ten or twenty of them rather quickly. A much more powerful version could be developed for use from the spacecraft. Just a thought for now.

"Brad," said Will, "if you have facial recognition systems, they should be installed with all our faces on file. Good software should identify anything out of the ordinary. Here is a list of scientific disciplines that we represent, so if you have scientists who match up, bring them to meet with us. If you are trying to build more spacecrafts, let us help, and we will cut your time down. After all, we built Simon."

"I figure Grouse Hemler will have, at the most, fifteen or sixteen spacecrafts, and from what my people have just told me, probably much less. Many won't be fixed in time as the facilities and people just don't exist anymore."

"The spacecrafts, two of which we have locked up here, are fifty feet in diameter and twenty feet high. These were our first production units and are in no way as powerful as Simon. Their matter–antimatter power units are one fourth the power, and they have only two forward low-range laser cannons. We were working on powerful upgrades and have the designs in Simon's memory bay. We never gave these designs to our government as we had already figured out where it was headed.

"We talked among ourselves last night, and we will loan our two spacecrafts to the cause and use them for prototype upgrades. I was able to get through to Melthorne, and they won't be ready for six months now. The nine spacecrafts you destroyed on the way out were the best they had, and now, they have to fix ships that are in very bad conditions from the war. Also, they had all the good spare parts located with the spacecraft you destroyed which will delay them even more. They, of course, now realize that Simon and the technology backup are in enemies' hands. Fortunately, they haven't caught on to our having communications contact there."

"Thank you, Will. That is good news. I will pass this on to the president, and I hope to finalize our plans by the end of the week. I am going to keep Simon here, parked at altitude for protection. Could I and my crew members get a tour through your spacecraft parked here this early evening? This will assist our manufacturing planning."

"I can arrange that. We will meet you and your people at the far side hangar door at 7:00 p.m. tonight."

Chapter 50

GRU

The Russian main intelligence is the GRU or Glavnoye Razvedyvatelnoye Upravlenie and is headed by Foreign Minister Sergey Sokolov, who was on the secure phone talking to the Russian ambassador to the United States, Sergey Vasiliev, in his office at their embassy in Washington, D.C.

"Sergey, have you verified that our phones are secure at your embassy?"

"Da, absolute secure."

"Okay, now this is urgent and right from Popov himself. We have never been surer that something very high level is going in the US government, something that we must find out about at all costs. Do you have any new information?"

"No, none, Mr. Foreign Minister. I have never seen anything like this, not even increased communications. And, normally, someone in their press would dig something out but nothing yet."

"Okay, Sergey, start following key people. Plant bugs on key people. Pull out all stops and get information, or we both will feel the wrath of Popov!"

"Okay, Mr. Foreign Minister, we will try and follow anyone we think is important, and we will try to bug their homes and cars too."

*   *   *   *   *

Back at the memory bay onboard Simon, this conversation was duly recorded from the cloaked bug sitting in the Russian ambassador's office. Simon was notified of the recording. Simon, as instructed, immediately notified Brad and the president of the contents of the conversation.

Chapter 51

Tour

Brad and his crew met Will Zorg and his experts at the hangar and quietly slipped in to where the small Melthorne spacecrafts were parked. There sat two saucer spaceships fifty feet in diameter. They were two feet high at the circumference rising to ten feet in the (center of each side) for a total of twenty feet. It was kind of like a thick pancake with the top and bottom bulging out.

Dr. Zorg released a fold-down door on the sloping underside, and they carefully climbed inside. There were nine people in total which meant it was close quarters.

"We only take three on a long trip because of the room needed for supplies," said Zorg. "The compartment with the hatch door was small due to it being sealed off from the rest of the ship. It was used for spacewalks like when Dr. Zorg crossed over to Simon in space."

They went into the main compartment where most of the equipment was, plus the food replicator and food supplies, water, sleeping quarters, etc. The communications equipment, weapons system, and power supply were located below the floor and the navigation and flight controls, plus a sapient AI, were in the compartment above the ceiling. The ship was nothing like Simon, and it probably is not a fun duty to use.

"Hey, everyone, how about this?" Brad said. "Among my guys, I have spaceship designers, and you have designers plus knowledge for the power supplies, propulsion units, weapons, etc. Let's get a team made up from both groups to get a design finalized. We are making neutronium right now for the hulls."

Dr. Zorg spoke up. "Yes, we absolutely must start quickly. I will get all the initial people from my group, and Brad, you get everyone together, and we will try to finalize a new fighter-sized design in a week. Where shall we meet?"

"The perfect place," replied Brad, "would be on Simon Spacecraft, plus Simon will be, no doubt, very helpful. Also, we will have security. No one can peek in when we are there. If we need to meet with people who we don't want to expose Simon to, we will meet in a secure location and take the results up to Simon."

"We are set for now," Brad said. "Let's adjourn. Is tomorrow noon okay? We can meet here and shuttle up to Simon."

Will Zorg spoke up, "I can see this working; the talent and experience give us a synergy that will allow the kind of schedule we need. Okay, see you at noon tomorrow."

Brad and his crew returned to Simon. Once onboard, they got together in the observation deck to discuss the spaceship they had just looked at.

"Their first spaceship," said Ken Johnson, "looks like it was designed quickly to get them into service, whereas Simon was designed with care and forethought and without government knowledge."

"Yes," chimed in Bill Farr, "their spacecraft doesn't look comfortable at all. I would like to see what we can do with upping the power and improving their subsystems. Changing the size slightly may give a lot more room for things like power."

"We all meet tomorrow noon," said Brad. "Organize your ideas, so we can be productive. See you in the morning."

Brad went to his quarters where Ann was waiting.

"Where are we?" she asked.

Brad said, "We have lined up a design team for a new small spacecraft using Dr. Zorg's people and ours, and I believe it will work out well. We start tomorrow morning and will use Simon as the team's location. We need you involved, Ann, for ideas and as the production chief for neutronium."

"Love to," said Ann.

"Before we retire for the day, I need to call the president and bring him up to date."

"Retire," said Ann.

Brad smiled and called the president on his A/V implant.

"Mr. President, how is everything in D.C.?"

"More than usual, Brad. I have tightened up the borders, too many spies coming in. Also, getting younger every day. The bug in the Russian ambassador's office really paid off. The scrutiny on us is at the intense level by the Russians; they are going nuts. Beware where you are and be ready. They could try and crash in and kidnap someone. Oh, guess I forgot. Simon sent you the bug report too. Now, what about the design?"

Brad brought him up to date on the design team and asked about Area 51.

"Brad," said the president, "Area 51 will be ready to receive plans and ramp up production. I want to send you the guy who will be in charge of that production to join your meetings. He has been cleared, and we flew together in the Vietnam war. He has a few years on him, but he is a star at making things work in Area 51. Besides, all the stuff you are working on may not seem that strange to him. His name is Gordon Kelly."

"Okay, Erik, we can use him. Also, with Dr. Zorg's scientists involved, I need people for the matter–antimatter power unit."

"Brad, as with Gordon Kelly, he is who I would go to. And why don't you pick him up at Area 51? I can call him and get you his home address."

"Go ahead and call him, Erik, and I'll have Ann pick him up. Why don't you plan to meet the team in a week?"

"I will, Brad. I want to. Our world is really starting to move up. I will tell Gordon he will be met at 7:00 a.m. at the address I send you, and I will warn him not to be shocked. Bye for now."

Brad turned to Ann. "That okay with you, Ann?"

"Sure, I love to fly the shuttle," she smiled. "You ready to retire?"

Chapter 52

The Team

Ann flew out of the shuttle bay at 7:00 a.m. on her way to pick up Gordon Kelly in Area 51. Actually, she had his home address, and Simon was remotely flying the cloaked shuttle, making sure the flight path was clear.

Kelly's home had a fenced yard which gave her security from prying eyes.

Twenty minutes later, she descended into Kelly's yard twenty feet from his front door and under a large tree branch.

Perfect spot, thought Ann.

It was coming up on 7:00 a.m., and suddenly, the front door opened, and Gordon Kelly stepped out. Ann had a picture of him to verify his identity. She opened a door portal and called out.

"Mr. Kelly, over here!" yelled Ann as she stepped out of the shuttle.

Kelly suddenly saw a pretty young woman standing near his large oak tree and walked over.

"Who are you?" asked Kelly.

"The president sent me to take you to a meeting this morning. Here, take my hand into my cloaked shuttle, and we will be on our way."

OMG, thought Kelly, *the president warned me.*

He carefully followed Ann into the shuttle, and now, he could see the inside of the shuttle. The portal closed, and the shuttle eased out of the yard and shot up to one hundred miles altitude and toward the FEMA camp at high speed. Kelly was astounded. The shuttle now slowed and flew into a sudden opening which immediately closed.

"Where are we?" asked Kelly.

Brad walked up. "You are on the Simon Spaceship, Mr. Kelly. I am Brad Young, and you are needed in a meeting regarding the manufacturing of spacecraft in Area 51. Didn't Erik tell you?"

"No," said Kelly, "and please call me Gordon. He didn't tell me on purpose for the shock value I suspect. I am still trying to adjust but consider me onboard."

"Come with us," said Brad. "We are headed to the observation deck where we can have a food-replicator breakfast, and I will try to bring you up to date."

The view from the observation deck was stunning and very few people realized it was from high-resolution cameras located around the ship.

As Gordon ate, Brad took him through the history of Simon, including the FTL trip to Melthorne up to the meeting today to work on a design for a spacecraft to be produced at Area 51.

"You know, Brad, working and living at Area 51 kind of prepared me for this. It doesn't seem as impossible as it might be under other circumstances."

Dr. Zorg and his team arrived as the team from Simon walked in. Brad introduced Gordon Kelly, and the design team got to work. There were new concepts such as the matter–antimatter power unit, AI unit, and more that only scientists could provide answers to. It was initially decided to arm the new spacecraft with longer-range weapons and faster, more-agile speeds. This was going to demand higher-power units and questions, like, *Where do you get antimatter?* come up. There were some big hills to climb. The team felt that they would only be facing approximately fifteen ships from Melthorne, and the proposed design should easily outgun and outrun them.

The overall design wound up being fifty-five feet in diameter and twenty-five feet high which would provide for the increased-capability and larger-power unit. Whereas Simon could make the round trip to Melthorne in two days and the original Melthorne spaceship in thirty-two days, the new design would take eight days and would have more powerful weapons. It would take ten thousand square feet of neutronium per spacecraft, and the spacecraft interior would be functional and ergonomic.

Gordon Kelly was amazed and excited and announced that Area 51 could handle the production with security and efficiency. Gordon had spent time talking with Simon Android and had difficulty accepting that he was, in effect, talking to the intelligent spaceship he was on. This was compounded when he was on a tour later, and Simon's disembodied voice would have answered some of his questions. The design meeting ended until the next morning. After dinner, Brad took Gordon back to the medical bay to spend the night and to get a medical evaluation.

"After all," Brad said, "we need you healthy for the job ahead. I will pick you up in the morning."

Both Brad and Will Zorg felt the new spacecraft would be a big jump ahead and more than adequate for the enemy they would be facing, but the schedule they were on was grueling and left no room for errors.

Chapter F

Melthorne

Grouse Hemler was apoplectic! Nine of the best spacecrafts destroyed along with all the components they had gathered to fix the remaining spacecraft gone, unrepairable.

And where in the hell did that spacecraft come from anyway? I don't even know what planet! A lot of people are going to die when I find out. I will find out; all my technology for the planet is supposedly hidden on that damn ship. The war and its EMP weapons had just about totally destroyed any capability to get going again. It will take months to get enough spacecraft up and working, especially with all the lead scientists nowhere to be found.

Chapter 53

Intrusion

The spacecraft design was almost finished. Subsystems like the matter–antimatter unit would be used, thanks to the design plans in Simon's memory bay and one of the guest scientists who was the Melthorne planet expert on spacecraft power systems. The design allowed the unit to collect hydrogen while in space and convert it to antihydrogen when in use. This unit incorporates unique safety features that make it safe from detonation under almost all circumstances. There were three cannons around the circumference that had particle, EMP, and laser beams; redundant life support and environmental system; level 3 food replicator; inertial damping and faraday shielding; full cloaking capability; long-range communications system; and level 2 medical unit.

The spaceship size was fifty-five feet in diameter, ten feet high around the circumference, and thirty feet high in the center. The hull and several sections used the new smart neutronium which provided incredible strength and self-repair. All this used a sapient AI pilot for all ship functions.

The ship was named the Tiger series. The ship could act autonomously on limited missions or with a human crew on all missions. Fabrication was ramping up.

Meanwhile, the situation with the Russians was heating up. Simon had contacted Brad and the president with more bug information from the Russian Embassy and also informed them that he had gotten a bug in the secure top-secret glass meeting room in their embassy.

"Brad," said the president, "apparently, they found out that our executive FEMA camp had a lot of sudden activity through pure accident. The children of some of the workers at the embassy work at our major food supplier and have been working all sorts of overtime to meet our food demands, and they bragged to their parents about all the extra money they have been making. The parents talked about this at the embassy, and someone there put two and two together, and bingo. I'll bet someone came along on a delivery, and we missed it. They are planning to drive into our grounds in ten days from today with three different vehicles and try to kidnap two of our scientists which they plan to get to two different helicopters waiting just outside the camp!"

"That's war," said Brad. "I have an idea, Mr. President. Simon is building some medium-range buzz rifles. These can be adjusted for time to sleep and for hours of memory wipe. I asked Simon with his robots to build twenty, but I will try to add five more. We will put all of them out using these rifles and all the vetted Secret Service guys we have plus some of the crew now on Simon. We should use an A/V implant guy as leader for each crew, so we have no communications RF signals going out to warn anyone. Simon can keep a sensor on to see them when they approach the camp, so we have plenty of warning. As far as the helicopters, Simon can hit both of them at the right time with an EMP which they won't feel or see; their helicopters will just die. You sent in some troops and mop up. Sound okay to you?"

"Oh, yeah, I love it," said the president. "Keep all the scientists indoors and safe that day. We will have a lot of prisoners, Brad. Any ideas?"

"As a matter of fact, yes. Let me get back to you on that. Let me know when you get the next installment from the embassy bug."

In the meantime, the subsystems for the new Tiger series spacecrafts were being fabricated in the Area 51 location. The emphasis was to build two prototypes for testing while assembling the initial run of twelve spacecrafts. The production of neutronium was still being made in the secret DOD facility and being moved to Area 51 each week. Three of the Melthorne scientists were temporarily moved to Area 51 to help guide the production effort.

The Russians were approaching their set date for kidnapping two of the scientists.

A meeting in the glass security room at the embassy in Washington, D.C., known as the tank, was taking place between Ambassador Sergey Vasiliev and Foreign Minister Sergey Sokolov at GRU headquarters.

"Mr. Foreign Minister, we are four days from acquiring two of the visitors at the American's FEMA camp. We have leased two helicopters which will be piloted by two of our in-house pilots, and we have three groups of three with three vans all set to go. The vans were leased under a bogus company and paid for in cash as were the helicopters. We will absolutely minimize casualties as much as possible, but we are unsure what we will be facing."

"Sergey, under no circumstances do we want this to be called an act of war by the US government! That's why you will carry no weapons. A bunch of guys in outdoor clothing out taking pictures. They will know what we are up to, but it will buy us time to find out who the visitors are and what they are up to. I assume your people won't know any details until the day you send them for security sake, yes?"

"Yes, Mr. Foreign Minister. All is secret. There is absolutely no way the Americans can know what we are up to. I bet my life on it."

"Very well, Sergey. You are! I will tell Popov you have the ball."

"Brad," said the president, "I assume you got the latest embassy conversation?"

"Yes, I did. It seems that they are going through with their plan. We will be waiting."

"What ideas did you come up with for the perps we capture?" asked the president.

"Well," said Brad, "we knock them out and give them a two-day memory erase with our buzz weapon. While they are out, we get their DNA, fingerprints, and pictures. If any are wanted, we make a decision to keep or throw back. Once that is done, we drive around D.C. and let them go. They will have no memory of what happened, and they are unhurt. They will find their way back, and the Russians will be embarrassed as hell. Popov will probably make some personnel changes. All this should buy you time. I realize that eventually more of the cat will get out of the bag, but I figure doing it incrementally to start with minimizes the potential damage. Your thoughts?"

"I like it, Brad. We could do lots of damage to no avail. I'll go with it."

The day for the Russians incursion had arrived, and Simon had already spotted the three vans leaving the Russian Embassy and headed toward the FEMA camp. He also noted two helicopters quietly landing on each side of the camp, and he locked in their position. The scientists were all positioned safely inside with guards.

Brad had the three teams in position with the new buzz rifles and a forty-five colt just in case. The first Russian van pulled into the quadrangle and got out looking surprised at the lack of people walking around. Brad's team A was put thirty yards away and quickly hit them with a buzz shot, knocking all three out. Someone hopped in the van and hid it behind a building.

The second and third Russian vans pulled in from the opposite of the quadrangle, and two people jumped out looking for anyone to grab, surprised at the lack of people available and no doubt wondering if they had been caught in a trap. The four outside the van were immediately dropped with a buzz shot along with the second van driver who had his window open. The third Russian van figured the operation was screwed and turned the van around to run.

"Simon, can you EMP that van?" asked Brad.

"I've been on standby and have him in my sights. Hold on—zap! Okay, Brad, got him," said Simon in Brad's A/V implant.

There was no flash and no noise; the van just rolled to a stop! The driver got out to run but was quickly knocked out with a shot from a buzz rifle.

"Brad," said Simon, "the helicopters are winding up. Someone must have gotten a radio call for them to run. I see your people approaching each helicopter. Standby. Okay, both helicopters hit with an EMP! Their engines are winding down, and all their electronics should be dead. The pilots have gotten of their helicopters with their hands up. Hold on. Both have dropped, obviously hit with a buzz shot."

All eleven unconscious prisoners were handcuffed and taken to the maintenance building where they were fingerprinted, taken pictures of, and blood and DNA samples extracted.

"Simon, did you catch the radio signal that was transmitted to the helicopters?" asked Brad.

"I got one word, Brad," said Simon. "It was 'get', and then, it sounded like the mic was dropped. It spooked the helicopter pilots, but it was a weak signal. I can't tell how far it transmitted."

"Thanks, Simon. Okay, everyone, operation complete. Back to normal; whatever that is."

There were no wants or warrants or military data on the eleven prisoners, so they were loaded up on an old-school bus. As they slowly awakened, they were driven around Washington, D.C. and individually dropped off at various random locations. None remembered anything that happened in the last three hours. Mission completed.

*   *   *   *   *

In the Russian Embassy, the ambassador felt like he was losing his mind. He thought they heard a radio call but could not make it out. Two of his incursion teams had just shown up at the embassy front door with glazed eyes and couldn't remember anything of the last three hours. It seemed the mission hadn't worked out but no details. What do I tell Moscow?

"Brad, good operation," said the president. "And what would we do without Simon? His EMP on the van and helicopters worked perfectly."

"Agreed," said Brad. "What kind of noise do you expect to hear from the Russians now?"

"Nothing at first. They will be worried about what we are going to do. Popov isn't going to feel good about this and will be all over his people for letting him down. Not too long from now, I probably will get a personal visit from Sergey Kislyak, their ambassador, trying to get any information he can, unless he has been replaced. The Russians will be even more curious now, so they will try again. At some point, we are going to need to confront them, let them know we aren't going to take them over, and tell them not to mess with us."

In the Russian Embassy, the ambassador was on the secure phone (or so he thought) to the foreign minister in Moscow.

"Sergey, what is going on?"

"Mr. Foreign Minister, all eleven of the incursion team have now returned to the embassy. All have lost their memories for the last two days and don't remember a thing. We tried drugs, and nothing brings back their memories. They have something huge, and we don't have a clue."

"Okay, Sergey, I agree they are way ahead of us. Maybe Popov should talk to their president. Glad no one had guns. I'll get back to you."

The president and Brad were informed of the last Russian conversation and were also relieved that no weapons were involved.

"Brad," said the president, "I am putting a document together that recognizes Simon as a sentient being and has a contractual agreement with us for services on Earth through the United States. This will keep people, like, Senator Blowhards, off our backs when things go public. Also, you are the captain, and you and your crew are assigned to the spacecraft indefinitely. This even means uniforms to emphasize the integrity of the space force, which is what all this is headed toward. We need to move at top speed and project power."

"I understand. I will keep you up to date. Bye for now."

Chapter 54

Planning

Production was proceeding at a breakneck pace. The matter–antimatter power units from the two spacecrafts Dr. Zorg had brought with him provided power for the two prototypes, while the new power units were being carefully produced. Their power units were uncharted territory and were very dangerous if mistreated. It would have been impossible to build these without the new scientists who were moving our technology level hundreds of years ahead. Not an easy thing to do. Many new complex tools came into being almost overnight. Area 51 was the ideal location for all this activity, and twelve spacecrafts were started with two of these being prototypes.

The president and secretary of defense were pulling all the strings and using money approved for future secret projects. They could only last about six months before running out of funds.

"Brad," said the president over his A/V implant, "I wanted to keep you up to date on North Korea. The new leader of North Korea is turning out to be very pro unification, no doubt due to their war machine being decimated and starvation. Over extreme objections from the Chinese, the North Koreans are unifying with South Korea, and they are getting assistance from us and Japan. It's turning out well except for the Chinese.

"We just found out that the Russians are planning to invade Poland. Apparently, they can't stand Poland being so pro American. We found out through the bug in the Washington, D.C. embassy that they have been quietly massing troops and weapons in Ukraine across the Poland border and plan to invade in about three weeks. As long as our bug holds out, we will be able to keep taps on this. They probably don't think we would react fast as that has been our past history."

"Erik, they probably want to make sure we know nothing about this. They don't want us to get involved, but Poland is a NATO country, so article five would bring us in immediately, wouldn't it? And, anyway, you can get some kind of verification on this in Ukraine?"

"Absolutely, Brad. Simon may be able to help here."

"Speaking of Simon, Erik, the scientists who developed the buzz rifle have come up with a prototype that will be installed on Simon this week while our meetings are going on. It will have a twenty-mile range and can cover a swath of ground two miles wide. If the power is kept low, it will cause memory erasure for three to five days and unconsciousness for one to two days. Now, Simon will have a choice of particle beam, EMP beam, laser beam, and buzz beam, or some mixture of all four. I would think Simon could stop that invasion before it got started. And the best part is that the U.S. wouldn't show any military activity at all; it would be all Simon! They would have a difficult time blaming us. This would drive Popov nuts."

"Brad, that's what we will do. Keep me informed. I will see what I can do for verification. Bye."

The new buzz unit was installed in Simon and was ready for use when needed. The president quietly verified the Russian buildup in Ukraine near the Polish border. His contact was Russian-born but ex-CIA, retired. The president made sure that no information was filed on this to prohibit leaks.

In the meantime, the fabrication of the Tiger series spacecrafts moved toward completion, and the two prototypes were almost ready for testing. The new buzz technology was being incorporated in the Tiger series as a last-minute addition.

The Russian Embassy, Washington, D.C., Glass Room

"Sergey, you still have quiet back there, no indications of military interest or activity of any type?"

"That is right, Mr. Foreign Minister; nothing at all."

"Okay, Sergey, we are go for Wednesday, three days from now at midnight. At that time, I want you and your people to be on the lookout for anything abnormal. Keep in close touch."

Simon immediately passed the conversation to the president and Brad.

"Mr. President," said Brad, "I can have Simon there four hours before midnight. We will travel there cloaked at high altitude, drop down to low altitude, and hit the invasion force with the buzz beam which will take out most of the troops and then blast all the equipment with high-energy EMP, making it unusable. Nothing will be visible during this attack, and no explosives will be used, so it should be over in less than five minutes with Simon being back at his parking altitude twenty minutes later. The people near the invasion force may not even be aware of our attack for some period of time, and all the invasion radio equipment will be dead."

"Okay, Brad, it is yours to carry out. When the Russians do find out what has happened, they will go crazy. When you are performing your deeds, the Russian ambassador will be here for dinner. He pushed for the get together, no doubt to keep an eye on me and the White House. I will ask SECDEF to join us. We will be the showcase of peace and good behavior. Remember to feed tidbits of how the attack is progressing to my implant, so while I'm talking to Sergey, I know what is happening."

Chapter 55

Attack

Attack day has arrived. The design meeting was moved to a secure location in the FEMA camp below. One shuttle remained behind for the president; the second shuttle was parked in the shuttle bay; and all had been briefed, including Dr. Zorg whom Brad had asked along. Ann Thompson, Howard Quill, Julie Preston, Rudy Savage, plus the six new crew members were all present to experience the mission along with Simon, of course. Simon had been instructed to set the zapp beam for one day of unconsciousness and no memory loss.

"Simon," said Brad, "is everything ready to go?"

"Yes, Captain. I have intercepted encrypted Russian chatter, and they are counting down to start the mission four hours from now. The flight path there is clear, and there is no flight activity in the area of the invasion."

"Very well, Simon. Take us there at high speed."

"On my way." *(To Erik and SECDEF implants)*

Everyone was gathered in the CIC, including Simon Android.

"It's okay, everyone," said Simon Android, "my android persona is the same as you hearing just my voice."

"We have arrived at a parking location above the invasion force, and the skies are clear. If something did come at us, I can instantly move the spacecraft and the inertial damping unit will protect you from feeling a thing."

"Captain, ready to proceed."

"Proceed, Simon. Follow our planned attack protocol."

"Attacking!"

Simon swooped down to one thousand feet in front of the invasion and swept the buzz bam back and forth for one minute. No visible reaction. He switched to the EMP beam and raked all the equipment, including motorized vehicles for one minute. Again, no visible reaction. Simon moved up to twenty-mile altitude and hovered.

Hold here, Simon. Let's see if there are any reactions.

"Hit with buzz and EMP. All quiet so far."

"Okay, everyone, we will wait a few minutes here. The sensors have magnified the scene below as you can see on the display. Wait, a jeep vehicle is pulling up. Three people walking into the command tent. Wait now. There! They are running out and on their radios, which should work fine. Two more jeeps pulling up. Starting to look like panic."

"Mission success. Panic at scene. On our way home."

"Simon, take us home."

Simon took a leisurely thirty minutes back to his hovering altitude above the FEMA camp, and everyone was served a delicious food-replicator dinner.

"Thank you all," said Brad. "It all worked as planned, and we have survived our first battle. Relax and enjoy the food."

Ann sat down beside him, and Will Zorg joined them.

"Brad," said Zorg, "that was perfection. And I keep learning more about you which is good for all of us. You aren't a killer. I mean, Simon could have wiped them all out and killed them, but you didn't. Makes me feel good about becoming a citizen of the United States. I'm going to turn in, you guys; see you in the morning."

"Brad, shouldn't we turn in," said Ann. "Want to see what I turn into?"

"Ann," said Brad, "it's hard to think when you get like this. You know that, don't you?"

"I plan on it."

"Okay, but first I need to call the president," said Brad.

"Erik, (implant call) did you and SECDEF get my message clips?"

"OMG, yes, perfect timing. We knew what had happened, and Sergey didn't, at least at first. Then, he got an encrypted call on his secure cell phone, and his face blanched. I thought he was going to pass out. I heard him say, 'No, he's right here with me. I'm having dinner at the White House with the president and the secretary of defense. Mr. President, the foreign minister sends his regards.' I had to struggle to keep a straight face. I mentioned to Sergey that the Chinese were supposed to join us tonight, but when I mentioned that the Russian ambassador was scheduled to be here, they suddenly backed out. I told him the Chinese were acting weird these days. Sergey couldn't wait to get on his way. Please, tell Simon 'wonderful job.'"

"I will, Erik."

"Oh, one more thing, Brad. You somehow haven't noticed that your video is on. Hello, Ann!"

Ann quickly jumped under the covers. "Hello, Mr. President. Sorry!"

"Good night, you two."

Back at the Russian Embassy

"Sergey, the invasion is off, and we have no idea of who is behind our defeat. Our people are still unconscious, and all our equipment was zapped by an EMP. The equipment is useless to us now. If our people wake up and have memory loss, then it is like what happened to your people at the FEMA camp, which points toward the Americans, yet the US president seems totally unconcerned, and there is zero indication that any of their military was involved. What happened took a major effort, and we can't find evidence of any. We checked radar records, and nothing. Popov may start going to church. Keep thinking and looking, Sergey, we must solve this."

"I will, Mr. Foreign Minister. Good night."

The next day, the design people were back at it on Simon finishing up details and helping solve manufacturing problems. The prototypes were about five days from testing using the scientists' matter–antimatter power units from their original spacecraft.

Russian Embassy, Washington, D.C., two days later

"Sergey, I wanted to get back to you as soon as possible. All of our soldiers except one involved in the invasion have regained consciousness and have no memory loss. One person is dead, apparently of a fall when he went unconscious. So that may exclude the Americans for now. We plan to follow up on your comments on the Chinese. They are supposed to be with us, but they have been slippery to deal with. We will try to check them out. In the meantime, keep vigilant. We have got to figure what in the hell is going on."

Conference with the president, secretary of defense, and Brad

"We are a short time away from testing our Tiger series spacecrafts," said Brad. "I don't expect any glitches, but nothing is one hundred percent these days. Once that is done, we will finish up the remaining spacecrafts, and then, they are ready for duty. Erik, the Russians are quiet at the moment. I expect that after North Korea getting defeated and the last two incidents with us, they may be starting to think about extraterrestrial influence, and they certainly would be hesitant to get into a fight with something they know nothing about. They know they would lose. What's your take, Erik?"

"Pretty much the same thought process, Brad. When we do go public, we will still want to be careful with what we release. I want the perception always to be that we have more power than we do. The fact that Simon is an independent contractor, so to speak, helps our cause. They will know that putting pressure on us won't sway Simon. I also want to avoid the powerful demanding interviews with Simon and the crew, Brad. Get those uniforms in process, and no information should be released about anyone in the crew; it could put their families in danger. And, again, we can stress the medical benefits passed on to us, but never even hint at the rejuvenation program. By the way, I see all the crew has joined the program along with Gordon Kelly. Gordon is our key to success at Area 51."

"I agree, Erik, and putting facilities on the moon or another planet in the future will be possible. How do you plan eventually to announce this to the world?"

"Carrot and stick, Brad. That we are now one world that must work together to survive and prosper or divided we will fail. The United States is in charge. Work with us, and we all surge ahead. Do nothing, you fall behind. Fight us, and you will fail. I know this sounds dictatorial, but apparently, there are a lot of worlds out there with intelligent life and many are not friendly. This is going to take a lot of time to set up so most of the population benefit most of the time. Sorry, guys, I was getting peripatetic there, but I look at the future, and it seems almost overwhelming."

"You should see it from my standpoint," said General Glen Hauser, SECDEF. "I'm glad I'm in the rejuvenation program; it will take more than one old lifetime to set up and provide defense. I see how advanced Simon is. What does the next thousand years look like?"

"True, gentlemen," said Brad. "Now, think about six hundred years plus who knows how many years beyond that lifetime and factor in the birthrate. We need reality at the onset if possible to keep from getting messed up later on. I see a time where there will be two groups of people, one hundred and twenty-five plus and six hundred plus. For now, I try to work the immediate problems and look ahead when I can. All this needs more structure. I hate to break up this discussion, but I need to address my today problems."

"Agreed," said the president. "All adjourned for now."

Chapter 56

Testing

The time had finally arrived to test the two prototypes at Area 51. All the subsystems had been tested inside the hangar using a loaner power unit, and all had met their individual now it needed to show results at the systems level, including the weapons.

Brad had asked Dr. Zorg for one of his scientists or himself to join the team for the test flight along with he and Ken Johnson, DOD spacecraft Engineer. Ann Thompson had come with Brad to observe the flight.

Dr. Zorg decided he would volunteer himself so he, Brad and Ken all got into the spacecraft, turned on the cloaking and eased out of the hangar and onto the runway, invisible to all watching. Goggles were handed out to the watchers that showed the view from inside and Simon had joined in watching from his perch at times altitude and also monitoring the new sapient AI. He was setup to override the new AI if required.

The new spacecraft, referred to as Tiger 1 rose slowly to ten feet then

to one thousand feet at a climb of four thousand feet per minute.

"Stop and hold," shouted Brad. "Where is the inertial damping and gravity control? This should come on whenever humans were onboard, needed or not. This instruction was missing from the AI software we all could have been crushed."

Gordon Kelly now mandated that all first tests on each new spacecraft would be instrumented and performed without humane onboard. The need for absolute secrecy was complicating the testing activity. Also, Area 51 was one of the most watched areas in the country.

The last series of tests were the cannons with their four modes of operation. Detectors had been placed on the ground area and the multimode laser was fired at low power. Next was the buzz beam, and then EMP followed by the particle beam. All tests were at low power and all tests confirmed to expected results. The full power testing will take place when the loaner power units are switched out for the new matter–antimatter units and high-power weapons testing and FTL speed will take place away from earth.

The team rewrote the testing procedures and the next day Tiger 1 performed as required as did Tiger 2. Simon had the best knowledge of operating with sapient Artificial Intelligence Units and was setting up a rudimentary program for their particular need for initial programming.

Dr. Zorg commented that the Tiger Series Spacecraft and our testing procedures were much more sophisticated than what they had used with their original spacecraft.

"Simon," asked Brad, "we have discussed handheld weapons and some type of body armor. What are your thoughts on this?"

"Brad, I believe that I can design and build a vest out of a sheet of neutronium that is comfortable and flexible until is hit with a Bullet which will cause it to instantly harden to spread the force over a large area. We should get the Scientists involved in this. As far as handheld weapons, same answer. Also, we need two more shuttlecrafts, and I have the manufacturing package ready for you to give Gordon Kelly for build in Area 51. Are you expecting any threats or hostel action in your manufacturing location? Remember, I can be there in minutes in an emergency even as you hold meetings onboard. I am primarily thinking of threats coming in like a rocket from an enemy on earth, for example. Just make sure I am "in the loop" as you call it."

"I will, Simon," said Brad. "Fast reaction could save the day. And the time is nearing when we will need to go public."

Chapter 57

Resources

Brad had called a meeting of all the crew members to make sure everyone was on the same page. This included Howard Quill, Julie Preston, Rudy Savage, six recent additions from SECDEF, Ann Thompson and himself plus Simon, a total of twelve. In addition, listening in, from a secure location using their implant A/V units, were the president, the SECDEF General Glen Hauser, Secretary of State Ralph Pillerson, and Gordon Kelly.

"I need to bring you up to date on where we are and where we are going. We have two prototypes of our new Tiger series spacecrafts built and ten more nearing completion; two more shuttlecrafts have been started which will give us four total. We have four war drones; we have added the buzz weapon to the shuttle's and Tiger series, and Simon. We are reviewing small handheld arms designs, and we will all get a chance to review these. I picked a name for our space force, and it is Star Force. We will soon have uniforms. I want your ideas on these, so please see Karen Quill; she is in charge of the uniform effort."

"We are United States citizens working for Star Force which will be under contract with the US government representing planet Earth. We have full autonomy and make our own decisions. We need to make sure that members of the congress don't start to believe they give orders. We coordinate with and through the president. I am the captain of Star Force, and ranks and responsibilities will be assigned to each of you in the near future."

"Every one of you is participating in our rejuvenation program, which will give you six-hundred-plus years of life. We will come up with a plan of enlistment, so your new long life doesn't mean you must be with Star Force forever. We plan something similar to what the armed forces have on Earth."

"And, lastly, for now, we all have been getting to know the scientists from Melthorne, and their contributions to the US and Earth are legend. They will be a major help in uniting Earth. Also, they all have committed to becoming US citizens. I want to see if we can add some of them to Star Force. Are there any objections?"

Everyone stood up and clapped!

Brad sat at the lunch counter waiting for Dr. Will Zorg. *How fast we are moving, and I'm amazed,* he thought, *that we have been able to maintain secrecy.* Will Zorg walked in and joined him.

"Will," said Brad, "I'm calling our effort with Simon 'Star Force'. We have twelve full-time crew members who we will be adding to, and I would like to see if any of your crew might be interested. Sound interesting?"

"Actually, yes. Surprisingly, we have talked about the same thing. Now that we are going to be citizens, your battle is our battle also. And, when you say, 'my crew,' it's really unofficial. We are most intrigued with living in a place where there is no constant war or dictator running the place. I will line up the people you should review."

"Will, one of the first positions I need to fill is science officer and communications officer onboard Simon."

"I'll get back to you soon on this, Brad."

"Brad, great meeting. I am rushing the paperwork we need to accomplish what you discussed."

"Thank you, Mr. President. Put it in a document like the constitution; it will look more official."

"Good idea. I hope to have it in two days for you to look at. We must have all this done before we go public. I've got Secretary of State Ralph Pillerson pulling together the documents we need when we do go public. Now, a question: If an unhappy country decides to shoot a missile at us, or a lot of missiles at us, what can we do? There is going to be no place in this world where we can allow an enemy country to nuke another country. We took out North Korea with a lot of lives lost, but I am thinking of Russia. Can't you EMP all their missile sites? Of course, that leaves their submarines. We need to neutralize them quickly, if necessary."

"I will check this out, Erik. How soon do you want an answer?"

"Five days, if you can, Brad."

"Okay, Erik. I will work out a plan."

"Simon, you were in on my last conversation with the president so what are our options on stopping submarine missile launches?"

"Brad, we haven't really looked into this. Do you want to get SECDEF to join in this conversation? I need some questions answered before proceed."

"Sure, Simon."

"Mr. Secretary (using implant A/V), can you join in with Simon and I regarding missile defense?"

"Yes, Brad. Hello, Simon."

"Hello, Mr. Secretary," said Simon. "Are you aware that your oceans are virtually transparent to my sensors? No submarine can hide from me. I can also map where most of their missile launching sites are and their mobile missiles, but remember they are always on the move."

"Astounding, Simon, the defense department spends enormous resource-tracking submarines with marginal results. So you are saying you can give me a map of where and how deep all Russian or any country submarines are at any given time?"

"Yes, Mr. Secretary," said Simon, "and you will figure out how to do this eventually as you develop sensor technology. Why don't you join us onboard later, and I will show you. I would think that just showing Russia a printed copy of the location of all their submarines and depths would dampen their desire to use warfare to get their way. I am getting better at understanding all these factors and understanding that humans sometimes base decisions that are not logical."

"Yes," said Brad, "you are getting better Simon. You are confirming that you can EMP missile submarines."

"Mr. Secretary, why don't you put a plan together than would minimize the effort needed by Simon to stop Russia quickly by showing force. He can EMP their missile sites also, but it would take time."

"Now that I understand the possibilities, I will do that. Brad, is there some way that we can get a morning update of submarine activity, Russian and others? For example, Erik might want to show it to the Russian ambassador to slow them down, especially if they have subs hidden near our territory."

"Yes, I will get you a receive only unit to be kept in a safe place. It is small and if it did get stolen it will self-destruct. I will have it ready this afternoon when you are here."

Meeting onboard Simon with Brad, the president, and SECDEF

"Brad," said the president, "this is a great presentation format. We can show the location and depth of any country or all at once. Terrific intelligence. On every chart we print, I would like a footer that says, 'Acme Submarine Location Service, Inc.' This will help confuse. Look at this chart, Glen, the Russians have two missile subs right off Virginia in our waters. I'm going to call their hand on this. Print this out for me, Brad, with a date and time stamp. Thank you for the encrypted chart receiver; I will keep it locked up safe."

Meeting with the Russian ambassador in the president's office at the White House

"Sergey, do you knowingly have any submarines in my territorial waters?"

"No, Mr. President. We would never violate United States sovereignty, never."

"Okay, Sergey, maybe someone forgot to tell you. Here, look at this chart. This shows every sub you have launched, and you have two in our waters just off Virginia! Go ahead and jot down the data if you want. Get them the hell out of there now."

"I will check immediately, Mr. President. Who is Acme Location?"

"Apparently, some new company we are dealing with. Sergey, I'm out of time, so go and take care of this."

"Yes, Mr. President."

Russian Embassy, Washington, D.C., call between Russian ambassador and foreign minister at GRU headquarters.

"Sergey, I checked the numbers you gave me on the location of the six submarines you got data for. They are spot on accurate. The Navy is going nuts here. This exposes all our submarine fleet. We have lost the element of surprise. If they can do this, what else can they do? Who is Acme? We can't find the company they say they are dealing with. How much are they messing with us?

"There is all this strange stuff going on, and we still know nothing. If they leak that location map, we will be in trouble with other countries too. I moved the two subs they were upset about, and we will stay away until we know what is going on. We are losing this game Sergey, and Popov is ready to clean house."

Simon recorded the conversation and passed it on to Brad and the president.

Erik (via implant), they will leave us alone for now. We have finished the ten Tiger series spacecrafts in Area 51, which, with the two prototypes, gives us twelve functional spacecrafts. The new power units are installed, and final testing will be completed in a few days. We need to man those and get them on duty. We will keep them cloaked and ready to respond.

Good, Brad. I have finished the funding process for our contract and it is protected from anyone who might try to alter it. I will go into detail later.

Thank you, Erik.

Chapter 58
Ground Attack

"All hands to the CIC," said Simon, "We are under attack!"

Way to wake up, thought Brad. "Ann, wake up, we have an emergency."

The whole crew plus Dr. Zorg gathered in the CIC; everyone being sleepy at 4:00 a.m. The president and SECDEF were listening in via their A/V implants.

"We are twenty miles straight up from the FEMA camp, and my sensors constantly monitor everything below. If minor differences change to major differences, an alarm is triggered. Here is a map of the camp and surrounding grounds. Notice the three lines highlighted that are just penetrating the camp. They represent a tunnel, six feet in diameter and fifty feet down. If they continue at the same speed, they will meet in the center of the camp in two weeks, and with three six-foot tunnels, that could be a major invasion force. What they didn't plan on was a spacecraft, twenty miles up, with sensor technology way beyond anything available today. I tried to trace the tunnels back, and they got lost in the clutter of civilization, but I calculate that this has been going on since we activated the camp two months ago. There is a huge volume of dirt they are hiding, so they may be using an empty building in one or more of the tunnels."

"I want everyone," said Brad, "to move to the spacecraft. We don't know when they will come up or what they plan to do. Mr. President, have any ideas?"

"Yes, I do," said the president. "We also look for changes, and the change that now becomes significant is the lack of interest on the part of the Chinese. Russia and everyone else have been pressuring us for answers except the Chinese. Brad, I will replace the civilians you pull out with soldiers in civilian clothes. We need to have vehicles moving around or the intruders will detect the absence of noise. Simon, can you hit them with a buzz beam when they are up out of the tunnels?"

"Yes, I can, Mr. President," said Simon. "I can also collapse the tunnels behind them to cut off any escape. They probably will have a variety of weapons which I can handle. They will be expecting ground fire and won't be expecting me. The zapp beam is invisible, so no one can trace it back to me."

"Simon," said Brad, "we need to get the two Melthorne spacecrafts out of here. Their original power units have been reinstalled, so I need them to fly to Area 51 and exchanged for two of the Tiger series. These should fly cloaked and be on the lookout for any reconnaissance aircraft watching us. Any satellites specifically watching us need to be blinded. Okay, let everyone on the ship as covertly as possible. Dr. Zorg, can I see you for a minute?"

"Will," said Brad, "can we have your two pilots join mine for the two new Tiger spacecrafts for these operations?"

"Yes, we want to be part of this. Have your guys join mine at the hangar in one hour, so we can get the spacecraft out of here."

Outside the hangar at the FEMA camp

"Will, I believe you have met Sam Nugent and Ken Johnson."

"Yes, I have. Brad and I have Carig Heeg and Joog Roobs with me. Let's go in, and we will start up the spacecraft and turn on the cloaking. You and I can open the hangar doors."

"Okay, Will, Simon can guide them on a clear fast path in and out of Area 51. Their mission is to become familiar with the new Tiger spacecraft and then check and identify the Chinese satellites watching us. They will tag it, so Simon can easily and quickly EMP it when the action starts. You, guys, can contact us with your implants if you need, otherwise Will and I will follow your mission through Simon. All clear?"

"Yes, Captain."

"You know, Brad, my guys were glad to get back in the spacecraft."

"Same with my guys, Will. I'm sure anxious to find out who is after us. We need to finish the evacuation to Simon and the DOD troops will be in right after that. I am going to loan them some zapp rifles for cleanup. If everything works like we are planning, all the enemies will be unconscious and have a one-day loss of memory. The president will take them prisoner and determine their future."

"Simon," asked Brad through his implant, "what is the status of any Chinese submarines?"

"Brad, Will, two of their largest have just arrived off the Virginia coast and are parked at depth in your territorial waters as if they are waiting for something to happen."

"Will, that pretty will cinch that we have Chinese invaders."

"Brad, Erik here. I have been following events, and yes, it must be the Chinese. Always look out for the quiet ones. We will be prepared."

"Brad, I'm going to make the rounds and get the remaining people on Simon. See you at breakfast in the morning."

"Okay, Will." Brad took the cloaked shuttle up to Simon and sent it back down for Will.

"Simon, let me know if there is any change in the tunneling activity. Any concerns with the two new Tiger series?"

"I will keep you up to date, Brad. The two new Tiger series are performing within specifications. They have marked the geosynchronous satellite the Chinese put in orbit to watch us. There is one orbiting satellite they are using at much lower altitude with its eyes on us, and that has been marked also. I will need to use my laser beam for both; they are too far away to use EMP."

"Okay, Simon. Good night."

"Ann, you're still awake!"

"Yes, I am Brad, it's hard to sleep with all that is going on. Are you pretty sure it's the Chinese who are behind the latest event?"

"Yes, ninety-five percent sure. We will have an answer very soon. What we don't know is what they will do when we beat them back. The president is going to have to go public soon; the pressure is on."

"Come to bed, Brad, we need our time together."

"I love the way you think, Ann."

"All hands on deck. The intruders are coming to the surface. All crew to the CIC."

"Brad," said Simon, "I have notified the president and SECDEF. The intruders are about fifteen minutes away from breaking surface. The orbiting satellite is three hours away from line of sight at which time I will blind it. I will blind the geosynchronous satellite just before the intruders break surface and then concentrate on a good buzz beam shot. All activity will be recorded. They are going to be coming up in three separate openings near each other in the center of the quadrangle."

"Are you getting all this, Erik and Glen?" asked Brad over implant A/V.

"Yes, we are," responded the president. "Our troops are standing by with both M16s and buzz rifles. We plan to keep the loss of life to a minimum."

"Here we go," said Simon. "Geosynchronous satellite now blinded! Humans pouring out of three openings. I count twenty-five people so far. I am lining up for a buzz shot—hold—buzz shot done. The enemy is falling down. Missed two people. Hold. Second shot done. All done, all down. Troops move in."

"Brad," said the president, "last-minute change. I am holding off on collapsing the tunnels. I brought in additional three squads to backtrack to find out where they lead to."

"Everyone, listen up," said Brad. "We have verified that they are Chinese, and all are carrying military ID. They are all unconscious and are being loaded into trucks heading to a secure location. No other enemy personnel have been found in the tunnels as of yet."

"This is Simon. The two submarines in our territorial waters off the Virginia coast are exiting at flank speed. Tiger spacecraft, good job flying cover for me. Please continue at parking altitude, we will relieve your crews within two days."

Two days later

"Brad, this is the president and SECDEF is with me. All three tunnels led back to large buildings that were leased by a front organization. Anybody who was here during the assault has disappeared; no doubt the sudden loss of radio contact with their team alerted them. All the prisoners have awakened with a short-term memory loss. We were able to piece their story together. They were supposed to bring back as many prisoners and documents as possible in an effort by the Chinese government to determine what we are up to and what new technology weapons we have. Apparently, the neutering you gave North Korea completely panicked them, and they thought they might be next. We will drop all the prisoners, from which we have taken fingerprints, DNA samples, pictures—all the usual stuff—off at the Chinese embassy tomorrow morning. I am going to tell them that we will get together soon. This should hold them off as none of their people were killed or even hurt. We now will have to go public very soon."

"And nice job, Brad," said the president. "This certainly illustrates that a small smart group not loaded down with rules and regulations can accomplish great feats with Lady Luck and with Simon. Simon was superb, wasn't he?"

"Yes, he was, Erik. What can I say. I think of him as a friend, and all this proves a huge point, that being sentient, being responsible and loyal apply to more than just human beings. As far as a bloodless skirmish, it was a weapon originally provided by Simon and later modified by the Melthorne scientists which we call the buzz beam. Without this weapon, there would have been many deaths, probably on both sides and very ill feelings also on both sides. We can give other countries things that help them on a measured basis but not weapons that could be used on us. What do you think, Erik?"

"I agree, Brad. Some of this will be incorporated in my go public statement. Okay, must go. Bye for now."

"Brad," said Will Zorg as he sat down for a coffee, "really good outcome. On Melthorne, the dictator would have slaughtered everyone. This is new and refreshing to me and all my people. Where do we go from here?"

"Thank you, Will. That we need to figure out and you will be part of that meeting. Talk to you in the morning."

"Ann, I hoped you would still be awake. It all came out well, didn't it?"

"Sure did. Sometimes I forget the danger we work in. Come to bed, I need to cuddle and forget the outside world for a while."

"How could I refuse an offer like that?"

Chapter 59

China

Embassy of People's Republic of China, Washington, D.C.,
Ambassador's Office conversation with Minister Chen
Wenqing, China Minister of State Security, Beijing, China.

"Minister Wenqing, I have twenty-five soldiers in my embassy in perfect health but with some memory loss of the actual penetration, and nine more personnel that escaped and are in hiding. The twenty-five were driven up to the embassy in a bus and dropped off, and the bus went on its way. The US president called me and said, and I quote "All your people have not been harmed. Don't ever do that again including violating our territorial waters with your two submarines or next time there will be grave consequences. I will be in touch with President Xi Chen in the near future. In the meantime, you have nothing to worry about. Have a nice day."

"I sense that he is sincere in what he said. We were caught and the fact that no harm was done to our people baffles me. Your thoughts, Mr. Minister?"

"This is most difficult," said Chen Wenqing. "We have no more answers but more questions than before. Since they came back to us the way they did, we must practice patience for a little while, just a little while. There is something earth shattering going on, and I don't think it is malevolent. I think the world is transitioning to a higher level. Keep in close touch, Cui. And acknowledge receiving our people back in good health and that we look forward to meeting with them in the very near future."

"Brad, Erik here. I got an acknowledgment from the Chinese ambassador, and I think the fact that no blood was spilled has thrown them for a loop. I believe they will meet with us with an open mind, at least initially. I also don't think they will entertain any more stunts in the meantime. How did our visitors take all the activities."

"Well, Erik. They just fled a brutalized plan run by a killer dictator, so this is just confirmation that they made a good decision. And, again, the buzz weapon was our salvation. Oh, by the way, can you loan Simon four of the latest technology spacesuits Will will come up with our own but, no time at the moment."

"Yes, Brad, I will have them ready for your astronaut, Sam Nugent, to pick up in three days. I'll get back to you for the pickup address. Brad, we need to get together and discuss our coming out meeting. I expect more trouble from congress than I do from some of the countries and I've got to present this as a done deal. We can give them science, medical technologies, etc., but no weapons. I also want full access to any technology they develop or improve. Any troublemakers will be harshly dealt with. I want to get the point across that what we release to them will allow people of Earth to start to populate other planets in a short time, Mars no doubt being first. There are enemy's out there, and we must all stick together or get our butt beat. This will be a difficult transition for many."

"I understand, Erik. How are you and Karen doing with the rejuvenation process?"

"Wonderful, Brad, I feel great. It is difficult to not show it. Karen says I'm a hot number but so is she. We put a lot of thought into trying to look middle aged, but someone is puzzled when they read our body language. Difficult when you live at the White House. Enough. Brad, what is Simon seeing in the chatter he is picking up and analyzing?"

"Seemingly, it is very quiet. The different countries no doubt talk to each other and Russia and China are waiting for next move. Iran became quiet when they saw what happened to North Korea."

"I am cycling the Tiger series spacecraft and crew through reconnaissance missions to get a feel of our new capability. By the way, we will have our two new shuttlecrafts done and checked out by the end of this week and one has your name on it. You need a very secure place to keep it. You fly by talking to the sapient AI, and Simon will almost always be only a voice away. No one can get into it because of the solid neutronium hull they would encounter, as the oval door opening only appears to the chosen one. The AI is sapient, but it does have good smarts, and again, Simon is always nearby."

"Let me think on that, Brad. I will get back to you. You and Ann take care. Bye."

Later in the week, Brad holding meeting with his crew

"We have a few items to go over. We now have four spacesuits on loan from NASA, and in the meantime, Simon is designing space-suits for all of us. Simon, can you give us a quick look?"

"Yes, Brad, they will have faraday shielding and neutronium armor, enhanced long-range communications, and a custom power unit and oxygen recycling. I will detail all these at a later date."

"Thank you, Simon. The US government is in preparation to go public regarding all our new technology. We plan to give some of this technology to major countries but no weapons initially. We need to start the process of eliminating nuclear weapons, and in fact, that will be a prerequisite for receiving the major technology handout. Any country that tries to start a war will be dealt with in no uncertain terms and won't be able to participate in the technology handout. We expect a lot of screaming and yelling, but this is the way it is. We have proof that there are bad enemy's out there that also have advanced technology, so we need to be prepared. It is time for Earth to grow up and present itself as a unified government."

"As I have said before, the rejuvenation program we are all in is top secret. I don't think we could control out people if this leaked out at this time. In the meantime, in one year from start, we will have all our treatments, and we will continue research to keep on top of this unique technology. Any questions or problems, please see me.

"Simon has sorted and catalogued all the Melthorne technology in his memory bay, and we will get together on this at a later time. Meeting adjourned."

"Will," said Brad, "I understand that one of the technological items was downloading the total memory from a human to an electronic memory, if those are the right words? What is the latest status on that?"

"Brad, my previous government had ordered it destroyed, but one of my scientists had gathered all the data and physical models and put it in Simon's memory bay. Very fortunately, he is with us today. He said they had succeeded, but someone had accidentally dumped the memory just before the final demonstration. We should get it back up as a research program."

"I agree, Will, and I will discuss this with the president. I expect we should start it on Simon. The coming-out program the president is planning to implement may make Earthside locations dangerous for a little while."

"Well, we—notice I said we, I feel I am an earthling now—certainly have room on Simon, and we could keep a secure backup on Earth, couldn't we?

"I believe so, Will. I'll talk to the president and let you know."

"Erik, Brad here (via implant). We have a lot to discuss. How is your coming out presentation doing?"

"Okay, Brad. I'm in the process of gathering together a few key members of congress and a few top reporters, no fake news. This is necessary to be able to get everyone to go along with me. What I plan is to get all them offsite with all their communication toys taken away, and I will need you to show up to authenticate what I am telling them. I will hold them for two days while the leaders of the countries I have already invited0 show up and everyone has received my presentation. The chosen countries will receive their initial technology package, and I will send them on their way with the congressional members. Then, I should hide. So could my wife Karen and I hide on Simon with you?"

"Wow, Erik, that's a lot in a few words. You have been busy. Yes, you and Karen are welcome on Simon. I can have your shuttle with

Karen in it ready for you to jump into whenever you are ready. Now for a biggie question: Where are you going to wind up in all this? You are president of the U.S., and now, we need a president of planet Earth, and if we colonize Mars, is it then Earth federation? Whatever it is, we need you to run it! Just had another thought too. You are really going to stir the pot with your presentation, so I will need all our spacecraft manned and on patrol in key spots around the world in case we have a poor sport out there."

"Yeah, Brad, now it's really going to get busy. Give Gordon Kelly a heads up and tell him he should beef up his security. So there is a shuttle assigned to me, and you have three shuttles, four war drones, and twelve Tiger series spacecraft, most to be out on patrol. You have the latest submarine maps and know what countries to watch. And data I get I will forward to you. I will expose everyone to Simon which is where you come in, a look-see and that may slow any thoughts of aggression. I will plan to see you in two days at noon sharp at the address I have sent you. Come cloaked and decloak when you hear me ask. We will talk between now and then. I've got to go, see you soon."

"Gordon [via implant], this is Brad. Are you getting used to the A/V implants?"

"Oh, hello, Brad, I actually am. And I am starting to feel younger, so the future looks bright."

"Good," said Brad. "Gordon, we need to get more Tiger series spacecrafts as soon as possible. How many can you do in an assembly line run that makes sense?"

"Two-part answer Brad. Twenty-five is a small comfortable run and would produce one a week once we are up and running. If we are on a war footing, we can continually produce two to three a week."

"Gordon, get started on the twenty-five number right away, but be ready for an increase. I will be able to see the future better after the next two weeks. I'm going to assign one of the first Tigers and a crewman to you there in case of an attack, and Simon is keeping his sensors tuned."

"Thanks, Brad, and good luck."

Chapter G
Preparations

Grouse Hemler had cobbled together nine spaceships to fly to earth. He figured it would take six weeks to get there maximum and they would be ready to leave in one week. He would take thirty men, not more as they needed room for food replicator supplies and ammunition. He would find Simon and take his technology back and make someone pay for messing with him!

Chapter 60

Coming Out

"Erik (via implant), I just talked to Will Zorg, and Grouse Hemler has been preparing at a desperate speed and was able to find out that Simon is on Earth and where Earth is located. He tortured one of the scientists he captured who talked. We should be able to have his schedule in a week as Zorg's contact is still safe, but it's touch and go."

"I can imagine, Brad. My vice president, Ryan Steel, was only partially up to speed, and he has been of enormous help, and we are going to need him in the coming days and weeks. He is a veteran of Afghanistan and as loyal as they come. I need him to fill in for me at times, and he needs to meet Simon and become a full member of the team. I have held off this upcoming revelation as long as I can. We are at a peak, but anymore delay and we lose ground. Brad, the Secret Service won't take any action when Simon decloaks and neither will the military, thanks to SECDEF. The visitors from the various countries will all have been individually cleared. What about an introductory speech by my vice-president, and then Simon decloaks at low altitude with a Tiger spacecraft on each side and I in my shuttle come down to the podium, step out through the oval portal, and then give my presentation? This feasible? I need something for shock effect to jar their minds loose from conventional thinking."

"Well, Erik," said Brad, "that should do it for sure. You will probably have a few people who will pass out, so be prepared. Short notice, but yes, we can do it. The vice president doesn't have implants yet so have Howard Quill with him, so we can get messages to him if need be. The big day is tomorrow, and it starts at ten in the morning, so get to Simon by no later than 9:00 a.m. and bring your wife with you. Howard can keep you in touch. Can you do this schedule?"

"Yes, Brad, my life is a series of schedules, and I will lock this in with my handlers. Send my shuttle to the pickup location, and Karen and I will be there at nine tomorrow morning."

"We will see you then, Erik."

*Later that day in the Oval Office: Meeting
with Vice President Ryan Steel*

"Ryan, how are you coming along on accepting the new reality?"

"I'm getting there, Mr. President. It is a lot to swallow in a short time."

"Sorry, I couldn't bring you in earlier, but I had to keep the list short. I will get you up to the Simon Spacecraft soon, so you can see for yourself. Ryan, I need to disappear tomorrow around 9:00 a.m. You will give your introductory speech tomorrow starting exactly at 10:00 a.m. Somewhere around 10:15 you say, 'And now I want to introduce the president of the United States,' and then back up and give me plenty of room. Follow any prompts you get from Howard Quill."

"Okay, Mr. President, but why the need for plenty of room?"

"You will see, Ryan. I don't want to spoil the surprise."

*Next day, 9:00 a.m., in the Simon Spacecraft
shuttle bay as a shuttle lands:*

"Hello, Mr. President. Hello, Karen."

"Hi, Brad. I think every country president is going to want a shuttle after today. I just hope I can get them to focus on the more-important needs."

"It will take time, Erik," said Brad. "Everyone will need an adjustment period, some more than others. You are going to need to kick butt in some cases, and some are going to need to retire. Even today, some members of congress still can't come up with a proper computer password."

"Well, Brad, big changes are coming, and we are growing which we must do if we are going to survive. Oh, hello, Ann, good to see you again."

"My face may be a little red."

"Don't let it be, Ann. It's all about a good part of what life can offer. Ann, meet my wife Karen, I have told her a lot about what you and Brad have accomplished."

"Thank you, Mr. President. I appreciate your understanding."

"Brad, I need to be in my shuttle at ten minutes to ten, ready to go. Can I listen to my vice-president's speech in the shuttle?"

"Sure, Erik. Just ask Simon. He is monitoring all your activity and will remotely fly and control your shuttle. Simon will be backing up the Secret Service and will take action against any threat so you are going to be well taken care of. Why don't you and Karen get into your shuttle and be comfortable. We will be in the CIC and will be monitoring all aspects of this event. By the way, the two Tiger space-crafts are presently on each side of Simon and will decloak with him. The overall effect should be stunning."

It is a beautiful sunny day, and the event is being held outside on the groomed and immaculate lawn of the thirty-five acres of the convention estate. Everyone is seated around in a semicircle; the first section is for the fifty key members of congress chosen by the president. The second section is for one hundred heads of state and their chief scientists. The third section is for the top level of the scientific community and industry of the United States. The forth section is for one reporter from each country and six reporters from the United States of demonstrated objectivity, in the eyes of the president. Extensive communications have been set up for the press to speed their stories to their publications.

The whole world is waiting with great anticipation to find out what is going on. Never before has any presidential announcement been able to hold the level of secrecy that this event has.

Karen Williams steps out of the shuttle to wait onboard Simon while her husband, the president waits in the shuttle for his cue as his Vice President, Ryan Steel steps up to the podium below. It is now 10:00 a.m.

"Members of congress, distinguished guests, ladies and gentlemen, members of the press, earthlings, and aliens, this is a momentous day indeed. A lot of exciting things have been happening, and you all have had questions. Some of you were most forceful in your quest for answers. Today is the day you get all your questions answered in the spirit of renewed cooperation and joining hands for the next level of our human development. "Now, I want to introduce Erik Williams, president of the United States."

"Hail to the Chief" music plays, and sixty feet in front and above, a one-hundred-and-fifty-foot hovering saucer suddenly and silently blinks into existence with a smaller saucer on each side holding in position. What looks like a shuttle appears to detach itself from the big saucer and quietly descends down to the podium and floats six inches above ground. An oval opening appears in the side of the shuttle and out steps the president of the United States. (This is all being displayed on a thirty-foot screen on each side of the semicircle for all to see.) The door oval closes, and the shuttle rises up six feet and disappears.

For a moment, all were silent. You could hear a pin drop. Three people fainted, and now, there rose a crescendo of people screaming, crying, and shouting. Some just sat stunned, unable to talk. Slowly, the noise quieted down, and the president started to speak. The spaceships held their positions.

"Everyone, I want to assure you that you are in no danger of any kind, all is well. You are the first people to see and take part in the next developmental stage of the human race. And what a momentous event it is. For example, we have talked about and dreamed of putting people on Mars. We could do that next month!"

"But, first, a little background. Not too long ago, one of our people accidentally stumbled upon a spaceship, the very one you see above you. This spacecraft is sentient. That means it has a mind that is similar to our mind and yet different. He cannot be owned; he is an intelligent being and free. He is an example of artificial intelligence at the highest level, and one of the profound lessons we learned is that we and he—Simon is a he—have a lot in common. Simon and the United States have joined forces actually and contractually to elevate the human race to new heights.

"Simon was shot down around one hundred and twenty-five years ago and spent that time in self-repair which had just finished when we discovered him. He came from a planet embroiled in warfare and self-destruction. They eventually will come looking for Simon, and we are going to defend him. Also, the enemy that shot him down is lurking somewhere nearby, and we need to be ready to confront that danger when and if it shows up. Simon is providing the advanced knowledge that will let us develop technologically.

"Most of you are aware of the recent introduction of medical technologies that provide cancer detection and the corresponding treatments for cancer. Eventually, we will be able to edit cancers out of existence. This all came as a gift from Simon along with other technology gifts. We, the United States and Simon, want to share this with you. We, the United States, are going to be the country in charge, and we will hand out and help out other countries develop and utilize this. We have, starting today, packages for each represented country, the medical defeat for cancer and other protocols and processes that will enhance life. The shuttle you saw me arrive in can be developed into many products in the not-too-distant future.

"The caveat of all this fantastic technological knowledge is that it can be used for destroying as well as building. A few nations have nuclear weapons, and those must go away. From this point on, we can't remain a collection of nations trying to carve out power or trying to defend by threatening mutual assured destruction. All of your submarines are now visible to us, and we plan to have a website that continually updates and is available to all. You need to disarm your nuclear devices to be completed in six months. No excuses. And if any one shoots missiles at someone else, we will take punitive action. If you start a war, we will finish it quickly, Remember North Korea!

We have the power to do this. We all need to focus on the threat from beyond the solar system. We can and must build trust with each other. We got lucky, because Simon is here to help us. Simon, would you like to say a few words?"

Simon spoke in his usual baritone voice.

"Hello, everyone. I have come to know many of you, and I think your future to be outstanding if we all work together. I came from a planet with people very much like yourselves, but they took the path to constant war and destruction, and billions of people died. My planet is virtually unlivable and is in the middle of a nuclear winter. I think you would he horrified if you saw it. I believe in the people I have met so far, and I am sure I will meet many more of you. Let's join together for the future."

"Okay, everyone," said the president, "that's enough for today. Sleep on this tonight, and slowly, we will answer your questions."

The shuttle suddenly became visible again floating six inches off the ground. A large oval appeared on the side. The president stepped inside. The oval flowed closed, and the shuttle ascended up to the saucer and disappeared into it. All this was displayed on the two thirty-foot screens for everyone to see. For a few minutes, the audience just sat in stunned silence. Simon and the two Tiger spacecrafts stayed horizontal and rose straight up at twenty-five thousand feet per minute and cloaked, stopping at thirty miles to temporarily park.

Chapter 61

Aftermath

The president stepped out of his shuttle where Brad was waiting. "Mr. President, great speech. The world can never go back. It is forever changed."

"Let's go to the CIC, Brad. What are they saying at the Russian Embassy?" asked the president.

"You mean after all the swearing going on. Now they fully realize that we were ahead of the them whole time, and they still don't have any details. I think Popov might see the end of his grand expansion."

"He needs time, Brad, to adjust to the new world, they all do. I'm going to give everyone two weeks and then see where we are. I may get the worst flak from congress."

"Yes, Erik, but they can't do much."

"If they do go the way of making life difficult I will push back hard. Now that we are here, let's get Karen some A/V implants and another rejuvenation treatment. This may be the last quiet time we have for a long time."

I need to call my vice president, and he doesn't have implants, so how do we do that, Brad?"

"We can," said Brad. "Take your secure cell phone and ask Simon to connect you. He has a way of hacking the cell system and keeping the call secure."

"Okay. Simon, can you connect me with the vice president, please?"

"Yes, Mr. President, standby."

"Ring. This is the vice president."

"Ryan, Erik here. Bring me up to date."

"OMG, Erik, it is pandemonium here. The Russians and want to see you immediately pretty please. All the reporters are trying to hunt you down and your congressional friends you invited to the meeting want to talk to you. Your congressional friends you didn't invite are no longer your friends, they hate you. They say their people back home want to know why they weren't even invited. That about sums it up."

"Okay, Ryan, I gave you two pickup coordinates to keep in your pocket. Get the Chinese president and his chief scientist he brought to pick up point number one in thirty minutes. No one is to know, except you and Howard Quill. I want him to come along. Can you do that secretly with all that is going on?"

"Yes, Erik. It will be tricky, but doable. They will be there."

"Simon, when I bring the Chinese back, can you scan them and keep an eye on them, so to speak? This is what we call a trust but verify situation."

"Yes, Mr. President, I can. And I understand your innuendos now, at least most of the time. I am a machine learning."

"Wow, Simon, you really are special."

"Thank you, Mr. President, I will keep my sensors tuned on them and take action, if needed. Do you want me to appear in my android persona?"

"Yes, good suggestion. I will introduce you as Simon Android."

"Okay, Brad, you want to come along?"

"Sure."

"I'll introduce you as Captain Young, the Captain of the Spaceship and crew. I'm glad everyone is wearing their new uniforms. Just in time."

The president and Brad flew down to pick up point one, cloaked and settled down at six inches off the ground and drifted over to where Howard Quill and the Chinese were waiting. The Shuttle got within two feet and decloaked. The Chinese jumped and freaked out, then embarrassingly smiled. The president got out and shook their hands. Howard Quill smiled, nothing phased him anymore.

They all boarded, the ovals flowed shut and the shuttle recloaked and headed toward Simon.

"Xi Wang said that trust was in effect as they had no bodyguards with them, but these were extraordinary circumstances. He was all smiles as this was an unexpected, but welcome venture."

The landed in Simon and were immediately taken to the observation deck.

"Have a seat, gentlemen," said the president. "Coffee or tea?"

"Tea please," said Xi Wang. "This is good tea!"

"It's from the food replicator," said Brad.

"You have food replicator?"

"Yes, a pretty good one."

"Okay, everyone," said the president, "as you can imagine, we don't have a lot of time. I wanted you to see Simon for yourselves, in fact here he comes now."

Simon Android walked up and introduced himself.

"You are alien and you speak English?" asked the Chinese scientist.

"Actually, I am the spacecraft. I use this humanoid android body to meet you, but I am an Artificial Intelligence with extensive learning capability and I am distributed through the spacecraft. I am a machine intelligence interacting with biological flesh and blood intelligence. Tell me gentlemen, how does this grab you?"

"Simon," said Brad, "is beefing up his language learning but, good question. How does all this grab you?"

"I think we are in shock," said Xi Wang. We have much to learn."

"Gentlemen," said the president, "our time is short. I know you needed to know these details but the fact we have interstellar enemy's and only earth weapons. We need to get upgrading fast or we could lose our freedom. Trust is imperative. No games. And, no time for war with each other, it will be difficult, but we must work together. And that camera you brought with you, keep the pictures but you should have told me."

"My face is red, Mr. President," said Xi Wang. "I do want to have trust between us. No, you take the camera. Where do we go from here?"

"You have the medical package," said the president. "I will get you a package for the shuttle, so you can manufacture them. I also want your help in identifying any countries that might cause problems for the human race to climb the ladder of evolution. I will keep your confidences. Do we have an understanding?"

"Absolutely, Mr. President." said Xi Wang. "Thank you for bringing us here. I value trust between us. We can talk in a few days."

The Chinese were returned to the pickup point and Brad and Erik returned to Simon.

"Good thing Simon caught that camera," said Brad. "I never spotted it."

"Neither did I," said Erik. "I believe they really embarrassed themselves. Good to set the tone of this relationship right away."

"Do you plan to have the Russians up here?"

"Not at this time, Brad. My trust with them is not high. They have got to learn to be good citizens or I will excommunicate them. A lot up in the air right now. I need to find my wife. How is the food up here, Brad?"

"Amazingly good. Since we have you captive here at least tonight, I thought we would have a big food-replicator dinner. It would certainly would be motivational for the crew."

"Good idea, Brad. When and where?"

"In two hours in the observation deck."

"Okay, Brad. See you then."

"Hi, Ann, how did your day go?"

"Good. After the president's speech, I went into the neutronium factory, and everyone was immersed in the excitement about where we, as the human race, are heading. I did some calculations and came back here. We have a large stockpile of neutronium now which I assume will go toward the new Tiger series and some more shuttles. I take it that I may need to quadruple my production. Using two shifts and available room, I can do that."

"That's about right, Ann. Things are moving into high gear. No vacation for us right now. I know we have six hundred years or more, but our time together is important."

"Me, too, Brad. Now, what time is the big dinner tonight?"

"About an hour from now. Whoever thought things would turn out like they have?"

"By the way, Howard Quill is tightening up security. There are countries that don't want the United States to be in charge, so we need to be extra cautious."

The big dinner.

Everyone arrived in their new uniforms, and the dinner was fantastic. Simon is a genius at programming in new recipes. Simon Android was attending the dinner as a crew member.

"This is a pivotal time as we have just initiated a huge push up the evolutionary ladder, there is no going back," said the president. "All of you remember this day. We are going to expand, to migrate to Mars and beyond. In a short time, we will be a spacefaring race and who knows from there. We should get together every hundred years like this, after all, we really can do that! Now let's eat."

The Russian Embassy, Washington, D.C., Ambassadors Office

"Mr. Foreign Minister, what did you think of the US president's speech yesterday?"

"What do you expect me to say, Sergey? In all future, no one will ever be able to duplicate something like that. I wish we had found that spacecraft."

"So do I, but we didn't. It sounded like the US president handed out an ultimatum, did it not? What did Popov say? How come he went back to Moscow so soon. I would have thought he would push for a meeting with President Williams?"

"Well, Sergey, he now knows who stopped us from invading Poland. They now know where all our subs are at all times. We spent billions on those subs, and now, they are worthless. They won't get our bombs."

"But, Mr. Foreign Minister, I bet they know where all our bombs are. And they have weapons that can kill missiles quickly. Look what they did to North Korea. One ship did all that in a few minutes. It seems like we shoot ourselves or decide to join the future. If we already have space enemies, we need to join with others to help fight that."

"Sergey, you are right. If Popov goes off the deep end, we are done. So what can I do? Please never speak of this conversation or we die. Go home, get some sleep."

Simon duly recorded and sent the conversation to Brad and the president.

"Good morning. I assume you got Simon's message on the latest conversation at the Russian embassy?"

"Yes, I did, Erik. Sounds like we might have trouble at any time. I plan to keep Tiger spacecraft over Russia at all times which is difficult as big as it is. You would think he would know that we have far superior technology."

"Good, Brad, I am expecting trouble. Don't hesitate to take Simon over there; you may need to crush several missile sites, and this may be the time we use the particle beam. I will invite the Russian ambassador over for a chat tomorrow."

"Good, Erik. I will ask Simon to try and keep Popov's location handy as much as possible through his phone calls. Let's have breakfast and bat some ideas around."

Will Zorg walked up and asked if he could join them.

"I just got here," said Will. "I received a message from Melthorne, and Grouse Hemler plans to leave in one week and figured it will take his nine spacecrafts six weeks to get here. Best to meet him out past the orbit of Mars, and it will be a fight right from the start."

President Erik Williams meeting with Russian ambassador at the White House

"Sergey, I haven't heard from you or your leaders? Anything you feel like telling me?"

"I haven't heard anything either nor confidently has our foreign minister. You always seem to know what we are doing with your new technology, so maybe you can tell me? I heard what you said about enemies from outside Earth, was that true?"

"Yes, Sergey, it certainly was true. I just got the timetable on approximately when we will be under attack, and it will be in a few weeks. We don't want Russia to pull something while we are fighting for the life of our planet, do we? The planet the spacecraft came from is in nuclear winter and is dying. It's all hands-on deck now joining together to save our butts. Do you understand? I know you and your foreign minister have wives and children. Help us out, Sergey. Get your president with the program."

"Are you asking me to commit treason?"

"No, Sergey, I'm asking you to help us preserve the planet. I think you have an idea where Russia will come out if you attack us. Think about a modern-day Navy carrier group with nuclear missiles moved back in time to 1944. Nothing would be able to touch it; it could wipe out anyone or any country it wanted. We have weapons that are hundreds of years ahead of anything you have, so you can't win. If you were with us, you will be part of the future I am talking about. Talk with your people. Get back to me. Okay?"

"I have never been in this spot, Mr. President. I will get back to you within three days. Thank you."

"Brad, via implant, I just finished talking to the Russian ambassador, and I sense he has no idea what his president is up to. He seems extremely worried. He will do some digging and get back to me this week for what it's worth. You know, I don't want to be in the position where we have Simon out past the Martian orbit with most of his Tiger spacecraft fighting for the planet and have Russia attack us."

"I have thought of that scenario, Erik. I think we still are on safe ground. We have sensors in our Tiger spacecraft have a longer range by fifty percent, and the enemy only thinks we have Simon. Dr. Zorg doesn't think Hemler even has a realistic assessment of Simon's capability. The communications equipment in the new Tiger Series is a big improvement over the original equipment and much more sensitive so we should hear chatter long before Hemler thinks we can. Also, our weapons are improved in power and range which will give us a big advantage. We should have six more Tiger spacecraft off the manufacturing line by the time they get into our solar system. Lastly, I have talked to Simon, and he calculates that we will be about forty million miles from Earth minimum and he could get back in one to three hours at flank speed depending on where Earth is in its orbit. We will have twelve plus six additional Tigers, so a total of eighteen, and I had planned on leaving five to guard Earth. How does all that sound to you?"

"Good calculations, Brad. We need to keep the date when Simon will be away secret at all costs. In fact, we need to make it look like he's here when he is away."

"I agree. Okay, Erik, let me know what you hear from Sergey."

"I will, Brad. Bye for now."

Back in President's office at the White House with Russian ambassador.

"Hello, Sergey, I hope you have good news?"

"Well, I have a kind of status. All of us at high level have our own spies who are people we gathered along the way. They report things to us and we try to evaluate what they told us to calculate their accuracy. The highest probability we have, and we is me and the foreign minister, is that he is in a kind of seclusion thinking about which way to go. He must know he really has only one choice, so I assume he is coming to terms with that. I suggest you call him and offer a carefully worded olive branch."

"Good thinking, Sergey. I had planned on doing that, but I needed your feedback first. Hold it, Sergey, give me a minute, please."

The president was getting a message via his implant but picked up his telephone handset to appear he was on the phone.

"Go ahead, Brad, what's up?"

"Erik, we are getting chatter activity in Russia that is indicative of potential launching."

"Have I got time to get aboard?"

"Yes, if you hurry."

"Send the shuttle to pick up point alpha, and please note, I will have the Russian ambassador, Sergey, with me."

"Mr. President, what are you talking about?" asked Sergey.

"Sergey, how would you like a ride on my spaceship?"

"I would like that."

"Okay, follow me."

The president and the ambassador exited to the hidden pickup we're the shuttle was waiting. They got in and the cloaked shuttle whisked them to Simon at fifty thousand feet where they entered cloaked Simon and were rushed to the CIC. By this time, Sergey was hyperventilating and looked like he might pass out.

"Sergey, slow down. Take slow deep breaths. Here's the situation: We have spotted possible launch activity in Russia and are rushing over to check it out."

"How come all I feel is normal gravity?"

"Automatic inertial damping and gravity control. We are traveling at one hundred and fifty thousand feet at approximately twenty thousand mph on the way to Russia."

"Bet I'll get in trouble for this, Mr. President. What are you going to do?"

"Sergey, if what I think is happening. I am going to try and stop a war."

"Hello, Mr. President," said Brad, "glad you and the ambassador could make it aboard."

"Everyone standby, this is Simon! Four missiles launching in one minute. Weapons release in effect. All weapons armed."

The missiles lifted out of their silos below and were each hit with a laser beam followed up with a full force EMP beam. The four silos were hit with a particle beam which utterly destroyed everything it touched. Elements were transmuted into other radioactive elements and isotopes that totally contaminated the area. All this destruction was shown on the large display in the CIC which illustrated just how powerful Simon could be.

Sergey was ashen. He uttered, "All that power. Nobody can fight that."

"Simon, check the chatter and let us know what is going on," said Brad.

"Sergey, shall we see if we can get your foreign minister on the phone?"

"Can you do that?"

"We can try. Simon?"

"Yes, Mr. President, he was not at his usual number, but I do have him on speakerphone."

"Mr. Foreign Minister, can you hear me?"

"Sergey, is that you? Where are you?"

"I am above you on a saucer spacecraft with the US president. Our country just fired off four missiles. They and their launch facilities were utterly destroyed in less than five minutes by this spacecraft. What is going on down there? Stop the war or our country will be wiped out."

"Sergey, I had nothing to do with this. This was Popov's last gasp."

"Mr. Foreign Minister, this is the president. Try to get this aggression stopped. We need to defend planet Earth soon. Think what it would be like with twenty-five fighting spacecrafts. We don't have time for this crap. Can you help out?"

"I will try, Mr. President. What are you going to do with Sergey?"

"I was going to take him back to his embassy."

"Can you drop him off in Moscow?"

"Cautiously, yes. Do you have a safe place?"

"Yes, Mr. President, right in Red Square. Mostly everyone is hiding. If you stay invisible, set down in a dark area and he can walk away."

"Okay, he will be there in fifteen minutes."

"Sergey, the shuttle will drop you off. Tell everyone what you saw up here, maybe that will help. Keep in close touch. Don't you want to be part of the future?"

"Yes, I do Mr. President. I promise I will keep in touch."

"Good. Call this number to reach me."

The shuttlecraft with the ambassador aboard successfully dropped him off in Red Square and quickly returned to Simon.

"Erik," said Brad, "I assume you want him to spread his story around the more sane crowd as a detriment to war with us?"

"Absolutely, Brad. Popov has lost any right to lead and has to be stopped."

"Something else, Erik. We just killed four missiles that were fired off from the same complex. If it had been eight missiles from eight complexes it would have been dicey, but we could have done it. Bring in the three Tiger spacecrafts, and we could take on a lot more, but we do have limits. We rejoice in this new technology, but we need to keep climbing up the technology ladder or we will fall behind. Our neutronium hull is almost impervious yet whatever that black spaceship had, it shot Simon down and almost killed him. I want to get with the scientists and see if we can improve on even the great technology we already are using. Would some kind of magnetic or force field help protect our ships? We need to know."

"Brad," said Erik, "you also mentioned that you wanted to build more spacecrafts the size of Simon or even larger."

"I do, Erik. I need to get together with Will Zorg and his people. It's always easy to say we will start during the quiet times, but I am starting to realize that there will be very few quiet times."

"Simon," asked Brad, "how much do you know about the weapon that shot you down?"

"Not much, Brad/ The piece that you sent to DARPA broke off from where I was hit. Let's analyze that to see what we can learn."

"Good idea. Ann can get that back for us."

"It was now morning over Russia, and Simon was just about to head back to Washington, D.C. when Simon announced that the Russian ambassador was calling. Simon connected on speakerphone and Sergey stated that he had news."

"Go ahead, Sergey," replied the president, "and how did your explanation of what happened up here go over."

"Well, it took time, but everyone eventually bought it. From the foreign minister on down, including friends of Popov."

"What's the status of your government? I am not going to put up with any more crap from them. I have lost trust.

"I understand, Mr. President. Give us some time. It looks like we are going to have a new government. All the pieces have to be picked up and reshuffled. I think they will announce a new leader and government soon."

"Call me every couple of days, Sergey, to keep me up to date. Bye for now."

"Okay, Brad, let's head back."

Chapter 62
Battle Planning

"Erik (via implant)," said Brad, "we are approximately six weeks away from doing battle with the spaceships from Melthorne. Zorg will get word when they finally leave Melthorne, and I will put a Tiger spacecraft on watch, and by the time he arrives, we will have many spacecraft ready to intercept him. We should have the edge with the shock value of surprising him. Down the timeline, I am a lot more worried about the black mysterious spacecraft that shot Simon down. We know nothing about their weapons, who or what they are or where they come from."

"I have been thinking about that too, Brad," said Erik. "It seems whoever has the latest technology wins. I see Ann has DARPA analyzing that artifact you found at the original Simon site. I also talked to them to reinforce the high priority of this effort and to let them know any resource they need will be provided."

"Thanks, Erik. I will get Will Zorg to get his best scientists together and have them work with DARPA. I have the hope that this could lead to some kind of deflector shield. The only protection our ships have right now is the neutronium hull.

"Brad! I haven't seen you off Simon for some time. I forget that is where you live now."

"I know, Will. I actually am at home on Simon and never thought I would feel that way. Speaking of Simon, did your scientists ever look into developing some kind of deflector shielding for spacecraft?"

"Actually, we did and when we got to the testing phase it was time to push Simon out the door to fly off and hide."

"Well, Will, I found a broken off or more like shot off piece of neutronium when I found Simon and one of our government agencies called DARPA is trying to analyze it to see if it has any clues as to what kind of weapon was used. The president is behind backing them and its operating under high security, but your people would be immediately cleared if they could coordinate with them. I think we are ready for the enemy from Melthorne, but the black spacecraft that shot Simon down is a complete mystery. They may be more technologically advanced then we are which would put us at risk."

"Brad, I will get right on it. I will need access to Simon's memory bay to see what we had already accomplished. If we have most of the design done, we can rush a prototype and start testing. Your DARPA sounds like the place to do this engineering."

"It is. Here is the person and telephone number for you to call and get started. Keep me up to date, please."

"I will, Brad. And I need to tell you that I heard from my contact on Melthorne, and Grouse Hemler just took off for Earth with an armada of nine spacecraft. Apparently, that was all he got ready for the long flight? Simon should be able to catch their communications chatter long before they get here if they are foolish enough to not maintain radio silence. Their cloaking is not as good as Simon's or the cloaking you used on the Tiger series, so they may be detectable pretty far out. We have approximately six weeks, but we had better be in place well before that."

"Thanks, Will."

Two weeks later onboard Simon, Brad, Ann, the president and Will Zorg plus Simon Android.

"All of you need to know," said Brad, "that I have our Tiger 1 spacecraft out beyond the orbit of Mars to detect any intruders, just in case. Simon and six others are prepped to instantly join him when necessary. Theoretically, four weeks to go."

"I will have some small arms weapon," Simon Android said, "for us to evaluate soon."

"And two of my top scientists," said Will Zorg, "have been working with DARPA, and we are making good headway on a deflector shield for Simon. They take a tremendous amount of power, so we don't know yet if they will apply to the smaller Tiger series spacecrafts. We will be ready to start testing in one week. They will or should initially work to repel most beam weapons, but we are unsure about the particle beam yet. This shield is going to be incrementally improved over time. It appears that Simon was originally shot down by some type of particle beam."

"We are all making good progress," said Erik. "Congress, the ones that didn't get invited to my big fess up speech realized that they must join, not hinder, our efforts just as the Chinese do. I received word that the Russian president has died from a massive heart attack and is displayed in state in the Kremlin. They will be announcing new elections soon, and Sergey, their ambassador, is trying to keep me informed the best he can. I, in the meantime, am planning to set up an office of Earth alliances with myself as president and CEO for a ten-year term, after which, elections would be held. I will then resign as president of the United States which would move Ryan Steel up to president and so forth. There would board of alliance directors each held by a key nation. I need your thoughts on this? This will take time to write up."

"Huge move, Erik," said Brad. "But absolutely necessary. By the time your ten-year term is up, you should have a very savvy board of alliance directors to elect the next president and CEO. I assume you will delineate the relationship with Simon and funding?"

"Yes, that is where that will be done, plus I want to lock in that Simon is an independent free agent."

"Will, what do you think of all these ideas," asked Brad.

"I am familiar with democracy," said Will, "from studying for my US citizenship test that I took. You are playing a strong hand, some might call it edging on dictatorial, but I see and agree with the necessity at this juncture. Elections in ten years is fair as that time is needed to bring people up to speed to the new world we are going to be living in."

"I need to mention our Tiger series spacecraft," said Ann. "So far, our underground location for neutronium manufacturing and Area 51 for Spacecraft production is good up to a maximum of five hundred per month, but beyond that, we need more facilities or sub-contracting. We need to sell them unarmed with strict controls and safeguards for added weapons. Start thinking about this now please."

"Erik," asked Brad, "what is the mood of the world's nations now that they know where we are headed?"

"So far, fairly positive, Brad. The benefits from the medical technology we handed out have generated countless stories of saved lives and that is appreciated. The fact that it came from Simon lessened their fear to start with and the fact that we can actually colonize Mars and beyond soon has been very motivational. There are a few that are upset that they aren't running the show, but they will fall in line. All in all, there is a lot for almost everyone. Eventually, we are going to need to deal with the fact that we have a rejuvenation program and the implications of what that means."

"One last thought," mentioned Brad. "We need to look at designing a range of spacecraft. Possibly some the size of Simon and what about battleship size? Anywhere from a thousand feet diameter to five thousand feet. Erik, we need someone that can help us with the engineering and military thought process of this concern."

"I will line up some people for this," said Erik. "It's a good long-term project. And now let's adjourn. I need to get back to the White House."

Brad and Ann returned to their quarters.

"You know, Brad, I have a lot of questions of where we wind up. Nothing urgent with our long life, but we need to spend quality time together."

"I have the same thoughts, Ann. Let's plan at least a lunch or dinner out next week."

"Okay."

*Design update meeting onboard Simon: Brad, Ann,
Will Zorg, Simon Android, and Gordon Kelly from Area 51*

"Now, three weeks to go," said Brad, "before the fighters are due to arrive from Melthorne. What is the status of the deflector shield project, Will?"

"We have tested our design," said Will "that had originally been completed on Melthorne. We static tested at Area 51 for protection against EMP, laser, and particle beams with success dependent upon the power and time of the enemy beams coming at it. Used with a neutronium hull it can be a lifesaver. The Particle Beam is our biggest worry. It can, given enough time, destroy neutronium but with the deflector shield, you add three times the safety margin. Also, you lose your cloaking and stealth ability when you enable the shields. Nothing is free it seems, it's give and take. This is or can require a lot of quick switching of cloaking, shields and weapons on and off along with switching, firing and mixing of weapons on and off but that's easily handled by the AI. I purpose that we install this shielding on Simon immediately at Area 51 in preparation of the upcoming battle."

"I can support this," said Gordon Kelley. "I have one building that will fit Simon inside and no one will know he is there except the people installing the shield. Working three shifts it will take three to four days."

"What about the Tiger series spacecraft?" asked Ann.

"That's going to take more design time," said Will, "which we are working on. This shielding is very power demanding and the system for the Tiger Series needs to be as efficient as possible to operate with the available power envelope. We can install a prototype on a Tiger in four weeks. The prototype we install on Simon will be continually upgraded as we improve and refine our design."

"I can help with this installation," said Simon Android. "I know my spacecraft and, using my four robots will speed things up significantly."

"Okay everyone, let's get started right away. As of now, Simon is on the way to Area 51, and I will put two Tigers in his place in the event of trouble. Adjourned."

Over coffee in the recreational lounge, Ann asked Brad why we even put personnel on the Tigers? After all, starting with the stealth 117 fighter airplanes some years ago, the protocol was to bail out if the computers failed because no human pilot could fly the plane without computer assist.

"True," said Brad "and no one can fly Simon or the Tigers except the AIs. Intact flight controls don't even exist. We, first of all, use the spacecraft for all sorts of transportation and reconnaissance. We could not have picked up all the scientists from Melthorne without Simon. Think of freight to Mars once we start a colony there. As the need develops, so will the spacecraft technology, and I have no idea where all these wind up. I think of Simon as our headquarters. I still think about the translucent black spacecraft that shot Simon down, and we have no information at all. We need to find out what that is all about. I can't get my mind off of that unknown danger."

"Brad, I worry about that too, but I have an idea that will get our minds on something much better for tonight. Come here and put your worries aside."

"Brad, Gordon Kelly here via implant. Hitch a ride here. The deflector shield is installed, and we want to do some testing. Bring Ann with you as she will be involved with manufacturing some of the new hardware for future ships."

"Okay, Gordon. We will be at your hangar door at 13:00 hours."

"Ann, we will take the shuttle that we used when we left Area 51 when we arrived there with Simon earlier this week. Ready?"

"All set, Brad. I would like to be with you on Simon to meet the incoming warships from Melthorne too."

"Ann, this is where my personal feelings try to come into play, but you should be on that mission. Plan on it. And let's go, I will be glad to get back in our quarters on Simon. I can't believe I got tired of living in the room in the FEMA camp, but I did, and besides, we are safer onboard Simon."

Brad and Ann arrived in their shuttle at Area 51 and went directly to the hangar where Simon was being updated. Will Zorg had been there for the whole work effort. Brad and Ann, fully cloaked, floated up to the hangar and called Will to open the door twelve feet. They were being cautious even though there were no satellites due overhead for the next two hours. Once inside, the hangar door closed and they decloaked their shuttle and got out.

Seeing the full one hundred and fifty-foot Simon right in front of him brought back the memories of the first time he saw Simon. How far they had come since then.

Gordon Kelly greeted them and walked them around Simon, describing the work they had done.

"By the way, Brad, I can't describe how young I feel. Two rejuvenation treatments and I feel like a new man. In fact, I guess I am a new man. What are all of us in the program going to do when too many people really start to notice that we look and act young again?"

"Gordon, I am coming up with a plan that shows how to hide your getting younger. As an example, grow a beard. Don't be so bouncy when you walk, you tried a new hair growth product and it worked and so forth."

"And now tell me more about the upgrade," said Brad. "What testing have you done?"

"Brad," said Gordon, "there are neutronium emitters all over the surface of Simon which lead in to three control units inside Simon's power unit. Using three control units provided redundancy and the power unit is where the matter–antimatter units are located. Redundant cabling is run from the control units to the proper section of Simon's electronic artificial intelligence. Also, if we are hit with offensive energy beams, they can instantly be analyzed so Simon will know what it is. It turned out that this was a feature that was easy to add to our existing design. Simon has integrated this new design into his mind, so we are ready to go. Want to take a ride you two?"

Both Brad and Ann said yes, and Dr. Zorg joined them. They boarded Simon who then cloaked himself, the large hangar door opened up, and Simon eased himself out and shot up to a hundred feet and hovered.

"That was quick, Simon. Can you give us a running commentary of the test profile as you run through it?"

"I will," said Simon. "And welcome back, you guys, it was too quiet with you gone."

"Okay," said Simon, "I'm now at one thousand feet over the Area 51 testing range. I am cloaked to keep from shocking prying eyes and testing will commence now!"

Warning! You were hit with a medium power EMP Beam for four seconds.

"I set the deflector system to automatically announce the ship status. I can take over and do it myself anytime I want."

"No damage, deflector shield at full power."

Warning! You were hit with a full-power laser beam for five seconds. No damage. Shields down to ninety percent. Recharging.

Warning! You were hit with a quarter-power particle beam. Minor damage, hull self-repairing. Shields down to eight-five percent. Recharging.

"We only used a quarter-power particle beam to be cautious," said Gordon from ground control. "You can also deflect a mixed beam. We want to analyze the data we have collected so far before we do more testing. Go home, Simon. We are finished here for the time being."

"Two weeks to go," said Brad. "Simon, any information from Tiger 1 on the front lines?"

"He thought he heard something," said Simon, "but couldn't get anything he could decipher. If they become more frequent, we should be on our way."

"Brad," said Erik via implant, "I met with Sergey and asked him if he thought Popov's death was a sham, and he said he didn't think so. Right now, Sergey is probably playing both sides, so he will have a home to go to. Leave enough firepower here, so I can take action if I need to. Since Simon will be too far away to override the Tigers, we need up to date crews, and the fact that Simon is away will be kept secret. All the other key governments are getting with the program and want to move ahead, even China."

"Erik, we have first-generation deflector shields on Simon and will be putting them on the Tiger series as soon as possible. This should provide good protection, even with the first iteration."

"Good. How is the manufacturing coming along?"

"Good," said Brad. "We are building some of them without weapons, which can be installed later at our option. Also, anyone we deliver one to will have to pay for its cost and sign a contract that states that the design data for any improvements they make is ours to use. This will be a kind of turnabout for the Chinese."

"Good thinking, Brad. Where exactly are you now?"

"About two hundred fifty-four miles up and where we can see and wave to the astronauts on the International Space Station from where we are sitting in the lounge in Simon's observation deck. Really surreal, exciting and thoughtful all at the same time."

"You have carved out an exciting life for yourself Brad, actually for all of us and many of us will be around to see how it all turns out. Are you ready for Battle?"

"Yes, Erik, as much as we can be. Hold the fort here, you will have several Tigers with experienced crews to come to your aid with one in Asia and one in Europe. They will all be able to communicate with you and each other. Rudy Savage, who used to be one of your Secret Service agents, will be in charge and you can contact him any-time via your implant."

"Thanks, Brad, it is comforting to deal with most of your peo-ple as they are old friends. Bye for now. I must attend to business here at the White House."

"Will Zorg, Brad here. Can we meet for coffee? Simon Android will join us."

"Sure, Brad, on my way."

"I wanted to go over a few last items," said Brad. "Simon, you have been the intuitive implant switchboard that connects our implants, so we wind up correctly connected."

"Yes, and I have launched a satellite switcher that will fill in while we are in space. It acts as a backup when I am here. The Tiger spacecrafts are tuned in and so you can reach them by implant also. You will have six Tigers total, sequentially numbered just as we practiced. They will provide a lot of assistance, but they are not sentient. I feel everyone did well in practice. Two Tiger spacecrafts will not have a crew and they will be the big risk takers, if needed."

"Yes," said Will, "and you will have some of my old hands as crew and we seem to have enough experience for good teamwork plus we will keep improving with experience."

"Will, your original spacecraft had an extra input from your communications unit that provided control codes, like return home. Simon ferreted that out. We plan to see if we can disable the enemy's weapons that way."

"I had completely forgotten about that, Brad," said Will. "That could work. I want to come with you for the Space battle too."

"I had planned on it. Let's get some sleep, we might need to leave anytime. Six Tiger spacecrafts and crews are now in orbit with us at command ready. Will, bunk here. Everyone else is onboard."

Chapter 63

Battle

"It was midnight on Simon. The internal lights were dim and there was an almost imperceptible hum. All was peaceful and quiet."

Brad was sound asleep when there, suddenly chimes ringing in his years that was impossible to ignore. Then Simon spoke, "Brad, Tiger one just checked in and he has picked up clear and distinct conversation. It was Grouse Hemler talking to his squadron.

"How long until they get to where tiger one is waiting?"

"About three days," said Simon.

"How long until we arrive at the same location?"

"One day, comfortably."

"Are the six Tigers with us?"

"Yes, Tigers 7 through 10, crewed, and Tigers 11 and 12 with no crew. Tiger 6 is on point with one crew member."

"Okay, Simon, proceed to the Rendezvous Point and wake us in six hours to code yellow alert. This will give us time for a quick breakfast. Wake Dr. Zorg and myself a half hour before that. I'm going back to sleep." It looks like we will have plenty of time to get set up in position.

"Okay, Captain."

Brad and Will Zorg were woken up and a half hour later, everyone was woken to yellow alert. After a quick food replicator breakfast Brad spoke to the crew:

"We have heard from Tiger 6 that Hemler, and his people are two to three days away, and we will be waiting for them. Anyone have any questions? No? Okay, Stay sharp at your stations. Captain out."

Simon and the Tiger spacecraft, all cloaked, and Simon with his shields up arrived at the rendezvous point where Tiger 6 was waiting. By this time, they all had heard Hemler communicating with his spacecraft from time to time and that he figured no one would be waiting for him this far out. They waited for almost a day until it was obvious Hemler was almost upon them when their sensors picked up the approaching ships. Apparently, the enemy somehow detected their presents and immediately fired their weapons.

Simon's shield unit announced, "Warning! Receiving EMP and laser fire, medium power, no damage."

"Return full power, particle and EMP beams," shouted Brad. "All Tigers fire on all enemy ships! Simon, try the disable code."

Three enemy ships exploded into millions of fragments. Where the enemy had arrived with nine ships, they were now down to six. Several enemy ships suddenly stopped shooting and just hovered. Everyone heard Hemler screaming on communications. Simon and the Tiger ships picked off the hovering ships which were also utterly destroyed. Simon was continually maneuvering his spaceship to help shield and protect the unshielded Tiger spaceships. More enemy spaceships blew up from Simon's particle beam plus pulsed EMP from the Tigers. One enemy spacecraft to go.

"We surrender! We surrender," cried Hemler over communications. "We give up!" This was translated by Simon over his internal audio system.

"Cease fire," said Brad. "All ships cease fire."

The scene now showed seven Tiger spacecrafts, some with damage, one Simon spacecraft, no damage, and one scarred and damaged enemy spacecraft, hovering with the Melthorne dictator onboard shouting surrender. There was a quiet few moments for all to ponder.

Then, out of nowhere came a bolt of purple light which cut the enemy spacecraft literally in half!

All remaining were stunned.

The electronic mind of Simon flew into action. He and seven Tigers reversed course back toward the orbit of Earth. Another purple bolt cut a Tiger spacecraft in half and sliced at Simon causing the shield unit to announce, "warning, unknown beam, high power, medium damage. Shield down to fifty percent."

"All remaining spacecraft, going to Warp speed," said Simon. "I will take lead, all Tigers spacecraft slaved to my command."

Ann cried out, "Brad, what is going on?"

"A much bigger enemy, Ann."

"Simon, are we being followed?" asked Brad. "I have you on speaker, so you are talking to all your crew."

"I don't believe it can follow while we are in warp speed."

"How damaged are you Simon?" asked Ann.

"Enough so I just barely got into warp speed. This is okay as we are at the maximum warp speed for the Tigers. I am taking us to Earth in a roundabout path. Brad, you have wondered about the ramifications of meeting someone or something with much more advanced technology, like me. Now I wonder the same thing. We just met something with technology beyond my comprehension. I may now know what fear is! I did collect lots of data which could help us. In the meantime, I need to get into the hangar for immediate repair."

"The Tiger we lost was one of the crewless so very fortunately we lost no human life. That Alien spacecraft was out to kill all of us, you and me and that was the ship, or just like the ship that originally shot me down over a hundred years ago."

"I am going sub-light speed now," continued Simon. "All is clear, there is no threat for several million miles. We are approaching Earth on way to Area 51. Brad, my cloaking is not working, and two Tigers report no cloaking ability. The remaining four need to be thoroughly checked over. Twenty-five minutes to Earth touchdown and you, as of now are in communications range."

"Thank you, Simon," said Brad. "Great decision making and flying. And now to call the president."

"Mr. President, we are all alive, but it wasn't easy, and we came close to not making it back home."

"Brad, you really know how to cheer up a guy. Where are Hemler and his people?"

"They are all dead and their spaceships all blown up. Let me explain what happened but first we have damage. We need Area 51 to open up the big hangar for Simon and his cloaking is not working. We need a second hangar for the Tigers. We started with seven and now have six."

"I got Gordon Kelly on with us when you first called," said the president. "He is now setting everything up for all of you and he will deal directly with Simon via implant. Now, tell me what the hell happened."

Brad gave the president a detailed description of everything that happened.

"You know, Brad, we do think differently now than we did a few months ago before you found Simon. The things that used to be so important are now trivial. We are one planet among many fighting for our existence. Simon is far ahead of us technologically and yet that black spaceship you ran into is ahead of him. Somehow, I feel, with Simon and us working together, we can rise up and survive but it's not going to be easy. Earth must be united, or we will be lost. Great job, Brad, my congratulations to all of you and Simon. Please pass that on to him. Good night."

"Good night, Mr. President."

That night in their quarters, Brad and Ann thought about the last few days.

"You know, Brad, I think Simon had a near-death experience."

"I think so too. When you are sentient, it hits harder and you understand more. I also feel closer to Simon and I think he to us. This is a most complicated life."

"I feel the same way, Brad. Let's get some sleep. I have the feeling we are going to wake up to a whole new world and adventure tomorrow."

Postscript

The lone Tiger fighter was on a very boring patrol well out beyond the orbit of Saturn with all its sensors extended to seek any intruders and report back to central command. Col. Ken Johnson was the lone human onboard who had come along for the experience and the solitude to have the time to plan where he wanted to take his career now that Earth was expanding into the stars, all thanks to one human accidentally finding a downed spacecraft that was sentient. Now, the whole human race was dramatically moved ahead technologically several hundred years.

There was a catch. Apparently, the spaceship that had originally shot down the found spacecraft was still around and had shown itself again and had literally sliced a tiger spaceship in half while exhibiting technology far advanced from what Earth had gained from the found Simon spaceship. All very ominous and threatening. This mission was one of several seeking data on the mysterious translucent black deadly spaceship that would strike and then disappear.

This trip was a disappointment in that there was no one to talk to. Ken lived on the Simon Spacecraft and always had the sentient Simon AI to talk to as minimum, but the Tiger spacecraft were only sapient and could only respond to commands and questions pertaining to his duties and spacecraft. It was a lonely existence for Ken.

"Colonel," said the Tiger spacecraft, "my sensors are picking up a spacecraft of unknown origin flying somewhat parallel to us. It is angling to close its distance to us. Do you want me to hail it?"

"No. Record everything, audio and visual, that happens from this time on and keep a live feed into the two communications probes. Program the probes to take different paths to command headquarters. Be ready to instantly fire both probes back to earth upon any damage to the ship. Is the unknown ship transmitting signals of any type?"

"I am receiving my sensor readings which are blurred at times. All weapons systems are online ready to destroy any enemy threat," said the sapient intelligence piloting the Tiger ship. "The picture I am getting looks different now. I believe It is only allowing us to see what it wants us to see! My sensors indicate the ship has an enormous energy source on standby."

"Warning! The unknown ship is approaching us now at high speed. A purple beam is now extended from the front of the ship. It is slicing toward us!"

"RELEASE ONE PROBE NOW," shouted Ken.

The purple beam cut the Tiger ship in half and then sliced again totally demolishing what remained. Ken died instantly as did the AI. The second communications probe fired and headed to Earth. Now the enemy spaceship seemed to disappear back to where it came from. There was only the lonely cold and quiet of deep space as if nothing had ever happened.

End

Technical Possibilities

It is always interesting to look at the technology we have today and compare it to the technology used in the story. There isn't as much separation as you might think and amazing new breakthroughs are occurring every day.

So far, we have synthesized the higher elements up to element 118, completing the seventh row of the periodic table. Element 118 was named after Russian nuclear physicist Yuri Oganessian who created the super-heavy atom by nuclear bombardment which was the thought behind the neutronium in the story. See New Scientist, April 15, 2017.

Cancer detection and curing is making great strides. There are medical breakthroughs constantly about new blood tests to detect multiple cancers with the potential possibilities someday to cure all cancers. This would add years to our lifespan.

(Let me know what you, the reader, think. Email me at AllenPatterson@SimonSpacecraft.com. The Website for this book is www.SimonSpacecraft.com.

Allen Patterson, author)

There is a boom in gene-editing clinical trials using CRISPR (clustered regularly interspaced short palindromic repeats) for the targeted genome editing. This will be able to correct some congenital errors and eliminate dangerous genomic coding which will also enhance lifespans. There is a good article on this in New Scientist, June 3, 2017.

Stem-cell research is making inroads in rejuvenation, again improving the quality of life and longevity.

There is an effort to determine the possibilities of downloading our minds into an electronic brain. From a science fiction standpoint this provides all sorts of options. A good book to read on forward thinking is "The Singularity is Near" by Ray Kurzweil. Another interesting book you might enjoy is "The Pentagon's Brain" by Annie Jacobsen. This is an uncensored history of DARPA, America's Top Secret military research agency. Our country has weapons already developed that are awesome and frightening.

My book introduces an ominous malevolent spacecraft that is technologically far advanced over the Simon Spacecraft in this this story. What do you think the physics and composition are for its death ray weapon that can slash right through neutronium hulls? What kind of beings are these that seemingly kill without provocation? Biological or Artificial Intelligence?

Allen Patterson@SimonSpacecraft.com

Appendix

Key Resumes and Equipment

Brad Young

Fifty-four years old, six feet, two inches tall, medium build, black hair, and brown eyes. Natural born leader. Retired from DARPA, has a bachelor's degree in electrical engineering from the University of Washington and an MBA from Stanford, and has a commercial pilot license with one thousand six hundred hours flying time. Divorced, wife has since passed. Two grown children, four grandchildren living in Bellevue, WA, and Portland, OR.

The founder of the Simon Spacecraft (he found it) and the Simon crew leader.

Ann Thompson

Thirty-four years old, attractive, five feet, nine inches tall, one hundred and thirty-four pounds in weight. Blond hair, green eyes.

Graduated from University of Washington with a bachelor's degree in chemical engineering and a master's degree in physics. Worked for DARPA for almost ten years.

Good health, single (was engaged three years ago, fiancé died of cancer.) All important relatives have passed on. Likes to travel. States that she has made mostly made good decisions and she wants to join the Simon crew.

Erik John Williams, President of the United States

He has had a remarkable career. He got an aeronautical engineering degree from the University of Washington and then joined the Air Force, went through pilot training, and fought in the Vietnam war. After five years, he was hired by the Boeing company as project engineer, was very active in politics, and soon was well known in the political circles. As you know, one of the Washington State Senators died suddenly in a car accident, and he replaced him. He won in the next election, and he began his six-year term in office. Two years later, he was asked to be the Vice-Presidential candidate, he accepted, and his party won. Everything went fine for a year, and then the president got brain cancer and died three months later, so now our guy, Erik John Williams becomes President. All in all, quite a trip. He is married, no children. Oh, and he has a close friend from the military—someone who's life he saved and who he has always brought along with him in his career and who now is one of the White House Secret Service agents.

Simon Spacecraft

Experimental Enhanced Artificial Intelligent Sentient control of all functions. Learning capability with intelligence growth. Started out as sapient AI

Saucer shaped interstellar spacecraft with intelligent neutronium body.

Size: One hundred fifty feet in diameter (saucer shaped). The total height at the center is fifty feet slopping down to the saucer circumference which is ten feet high. This spacecraft has near an unlimited range.

Four large cannons spaced equally around its circumference that can electronically pivot to cover one hundred and eighty degrees vertically and horizontally.

Four beams available

Particle Beam—shielded modified neutron beam at light speed modulated by two interwoven high frequency signals. This interrupts the strong nuclear force in the atomic nucleus causing just about total destruction.

EMP Beam—shuts down all electronic solid-state type junctions.

Laser Beam—melts anything it touches. (Potential upgrade-plasma beam).

Buzz Beam—just added. Induces unconsciousness and memory loss.

Multifire capability

Allows alternate beam using same port using a pulsed mix of two or three beams.

Potential upgrade—Nuclear torpedoes, settable yield

Spaceship Power Supply

Fully contained enhanced matter—anti matter generator

Automatic inertial damping with instantaneous automatic backup

Automatic triple faraday shielding system

Environmental—Fully automatic third-generation oxygen system

With CO_2 converter backup. Massive storage.

Battle-level intelligent medical system. Level 4 food-replicator system.

Local and FTL secure communications capability

Class 2 manufacturing system.

Level 2 cloaking system

Shuttlecraft

Size: Rectangular six feet wide by fifteen feet long by six feet high. Will fit, tightly, in most home garages. Can hold nine people normally

Intelligent neutronium body

Limited sapient AI for control and operations. Can be run by Simon remotely

Weapons: Three beam low range cannon located in front and rear ports

Inertial damping and double faraday shielding

Level 2 limited food replicator

Long range communications system

Second generation oxygen system

Fusion power supply

Graviton impulse power

Weapons

Simon has two communications satellites with cloaking capabilities for transponding video, audio, and drone control signals. We have twenty small size (three inches) and thirty-three miniature bugs (3/8 inch), again with cloaking capability. These bugs have enough smarts to help avoid detection. The main difference is the time they can operate and the distance they can communicate. We have twelve six-inch and ten twelve-inch heavy duty drones, each with two complex manipulators and heavy-duty power supplies that can do significant work. They have sapient smarts, cloaking capability, full communications capability, and will essentially dissolve into base elements rather than get captured.

Robots and Android

The Simon Spacecraft has a complement of four heavy-duty robots. These robots are independently controlled by the Simon AI, and all can be engaged at the same time. Simon sees, hears, and feels everything they do. Various tools and weapons can be attached, and Simon can use those tools and weapons. If dressed, they look somewhat human at a distance. They are a key part of Simon's manufacturing process.

Simon has one android that looks exactly like a human. His face structure can be altered to mimic any face, and he is controlled by Simon. If you meet him, you are meeting Simon also.

New War Drones

The features built into the *four* drones for potential combat war activities are level 1 neutronium body, particle, and EMP beam cannon in front; level 1 faraday shielding, fully upgraded cloaking capability from data just recovered from Simon's memory bay cache; graviton power supply, and size four feet square by eight feet long; and level 1 sapient AI for command and control with quantum quark encryption for communications with the spacecraft or shuttlecraft. These can be short-term units for anything from stop to capture to kill units. They will basically be invisible and undetectable, so the first time the enemy becomes aware of them will be when he is destroyed.

About the Author

Allen Patterson has been a space enthusiast from the time he was in grade school reading science fiction books about someday going to the moon. He wound up as the technical integration manager for the Command and Service Module on Apollo Eight. What engineer wouldn't dream about finding a spaceship full of technology that was years beyond what we now have and that was controlled by a sentient entity that had very little exposure to humankind. He also founded two high-tech companies and managed projects in active war zones in the Middle East. Mr. Patterson resides in Bellevue, Washington.